9/22

D0378728

Unleashed

ALSO BY CAI EMMONS

His Mother's Son
The Stylist
Weather Woman
Vanishing: Five Stories
Sinking Islands
Livid

Unleashed

A NOVEL

CAI EMMONS

DUTTON

DUTTON

An imprint of Penguin Random House LLC
penguinrandomhouse.com

Copyright © 2022 by Cai Emmons
Penguin Random House supports copyright. Copyright fuels creativity, encourages diverse
voices, promotes free speech, and creates a vibrant culture. Thank you for buying an authorized
edition of this book and for complying with copyright laws by not reproducing, scanning, or
distributing any part of it in any form without permission. You are supporting writers and
allowing Penguin Random House to continue to publish books for every reader.

DUTTON and the D colophon are registered trademarks of Penguin Random House LLC.

LIBRARY OF CONGRESS CATALOGING-IN-PUBLICATION DATA
has been applied for.

ISBN 9780593471449 (hardcover)
ISBN 9780593471456 (ebook)

Printed in the United States of America
1st Printing

Book design by Nancy Resnick

For My Hayati, Paul

would that we could wake up   to what we were
—when we were ocean   and before that
to when sky was earth, and animal was energy, and rock was
liquid and stars were space and space was not

at all—nothing

before we came to believe humans were so important

Marie Howe, "Singularity"

Unleashed

1

BY THE TIME they took Pippa to college, the rift between Lu and Pippa was already a year deep. The trip was marked by Pippa's tapping. She drummed her thighs, tapped her pinkie nail against the window glass, plucked the taut elastic strap of her backpack. *Ta-dum, da, da, da. Tsk-tsk, dum.* Lu could tell she was trying to tap quietly, so as not to annoy George at the wheel, who was easily irritated by his daughter's compulsive rhythm-making except when it was part of their special game, but Lu couldn't fail to notice—nothing about her daughter escaped her notice, especially since Pippa's hostility had set in.

When they hit the San Fernando Valley, the traffic turned rabid. Cars hurtled themselves from lane to lane as if their drivers misunderstood the laws of physics. Each was shiny—new or recently cleaned—their chrome serving as pilot lights that ignited the sun into blinding spears. Lu watched it all, aghast. It had been a while since she'd been to Southern California. She remembered the beaches, but not this endless concrete and asphalt, this hysteria.

"Welcome to the Wild West," George said, peering into the rearview mirror at Pippa, hoping to get a rise out of her. Any conversation would have been better than none, since their hours with her were numbered.

"Don't goad her," Lu said in defense of her daughter, though she, too, wished Pippa would talk instead of cocooning into herself, already gone. Didn't Pippa feel the zero-hour nature of this trip? Didn't she feel a need to come to some détente? Lu strained to remember what it had been like when she herself left home. Had her mother, Linda, been as bereft as she felt now? It was all so different back then. Lu and Linda had lived together, just the two of them in "The Nest," a six-hundred-square-foot house in Redding, until Lu was twenty and moved to Sonoma for a job at a spa.

Lu twisted to look at Pippa, who was staring out the side window, one hand on the traveling case at her feet, which held her cat, Alice.

"I was just remembering that time when you were four years old and you wandered down Sunset Loop stark naked. Remember? You made it all the way to Juniper Road before someone found you. Do you remember that?"

"No, Mom. I don't remember. You've asked me that a million times."

"You were adorable. You weren't the least bit embarrassed. You were so happy in your own little body."

"Okay. Okay. Can we not discuss this?"

Lu faced forward again, catching George's eye. The incident had humiliated George, who hated to have their neighbors thinking of them as derelict parents, but Lu had loved Pippa's feral quality. She had loved looking out the kitchen or living room window and seeing Pippa's bare body dancing around the yard, gathering sticks and stones to build structures, squatting to dig holes in the dirt, drumming on the tree trunks, and making hats of the broad catalpa leaves. Sometimes she would lie on her belly and put her ear to the ground to see what she could hear—she heard raccoons and mice, she said, once a cougar. When George objected, afraid of who might drive by and see, Lu put her foot down and made him butt out.

Along the side of the freeway, embankments of dry grass rose like hunched shoulders, some of the grass blackened from recent fires. They passed under digital signs flashing notifications of delays. Lu was no stranger to heavy traffic, but this felt extreme. Where was everyone going? Why such urgency? She held her breath, afraid for them all. Her daughter, her husband, herself.

Ta-da-da-dum. Ta-da-da-dum.

Pippa's withdrawal, after years of exceptional intimacy between mother and daughter, began with her saying she didn't want Lu texting her at school, and she wanted to be called Phipps, not the infantilizing name Pippa, a shortening of her full name, Philippa. She recoiled from Lu's hugs and no longer confided in Lu about her days, her fears, her obsessions. Lu had tried to take Pippa's moodiness in stride, inwardly hopeful that things would change, understanding that all daughters needed to establish identities separate from their mothers, but privately she was heartbroken. How could you begin to call your daughter a new, tough-sounding name like Phipps after years of thinking of her as Pippa, your very own Pippa, the girl from the poem "Pippa Passes," which George so often recited: "The year's at the spring / And day's at the morn . . ." Lu loved that poem and would have learned some of it herself if she'd had the talent for memorizing that George had. Now just thinking of the poem made her sad. With Pippa about to be so far away at college, it seemed less and less likely the two would ever get close again.

Worse, George was probably right: LA was not the right place for their eccentric, animal-loving daughter. He had always talked about what he called California's Great Divide. The northern part of the state, where they lived, was home to the best and the brightest, he said, home to the people with intellect and taste and savoir faire, like Back East, where he had grown up, or even Europe, but

Southern California was the Wild West, crass and lawless, a waste-land of concrete, populated by people committed only to hedonism and moneymaking. He would never have considered living there himself.

You're twisted, Pippa would say in response to his rants. She had insisted all along that she wanted to study in this land defined by sun, and Hollywood, and this meshwork of twelve-lane freeways, but she had no idea what she'd chosen, Lu thought. Who did at her age?

Lu had tried to support Pippa, pressing up against the veil of her daughter's unexplained hostility, but George, even now, had not made peace with her choice of UCLA. He had wanted her to attend college Back East, as he had, at one of the Ivies, maybe, somewhere small and genteel. Pippa had scoffed. *If you haven't noticed, I'm not genteel. And I'm definitely not Ivy League material.*

But you're from genteel stock. George was insistent that Pippa take this seriously. His ancestors, the Barnes family, had come from England in the 1600s, and they'd made various fortunes for them-selves, first in shipping, then in railroads; he wanted Pippa to feel proud to be a descendant of her brave and industrious forebears. Pippa would have none of this. She was a nonconformist, an outlier who needed to find her own path. She didn't care about George's fancy pedigree, nor did she care that her mother had no college degree. Lu applauded Pippa's rejection of status, even as she had accepted that this was an essential part of George, her husband of almost twenty years. Adaptation was a special skill of Lu's, almost a superpower, she thought privately, and she had discovered in her forty-five years of living that it was an especially crucial skill for surviving.

Dum-dum. Ta-da-dum. Dum-dum. Ta-da-dum.

"Have you been in touch with Evan?" Evan was Pippa's best and only friend at the private progressive school she had attended.

"Yes, Mom."

"He likes MIT?"

"Mom—it's been like *a week*."

"Right. Of course."

Alice, the cat, began to howl, an agonized, guttural sound. Confined to a carrying case, Alice had endured the trip stoically until this moment. But now she sensed something had changed. Was she aware of the crazy traffic? Was there something in the air she smelled? Pippa leaned over the carrying case to croon reassurances.

Riding shotgun beside George, Lu might as well have been a sponge for the way she felt her husband's blood pressure rising. The traffic, the howling cat, the gauntlet of driving through this parched alien landscape, was too much for him. She placed a hand on his thigh. "Calm down."

He turned to her briefly, his bear-like quality shifting from teddy to grizzly. With his heavy black beard and salt-and-pepper curls, people often mistook him for a young Francis Ford Coppola, which pleased him. *We're both vintners, after all*, he liked to say. He was a laid-back man until he wasn't, and now he was not. His face had reddened, and sweat had brought a sheen to his brow. "Who brings a cat to college?" he muttered.

Pippa was too immersed in soothing Alice to take the bait. The yowling continued. If the cat had been a human being displaying this level of distress, the car would have been stopped.

"Shut that cat up!" George yelled.

"I'm trying!" Pippa countered, fumbling with the travel case door to pet Alice.

Alice escaped from her case and leapt onto his shoulder. George jammed the brakes. The Porsche driver behind them leaned on his horn, pulled out around them and cut in front, missing the Odyssey's bumper by inches. Alice's back was arched, her gray fur bristling into cat-punk, her claws digging into George's back and chest.

"Damn it to hell! Get that cat off me!"

"Sorry, Dad." Pippa reached out to grab Alice, but Alice evaded her and dove into Lu's lap, then up to the dashboard, then down to the gearshift, before Pippa finally gained purchase around the cat's midriff.

"Back in the cage!" George yelled.

"She's going. She's going."

"Why did you take her out? What the hell were you thinking?"

"I was trying to calm her down."

"Well, you didn't."

Back in the case Alice continued to whine. The humans maintained a strained silence.

Animals had been a bone of contention between father and daughter for years. George was a lover of objects—art, books, wine—and devoted to what he called "the life of the mind," but he had no particular love for animals. He would tolerate them if they didn't get in his way. Pippa, on the other hand, was not herself without an animal to love and care for. There had been so many over the years—gerbils, snakes, guinea pigs, a tarantula—and they'd all helped to keep Pippa's superstitions and anxieties in check and get her through her rough patches—and there had been many rough patches.

It was the ferret, Emilio, who really got under George's skin. Emilio, a definite handful, loved to dance to the music of Michael Jackson. He tapped out cacophonous rhythms with measuring spoons just like Pippa. Lu enjoyed Emilio's hijinks because they

often led to uncontrollable communal laughter, but Emilio's unpredictability had put George on edge. The ferret often spirited away
sets of keys left on the kitchen counter, and once, when George
inadvertently left the door open to his third-floor study, Emilio ran-
sacked the place, scattering books and pens and pencils, chewing on
the potted philodendron, and shitting on his favorite Gabbeh carpet. The memory still made Lu chuckle, but George had not been
amused. That was it—Emilio had to go.

After Emilio, Pippa begged for a dog. George vetoed a dog of
any breed—they all required too much maintenance, he said, and
shed too much hair—but he finally consented to a cat. That was
when Alice came on the scene, a boisterous kitten at the time, but
downright tame compared to Emilio. In the four years that Alice
had been with them, she had mellowed, though you wouldn't have
known that from listening to her now.

The traffic stalled. It pained Lu to spend this precious remaining time as a family in anger. If she had been alone in the car—
alone with Pippa/Philippa/Phipps—she would have been laughing
and weeping and telling her daughter how much she would be
missed, even if Pippa only returned a stony silence. Lu couldn't
imagine how her life would be without Pippa in it. Over the years,
the two had spent so much time talking, Pippa reporting about her
days, her worries, her odd notions. Would Mrs. Marvel be there
when Pippa needed a listening ear?

Mrs. Ruth Marvel—what a wonderful name for a landlady. As
soon as Lu found the apartment being rented out by Mrs. Marvel,
she felt reassured. The pictures were charming. A bougainvillea-
covered outdoor staircase leading up to a one-room above-garage
apartment. A designated sleeping area with a queen bed. A bathroom with a shower stall. A cooking area with a microwave and hot
plate. The rest of the space was open to be fashioned however one

wanted. Though not large, it was bigger than a dorm room and, most importantly, Mrs. Marvel was fine with Pippa bringing a cat, which was central, because Pippa had refused to go to college without her cat. Lu made the arrangements via email. An image of Mrs. Marvel burgeoned: a warm, grandmotherly presence who would provide solace when Pippa needed it. Mrs. Marvel wouldn't *replace* Lu, but she'd be a mother *adjunct*.

George signed the contract and paid the deposit—not cheap, but they were prepared for that—and Lu gathered items that would make the place look cheerful. Colorful pillows and throws. Some artwork to fill the empty walls. Pippa said no to everything. She didn't want *stuff.* She would take the basics: sheets; a small selection of kitchen items; four or five changes of clothing, all jeans, T-shirts, and her omnipresent blue denim shirt; her computer, ukulele, and drumsticks. And Alice's needs, of course: litter box, food and water bowls, a scratching post.

Teetering between sad and proud, Lu had watched Pippa and George packing this small assemblage of objects into the back of the Odyssey. Pippa firmly believed the world might end any day now, and she knew *stuff* wouldn't protect her. She was right, Lu thought, but still, the stripped-down look surrounding her daughter as they packed the car—the scant number of possessions she deemed necessary, her unadorned style of dressing, the unevenness of her half-shaved head—suggested something might be wrong. How could Lu help but feel sorrow with her only child leaving home?

They slid auspiciously into a parking spot directly in front of a small blue stucco house on a tree-lined street exactly as quaint as Lu had imagined. With the ignition off, Alice stopped wailing.

They stood on Mrs. Marvel's front stoop. Up close the house

revealed itself to be in need of maintenance. The stucco was chipped in places to reveal the white dermis beneath. Paint curled off the wooden eaves. Lu was aware of the edges of her body, only inches from Pippa's, though the distance might as well have been oceans. They were the same height, but Pippa was more solid and given to stillness when she wasn't drumming. Staring at the brass knocker of Mrs. Marvel's red door, Lu pictured them as figurines in a doll's house, pawns capable of being lifted and removed and placed down somewhere entirely different. Surely Pippa must have been feeling a version of this too. Lu reached out and took Pippa's hand, and Pippa did not resist, though she didn't return Lu's smile. How desperately Lu wanted a smile from her daughter, that mischievous, sideways, slightly bemused smile. Lu's nasal passages and throat ached as she traveled a path from hope to despair and back. The to-and-fro of leaving. The cling-and-cut. A smile could not be commanded. The door opened, and Pippa dropped Lu's hand.

Mrs. Marvel looked out at them as if she had no idea who they were. She was not the grandmotherly woman Lu had imagined. She might have been sixty, sixty-five with tan, sun-damaged skin; paisley spandex clothing meant for someone Pippa's age; hair sprayed into a sixties-style flip and dyed a monochrome dark red. She smelled of smoke. Lu could already hear what George would say later: *Southern California in a nutshell—the ludicrous urge to remake yourself into the young movie star you'll never be.*

Mrs. Marvel went to fetch the key, and then, as if she was doing them a huge favor, she led them across the driveway and up the staircase to the apartment. Short of breath, she opened the door and stepped aside to let them in.

Furnished was a stretch. A bed. A hot plate. A faded, chintz-covered chair. It was nothing like what they'd seen in the photos. No curtains. No table. No microwave. No lamps or rugs. Their footsteps echoed over the linoleum flooring. Lu had thought from the pictures that the floors were wood.

"So here you go," Mrs. Marvel said, handing George the key. "Rent is due on the first of the month."

"It was supposed to be furnished," George said.

"You got furniture." Mrs. Marvel pointed to the bed, the chair.

"This isn't what we saw in the pictures."

"Dad, it's fine."

"We paid for a furnished place."

"Please, George, if Pippa—Phipps—is happy with it, it's fine," Lu said. "Thank you, Mrs. Marvel."

Mrs. Marvel disappeared quickly. No one else moved until the loud clopping down the staircase subsided. Pippa went to the bathroom. When she flushed, it sounded as if the entire apartment was flooding.

George, grim, had not moved from the door. "False advertising," he said. "This is a dump."

"We'll make it nice. She's a student—she doesn't need much. We'll go to Target tomorrow and get a few things."

George sighed. He hated being swindled.

It took only a few trips for them to ferry things from car to apartment. Pippa released Alice from her carrying case, and Alice made several sorties to the corners of the room, sniffing for signs of past inhabitants, returning each time to Pippa before sallying forth again.

Lu and Pippa made the bed. They'd been doing this for years, snapping the corners of fitted sheets into place, aligning the top sheet and blanket just so. They worked efficiently without having to talk. They were both too depleted for talk anyway. In addition to Pippa's favorite navy flannel sheets and navy blanket, Lu had brought four pillows and an Amish quilt in hues of blue and deep purple. The colors seemed too dark for this sunny town, but when they were done, the bed looked substantial, a perfect refuge, almost cave-like.

"You don't think these sheets will be too hot?" Lu asked.

"They'll be fine."

Lu lowered her voice to a whisper. "Will you really be okay here, honey?"

Pippa cut her a look. "You know I will. Stop asking."

Even after a year, Lu was still taken aback by these moments of open hostility from Pippa and too surprised to fire back. Pippa's peers had been doing this to their mothers since middle school—Lu often a witness—and their barbs, their impervious casual cruelty toward their mothers, had always engendered in Lu enormous gratitude for her own daughter. Those episodes confirmed that she and Pippa had a special relationship. Having felt immune, she was wounded when Pippa herself started being sarcastic, occasionally downright mean. George said it was normal, and maybe it was, but Lu could not accept that it had to be this way going forward. Wasn't a year of such punishment enough?

They would go to their hotel, get settled, and come back to take Pippa for dinner. But Pippa said no. "You go by yourselves. I want to explore the neighborhood."

"But dinner? You need dinner," George said.

"I'll get myself something."

"Then breakfast tomorrow?" Lu suggested. "And Target?"

Lu had been looking forward to the few days they planned to stay here, getting Pippa settled and using the occasion to repair whatever had gone wrong. George wanted to go to the Getty. Lu hoped to see the beach. And the campus, of course, they all wanted to see that. But now, with Pippa so withdrawn, it all seemed more complicated, less appealing. Still, Lu was loath to give up a minute of their waning time together.

Back in the car, George was cheerful. He adored Pippa, his only offspring, but recently he'd been a lot more sanguine about her when he wasn't in her presence. He was looking forward to being an empty nester, having the house to themselves.

"I'll buy you a good meal," George told Lu. "We'll relax, watch some schlock TV, and get a good night's sleep."

At Target the next day they wandered past aisles of clothing for kids, slinky polyester women's lingerie, pastel-encased shampoo and skin-care products. Pippa hooked Lu's elbow unexpectedly, and they ambled side by side. George walked briskly ahead of them. He had never been to Target before, calling it *merchandise for the masses*. They passed office supplies, electronics, tools, camping gear. Towels in every color of the rainbow, a display that drew Lu's attention.

"You're sure you have enough towels?"

Pippa nodded.

"You should have curtains. The sun comes blasting into that room. It could make it hard to sleep, not to mention hot."

"I love the light," Pippa said.

"You don't have to use them if you don't want, but let's get some and put them up and then you'll have the option."

"Okay, okay."

Pippa unhooked her arm, and Lu regretted speaking. She understood: Her daughter had grown up wanting for little, with a father who had always relished bestowing her with gifts, so rejecting *things* was a natural response, a healthy and admirable reaction—if youthfully naïve—in a world that was dying from too much consumption. Many of Pippa's peers were also happy to slough *stuff*. Why was Lu herself still drawn, like a magpie, to certain attractive objects? She wished she was more like Pippa, able to resist the allure of the shiny and the beautiful. She might not have been as object-focused as George was, but she wasn't as immune to the call of material things as she would have liked to be. She wanted to understand more clearly the line between *want* and *need*.

"Now we're talking," George said. He had found a boxed rectangular table with a faux wood finish. "You can eat on this and use it for your computer."

"Fine," Pippa said.

He selected a microwave and a toaster. Pippa shook her head as George dumped the boxes into an oversize cart. Lu found the cleaning supplies: broom and mop, soaps and cleansers for various purposes, light-blocking curtains. She grabbed a bath mat at the last minute. The cart was overflowing. Pippa's expression was vacant. She had slipped away and watched them from the stratosphere, saying nothing. Lu noticed but couldn't restrain herself. What else could she give?

"Where are you going to store your clothes? There's no closet."

Pippa shrugged.

Lu pointed to a bookcase. "This is small. You could use it for books *and* clothes."

Another shrug.

Lu fetched a second cart for the bookcase, and George added two standing lamps. At the checkout counter, George was impressed with how little the entire haul cost. Leaving the store, Pippa hung back, as if to say: *They don't belong to me, the objects or the people.*

"Maybe we shouldn't have done this," Lu whispered to George.

"She'll be happy we did. Once we're gone."

Once we're gone.

~

Mrs. Marvel watched from her open front door as they unloaded and humped the purchases up the staircase. Lu waved, but Ruth Marvel didn't wave back. Alice was whining again and didn't stop until Pippa stepped inside.

It took a couple of hours to unbox everything—George's pocketknife their only tool—and to assemble the table and bookcase, and cart the boxes down to the recycle bins, and mount the curtains, and scour the place clean. Alice was anxious, skittering from place to place as if she'd taken catnip, so they closed her off in the bathroom. It was late afternoon by the time they were done. Having had nothing to eat since breakfast, they were all sweating and irritable. George and Pippa sat perched at the end of the bed, Pippa immersed in her phone. George reached out and laid a palm on her thigh.

"Hey, Pips, give me a rhythm." It was their go-to game: She would tap a rhythm for him to replicate, which he could almost never do.

She frowned up at him, cowled and separate. "Not now, Dad."

"Last chance for a while."

"I said *not now*."

George shrugged. "Okay, but you might regret it."

"How about we get some takeout and go to the beach?" Lu suggested, thinking it might cool and calm them.

"Mom, can I talk to you?"

Pippa guided Lu into the bathroom and closed the door. There was barely room in there for the two of them plus Alice, and the towel rack jabbed Lu's back. "I think you guys should leave. No offense, but—I just . . ."

Lu hesitated. "If that's what you want . . ."

"I have to figure things out by myself."

"I know, honey. You're right. We'll go."

"It has nothing to do with not loving you. You know I love you."

"Of course."

"Thanks. And—"

"What?"

"Please don't be calling me all the time, okay?"

"Can I text?"

"Yeah. Sure. But not constantly."

Lu nodded, because what else could she do?

"Hey—where's your necklace?"

Lu fingered her chest and pulled the silver chain from under her collar. "It's here."

It was a modest, inexpensive silver chain with a tiny placket bearing her initials, LMV, Lupe Maria Vasquez, the name Vasquez having been handed down through generations of women, grandmother, daughter, Lu the granddaughter, and even Pippa, the great-granddaughter, though George had insisted on Pippa's last name being Barnes, so she had ended up with a ridiculously long name: Philippa Adrienne Luz Vasquez Barnes. When Lu was born, this necklace was given to her mother, eventually intended for Lu. Linda, Lu's mother, passed it on to Lu on her eighth birthday, when she decided Lu was old enough to wear simple jewelry, and Lu had been wearing it ever since. Even when she wore the showy ruby-, sapphire-, and diamond-studded necklaces George had given her, this simple chain hid beneath them, like a dog tag telling others who she was. She often rubbed it in times of stress, feeling it as a repository for memories, reminding herself: *This is who I am.* Once George had offered to have it embossed with Lu's new final initial B, for Barnes, but Lu declined.

What a disconnect. Pippa had brought her into this enclosed

space, where their bodies were only inches from each other, in order to tell her to back off, and yet she was concerned that Lu might have lost the necklace.

Pippa turned away and stared into the sink, exposing the unshaven side of her head with its tufts of pale brown hair drifting like windblown beach grass. Her head, Lu thought, was a powerful emblem of her personality, the shaven side evincing control, the unshaven side chaos.

When they left the bathroom moments later, Lu found herself still nodding, up and down, up and down, robotic and heartfelt. *Yes. Yes. Yes.* Whatever you want, however much you reject me, I will always say *yes.*

2

DESPITE THE LATE HOUR, they decided to head for home. A drive of six hours, maybe seven. George drove fast. Occasionally he reached out to touch her shoulder or thigh, but neither of them spoke. Pippa was born five months after they married; beyond those five months, they'd never lived alone as a couple. LA dissolved behind them, and she breathed more easily as they climbed up through the Grapevine over Tejon Pass. She thought of Pippa and Alice rattling around in that bleak garage room, knowing no one else in the vast city.

As night took over, the world shrank. There was only the car, the unfurling freeway, the oncoming headlights. They bolted through darkness. She sighed and rested her head against the seat back, longing to be home and longing to be back with Pippa, pulled between those two poles, filled with uncharacteristic torpor. Now would have been the perfect time to tell George about the D— she got in her summer physics class, a class George had encouraged her to take as the first step toward completing a college degree. The years following her high school graduation she counted among the happiest in her life. She'd worked at a number of hospitality jobs—barista, gallery receptionist, spa receptionist, once briefly in a gynecologist's office—first in Redding, living with Linda; then, when she saved enough, she moved to Sonoma, where she lived in an apartment with three other women and worked at a high-end spa called Nirvana. Her next job was at the winery where George hired her to work behind the bar, serving flights and individual glasses, educating people about the vintages. She was perfectly suited for all those positions, which involved getting to know customers, charming them, soothing the cranky ones. She loved the variety of people she met and, while she wasn't paid a lot, it was enough to cover her rent. Most importantly the jobs allowed her the time and cash to take classes: Zumba, Jazzercise, modern dance. She knew she'd made the right choice as she watched her high school friends suffering through classes they hated, strapped with student loans they'd never repay.

So many years had passed since then. Now, at forty-five, she'd forgotten how to study. Everything about the physics class had tripped her up: thermodynamics, electromagnetism, the laws of motion. She didn't have the concentration to remember the formulas, not to mention executing them in the real-life examples that appeared on the tests. She wasn't motivated to get her degree, but that didn't make her immune to the humiliation of having failed.

"Go ahead, doze," George told her. "I know this is stressful for you. I'm fine driving."

Sooner than she expected they had exited the freeway and were driving along familiar country roads, estates tucked in among the vineyards, everything artfully lit to simultaneously impress tourists and scare off nighttime intruders. Rows of undulant vines stretched over the semi-dark hills, neat as combed hair yet still sensuous, interspersed with copses of live oak, juniper, walnut, cypress. A landscape she never failed to admire.

They rose through the woods on winding Juniper Road to Sunset Loop at the crest of a hill where a handful of custom-built homes formed a small development, each house a personal aesthetic statement, constructed on a minimum of two acres with views out over the surrounding countryside. It wasn't the wealthiest neighborhood in those parts, not the choice for billionaires, but it was still very desirable. George was one of two vintners who lived there; the other residents owned various kinds of businesses or commuted to Silicon Valley.

Home. A contemporary structure on three acres with multiple glass facades that invited the outside indoors. She had always loved this house, which George had built before she met him, but now, on this particular night, it was an affront to the landscape. It didn't look like a place she belonged.

George went inside with the suitcases. He turned on lights, and the house awakened as if a live thing. Before she joined him, needing to move her limbs and breathe some fresh air, she began to walk.

She couldn't stop picturing Pippa as she had looked waving goodbye from the top of the stairs, cradling Alice, hair on the unshaved side of her head mashed down by sweat, her body listing forward, as if to say: *Don't go.* She was eighteen years old, too proud to tell her mother—close as they were—that she didn't want to be left. But Lu could already tell: Pippa wouldn't be happy in LA.

Lu walked to the end of the block near the Blackwell property, where a footpath that ran for miles descended the hill through sparse woods and meadows. She walked this path frequently, knew it intimately, and would have walked it now, even in the dark, but she felt George awaiting her. She paused at the top of the trailhead and inhaled what she thought of as the scent of the trees, though it was probably more than trees. Dirt. Grass. Various fungi. Animal scat. She knew too little, wished she could more accurately name what was out there. Nevertheless, the scent of this air was such a balm after LA's smog and heat.

In a few moments she would go inside, bed down with George, and he would reassure her.

3

LU, STILL IN BED, observed George through the open bathroom door as he prepared for his long day at the winery. Since Pippa had reached high school Lu had also been working there two evenings a week, and George had suggested she might take on more shifts now that Pippa was gone. Maybe she would; she wasn't sure.

He was moving quietly so as not to awaken her. This was his usual morning ritual, but she rarely had the occasion to observe it so closely, as it was her practice to be out of bed by now, waking Pippa then making breakfast for her.

George was more than a decade older than she, fifty-eight to her forty-five, but he was still youthful and attractive. Today, as always, his clothing was casual but chic: a dark red rayon shirt with an elegant drape, an unstructured charcoal blazer, no tie, as he preferred to style himself as an artist more than as a businessman. He combed his hair and shaved the edges of his beard and neck, splashed on aftershave, precise as he went about these rituals, maybe even nervous. It wasn't surprising; he was always a worrier, and now it was harvesttime, and the trip to LA had forced him to rely on his assistant, Tom. Tom was a longtime and trusted employee, in charge of agriculture at Barnes Vineyards, but still George couldn't resist micromanaging. He tiptoed out of the bedroom, shedding the scent of his aftershave.

"George!" she called on a sudden impulse.

He turned as if trapped. "I thought you were asleep."

"Will you be home for dinner?" It had been his habit for years to come home for dinner then return to the winery for a few hours.

"Of course. Why would today be any different?"

Why? She couldn't believe he was asking—of course things were different now. He disappeared down the hallway. She heard him downstairs puttering in the kitchen, making coffee and pouring it. He slipped out the front door and latched it behind him.

The house was plunged into silence. It mushroomed and swirled like smoke through all the rooms of the house, Pippa's room, her sewing room, George's third-floor study, and downstairs through the living room and kitchen, the library and the solarium. She lay on her back listening to the boisterous quiet, knowing more sleep was out of the question but unable to fight the lethargy that kept her in bed, the weight of decision-making in a life without clear direction. Did George really believe that all their routines and rituals would continue as they always had? Maybe for him it would be easier to hold on to the way things had been with Pippa in the house, but for her, the rhythm of her days would be entirely different. No making breakfast for Pippa and driving her to school. No fetching her from school and driving her to drumming lessons. No listening to her diatribes about insensitive teachers, or reacting to her unconventional school essays, or taking Alice to the vet. No last-minute dashes for school supplies Pippa suddenly realized she needed. No rubbing her back on the nights she couldn't sleep. No family outings on weekends, or making cookies together, or taking evening strolls around Sunset Loop. And in bed at night, what would replace all the time she and George had spent talking about Pippa?

She shot off a text, just a brief one so as not to cross any lines: *Just*

checking in. Thinking of you. Hope you're doing well. Love, Lu-Mom.
She waited for the ping of response.

It was almost 9:30 A.M. by the time Lu wrenched herself from
bed, made her way to the kitchen, and poured herself a cup of luke-
warm coffee. While she heated it in the microwave, she noticed
something on the kitchen counter: college brochures with a note
from George. *Have a look. Maybe you want to enroll full-time? The
first day of the rest of your life! (Also, can you bring some order to
Pippa's room?!) xo G.*

When George first suggested that she return to school, she had
been open to the idea, but the physics class had changed everything.
She would tell him about the D– tonight and shut down the discus-
sion. But she also needed to tell him that she had no need for physics, no interest, and that was why she hadn't been able to summon
the effort to succeed. Physics wasn't going to give her direction or
make her life meaningful, and it was doubtful any other academic
course would either. His expectations of her were misdirected; it
seemed as if he didn't fully understand her. He liked to think about
the ideas *The New Yorker* and *The New York Times* peddled to him,
the same endlessly discussed topics everyone else was obsessed with.
She quickly lost interest in those debates that, to her mind, went
nowhere. She knew she was smart, but not in any conventional
way—not book-smart, or test-smart, or *Jeopardy!*-smart, but body-
smart, people-smart, life-smart. Still, she took the brochures dutifully to the living room with her coffee and phone and sat on the
couch, where the two-story picture window looked out beyond the
terraced patio to a meadow studded with live oaks. A few robins
pecked for something between the patio's flagstones. The plaintive
call of a mourning dove issued from an invisible perch. She tapped
her silent phone to make sure it was on.

One of the brochures was for the University of California at

Berkeley, the other for Sonoma State. George had begun talking about her getting her degree since sometime this past winter, cognizant of their imminent empty nest, an awareness she had been trying to push from her mind. *It will help you figure out what the next chapter of your life will be*, he said. She hadn't considered a *next chapter* and couldn't help wondering if he saw her as insufficient.

The brochures featured smiling youths seated around seminar tables, lounging on grassy quads with stacks of books beside them, working at computers with furrowed brows, standing beside blackboards scribbled with numbers and symbols. She couldn't stand the thought of attending classes with people less than half her age, feeling dull-witted and unmotivated when she knew herself to be lively and capable of showing those young people what really mattered. Other than Pippa, she hadn't had an all-consuming passion since the end of ninth grade, when she had to stop her gymnastics classes. She'd had talent, all her coaches said that, but to continue to the next level her mother would have had to pay a lot more for classes in San Francisco, and she would have had to travel great distances, not only for those classes, but even greater distances for the competitions.

She trashed the brochures in the recycling bin where George was sure to see them and headed back upstairs to Pippa's room. The bed was unmade just as Pippa had left it, and the floor was littered with cast-off clothing. Pippa had never managed to keep her room tidy.

Lu stepped into the room and perched on the edge of the bed where she and Pippa had had so many of their conversations, Pippa stretched out on the bed or nestled at the center of her drum set, tapping the snare occasionally to punctuate something she was saying. How ugly those drums appeared now without Pippa in their midst. Taped to the walls were several unframed posters of Pippa's favorite drummer, Cindy Blackman, back arched and eyes closed in performance ecstasy. Beside Cindy was Tiamat, the Dragon Lady. It had taken Lu some time to adjust to this disturbing image when Pippa first printed and displayed it. Tiamat, Pippa explained, was a person who, after numerous surgeries, had made herself into a "genderless reptile." She had spent thousands of dollars to modify and transform the male body to which she was born: castration, ear and nose removal, tongue splitting, multiple tattoos, horn implants, removal of some teeth and sharpening of others, green eye staining, chin scarring. Lu could barely look at the picture. She worried Pippa might have the desire to mutilate herself like that. But Pippa said she simply admired the Dragon Lady, who had been abused as a young person and had finally taken control of her life and was happier than ever. As Lu had grown more accustomed to the image, she had also become more intrigued by this oddly re-created person, conceding there may have been something admirable in the Dragon Lady's focused path to transformation.

Still, the Dragon Lady signaled something: There was a deeply guarded well within Pippa she knew nothing about. You had a child, and early on you began to tell stories about the child. *This is a smart child. This is a child with a calm temperament. This is a fiery child. This is a tough child. This is a sensitive child. This is a child who adores people, whereas this one is a loner.* The stories often said more about the parents than about the child herself. They spoke to what the parents wanted that child to become, and often the child obliged by growing into the story, just as a plant grew toward the sun. What had Lu needed Pippa to be? Something, though she wasn't sure what.

L: *I don't mean to pester you, but are you okay?*

P: *Yowl (that's Alice). It's been one day, Mom!*

She remembered getting a call from the school when Pippa was in second grade. The school secretary wanted Lu to come and take Pippa home. *She's acting strangely*, the secretary said. When Lu pressed for details, she was told, *When the teacher talks to her, she barks back. She claims she's a dog.* Lu had been amused. Why shouldn't Pippa see how it felt to behave like a dog? Couldn't the school, which prided itself on its progressive attitudes, indulge her?

Lu picked her up and, for the rest of the day at home, Pippa barked. Lu fed her from a bowl on the floor and petted her and tied a necktie around her neck, pretending it was a leash. Pippa licked Lu's hands and barked some more. The next morning, to George's and the school's great relief, Pippa settled back into being human.

Lu rose abruptly. She was not going to tidy this hodgepodge; it was a perfect time capsule, awaiting Pippa's return.

4

GEORGE FOLLOWED TOM on an early-morning stroll through the vines, savoring how the morning chill sharpened the pungency of the ripening grapes. There was nothing more pleasant than these dawn walks down the rows, feet sunk in the dirt, dewy leaves brushing his torso, reaffirming the wholesome nature of his business, how it originated in soil and water and seedlings. Cultivating grapes was a noble tradition that had been going on for centuries, something that was easy to forget when he was immersed in the headaches of running a business.

George hoped the morning's cool air, the first indication of a seasonal change, might usher in some much-needed rain too, though there had been no rain in the forecast. The soil crumbled underfoot, and its color, even to George, was grayly anemic. But he tried not to worry about agricultural issues until Tom told him to worry—he had enough on his plate with production and marketing and the tasting room.

Tom, a laconic man with a beard that covered his chest like an artisan bib, had lived off the grid for years before he came to work for George. Trained as a horticulturalist, he knew plants and soil in an intimate way George never would. Today he had been pausing periodically to examine the underside of a leaf, to sift a clump of soil, to dig under the foliage to palpate the stalk itself. His way of knowing was tactile. George often thought Tom could have been blind and he would still have been an excellent agricultural manager.

What pride George felt as he looked out over his fifty acres. This was his doing—he'd had a vision, and he'd made it happen. Yes, he'd had financial help from his family in the beginning, but that had been it; the rest of the considerable effort of learning and building had been his. He would always be a New Englander in his soul, but here he'd found a second home three thousand miles from his birthplace. He loved the mild climate, the groomed landscape that connected him to his European ancestors. He loved the elegance of the homes and the restraint of the commercial developments, everything tasteful. It was a look and an atmosphere that was as close to New England as you could get on this coast. He certainly couldn't have built a winery like this if he'd stayed in New England.

Tom's harumphing snapped George from his reverie.

"*Bois noir*, I think," Tom said, pronouncing the French as perfectly as George himself would, surprising for a man who liked to pass himself off as minimally educated.

"No, please." It was a dreaded disease for viticulturalists, one that could radically reduce both grape yield and quality.

"I need to verify it," Tom said.

A low-flying hawk swooped up behind them, casting a shadow that made George duck. He tamped down an unnecessary spike of alarm. Tom was well versed in nontoxic, organic prevention techniques and had so far succeeded in heading off the major viral, bacterial, and fungal pestilences that had afflicted nearby wineries. And the newly planted vines had taken off much better than they'd expected. Tom would find a solution.

"We don't have to worry yet," Tom said, knowing George well enough to guess his reaction. "Sometimes *bois noir* goes into spontaneous remission."

"Really?"

"We'll see. I'm more concerned about the heat and the drought. And fires, of course. There's a lot of salt buildup in the soil. We should think about replanting some of these vines at an angle that protects them from the sun. It could be important going forward."

"Replanting?"

"After we finish harvesting. And we need to be using more drought-resistant root stalks."

George nodded. He understood these things to a degree, and he knew Tom was right to be making these recommendations, but he was loath to upset the current status quo, which had served him so well recently. The changes Tom was suggesting would take financial investment and major labor, and they would definitely affect the bottom line for a handful of years to come.

They stood in silence for a while, as was their custom. The sun sliced through a stand of live oaks and spread a triangle of pink light over the vines. Things were changing everywhere he looked. The whole damn country was going crazy—politicians behaving like two-year-olds, people throwing their lives away to cults, tempers frayed from extreme weather events—his own life no exception. Pippa had been gone only one day, and Lu was already acting as if something disastrous had happened. *It's the way of the world*, he wanted to say to her this morning, before he thought better of it. He wanted to help guide her into this post-parenting life, but he wasn't sure what would make her happy now. He had plenty of things to occupy him without active fatherhood, but what did she have? Nothing, as far as he could see, and it worried him. If only she were a bit more steely, like her mother, Linda.

~

He had told Lu he'd be home for dinner, but as dinnertime approached, he found himself stalling, finding one more task that seemed imperative to complete before heading home. The harvest reports had put him in a good mood, and he didn't want it ruined by having to reassure Lu. It was something he'd been doing for their entire marriage, something he'd been happy to do even when the grounds for reassurance were shaky, but couldn't he take a pass once in a while?

His watch said 6:15; dinner was at 6:30, and the drive home took ten minutes. He had to leave now if he didn't want to be late.

The timing of Marley Moretti's appearance was either good or terrible, he couldn't say which. She was sliding onto a stool at the bar, her sheer red blouse taking flight behind her. He had the feeling he'd hallucinated her, though she was far too tall and bright and substantial to be an apparition. Her neon reddish-orange hair. Her crimson lipstick. Leggings that evoked the paint-spattered work of Jackson Pollock. He lingered at the far end of the bar as she ordered her usual glass of Cabernet. What was it about her that riveted him? Her bright clothing and six-foot-two stature, certainly, as well as her flamboyant gestures, but it was more than that. It was the self-sufficiency she radiated. She was happy to talk to people, but she didn't appear to need anyone. She was content to be alone, perfectly entertained by her own thoughts.

Before this summer, he'd only known Marley by name. She had a reputation in certain circles around town for being an admirable eccentric, an independent woman who had given up a successful career in high tech to become an artist. She had moved from San Francisco to Sonoma twelve years earlier, transformed an abandoned barn into a studio and living space, and largely kept to herself. George had seen her around town occasionally, but he'd never spoken to her until she approached him in June to see if he was interested in purchasing some of her paintings. It was encaustic work, abstract backgrounds overlaid with shadowy figures and faces. He liked it immediately, found it quietly emotional, and bought three pieces, two for the gallery and one for home.

After he purchased the paintings, she began to drop by the tasting room. He had never felt quite so deferential to a woman before. Their conversations had begun in the most ordinary way, pleasantries about the weather, about California's politics and drought, the inevitable inquiries into where they each lived and where they'd originally hailed from. But it seemed to George that the subject took a different turn quickly, not to the more personal, as it might have with others, but to ideas. They were both lovers of art, of course, so perhaps this pivot was natural, but he'd never met anyone in all his years in California who was acquainted with the artists he had followed and admired over the years. She knew the New York art scene from the 1980s and 1990s. Jennifer Bartlett. Julian Schnabel. Robert Mapplethorpe. She knew the controversial work of Andres Serrano, whose work *Piss Christ* was composed of an image of the crucifix submerged in a plexiglass tank of urine. Also the work of Chris Ofili, the Trinidadian artist whose work *The Holy Virgin Mary* was made with elephant dung. Raised Catholic, Marley admired the boldness of these works, the way they called the Church to question itself. Throughout these discussions Marley questioned the value of art, even as she said to him, "It's my calling, so I'm doomed to do it whether it's worthwhile or not."

Marley's presence invited George to step away from the mundanities of running a business to think about the overarching considerations of human purpose, values, consciousness. He admired that she had been able to piece together a living as an artist despite not being a household name. It was a modest living, but she survived.

The minutes were speeding by. Feverish, he turned his back on Marley and all the patrons at the bar and went to the sink, where he busied himself drying glasses and placing them on trays, ready for the pouring of flights. Marley's red tunic fluttered on his vision's horizon like a hesitant setting sun. She didn't appear to have spotted him yet. He never knew if she came here explicitly to talk to him or if their conversations were incidental. Done with the glasses, no more obvious busywork before him, he glanced at her. As if she'd been awaiting his gaze, she beckoned, a definitive move of her arm that was almost impatient.

"What can I get you?" he said, laughing.

"You're a bit standoffish tonight."

"Standoffish? That's not what I meant to be. Can I get you another glass?"

She held up her full goblet. "Are you trying to get me drunk? I thought you might want to come to my studio and see more of my work?"

He'd lost his bearings. Did she mean now? "Sure." He waited for clarity, busying himself wiping the bar in front of her, straying a few feet in each direction.

"Text me a good time," she said, laying her card on the bar.

He picked it up, the time flashing up from his wrist.

5

FROM HER PERCH on the chaise in the dark solarium where she had been drifting in and out of sleep, she heard him padding from room to room, switching on lights. He liked to have every room blazing, even those that were empty.

"Lu? Lu?" He stood above her. "Are you awake?"

"I'm awake."

"Shouldn't we have dinner?"

In the solarium's dim light his heavy beard was the only thing she saw. She glanced at her watch. "It was ready over an hour ago." She spoke carefully, trying not to sound punitive.

"I'm sorry. I got caught up. You know how it is."

Yes, she knew. He had a million things to do at the winery, a million people asking him questions, depending on him. It wasn't the first time he'd been late, but didn't he understand how today, the first dinner with only the two of them, it was important to be on time?

"You could have called."

She rose, and he followed her to the dining area, brightening the rheostats as he went. He uncorked a bottle of red wine while she took the already-served plates to the kitchen for reheating.

"How was your day?" His voice scrabbled around in a higher register than usual.

She shrugged. "I took a walk."

He poured the wine and she brought the plates from the micro-wave and they sat, not in their usual places, with George at the head of the table, but directly across from each other, as if on a date.

He raised his glass. "To the future."

She raised her glass in kind, touching it lightly to his, wondering what future he saw that allowed him to speak of it so glowingly.

"Did you have a chance to look at the brochures?"

"I did."

"And . . ." He swirled his wine, sniffed it, swirled again. He did this so often it seemed almost robotic, an engrained habit shorn of original purpose.

"I've been meaning to tell you—I got a D minus in that physics class."

"Physics is a bear. I never did well in physics. You can take it again." He reached a finger into his glass and withdrew some sediment.

"But I don't want to. School—it's not—I want other things."

He swirled his wine again. "You haven't given your studies a chance."

"Listen to me. I don't want to."

"Okay then . . . I think you're making a mistake, but you know best. What else do you see for yourself?"

"Honestly? Right now I see nothing." Didn't he get it? For eigh-teen years she'd put all her energy into being a good mother—and he'd wanted that, encouraged that—and now, emerging from those years, the world appeared confusing and unreceptive to someone like her.

Swirling, swirling, what was so important about his wine? "You will. Give it time."

"George . . . ?" Her gaze was stuck on the dance of color and light in his glass, as if it held a prophecy. "Do you think she's going to be okay? She's never lived on her own."

"You have to stop worrying. It's a life passage everyone goes through."

He laid down his glass and turned his attention to his plate. Scrambled eggs and toast. She hadn't been inspired to cook anything elaborate. His judgment floated on the air between them, a tiny sliver of invisible, airborne glass.

"Breakfast for dinner?"

"I'm sorry." But she wasn't, not really. "I couldn't get motivated for anything fancy. It's not the same with just the two of us."

He appeared not to hear her, looking down at his plate again with an expression she could only see as despairing. He'd always loved the meals she prepared—lamb tagine, chicken piccata, chicken mole, prawns with garlic and mushrooms, filet mignon with béarnaise sauce—and he'd come to expect them. Sometimes he brought her recipes, which she was always willing to try. They were things she had never eaten before, ideas inspired by five-star restaurants in Italy and France, with ingredients she'd never heard of: mirepoix, garlic scape, Grana Padano cheese, Aleppo pepper. *You've got the cooking gene*, he often said of her, and he was right. Scrambled eggs for dinner was beneath his standards.

His laugh was brief and private. "Okay, I get it. You deserve a night off. You'll get back to it. Is there salad?"

"No salad."

"How about some parmesan?"

She fetched the parmesan, and he spread it liberally over his eggs as if it were transformative dust. Her mother loved to repeat the adage about a man's belly being the pathway to his heart. She studied his face: mouth parted, head cocked, eyes squinting as if readying himself. Why had she acquiesced to all that fancy cooking over the years, instead of serving, at least occasionally, the simple foods on which she'd been raised? It wasn't only for him. It was for Pippa too. She'd been introducing Pippa to foods that she herself had never been exposed to, trying to make Pippa more genteel just as George had been trying to remake her. A disturbing thought. But Lu reminded herself not to be too worried about this influence on Pippa. Pippa knew how to assert herself. In fact, in the last few months she had been avoiding the meat on her dinner plate, picking around it and opting instead for an extra portion of salad.

He ate suddenly, grabbing a breath then shoveling in forkfuls of egg then toast, barely chewing before he swallowed, pausing only to gulp his wine.

6

PHILIPPA HARDLY SLEPT. Traffic hummed off the boulevard, its droning interspersed with the syncopations of an occasional car in need of tire alignment. *Ka-chunk. Ka-chunk. Ka-chunk.* Lurid streetlight poured through the front window, and intermittent beams from passing cars arced through the entire room like searchlights, pressing against her closed lids. Every once in a while, Alice, asleep on the bed beside her, awakened, terrified and disoriented, and vaulted to the floor to cruise the apartment yet again.

It wasn't really Alice that kept her awake, or the changing patterns of light, or the incessant traffic—it was something else. An inexplicable ticking whose source she couldn't identify, sensation more than sound. A woolly feeling in her mouth. A quickening of her blood as if it was recalibrating to the new location. She had the weird notion that she'd left some kind of gathering and, as she departed, she'd accidentally taken up someone else's skin. Before dawn she identified the feeling more precisely. She was afraid. She was always afraid at night during fire season, but now the fear was intensified by being so far from home. A sharp-toothed dread, mostly coming from inside her, but also latched to the city's tumult. She pictured herself walking to campus, lost, cars barreling down the street and veering onto the sidewalk, mowing her down. She knew she was overreacting. Fear had never been her daytime habit—her superstitions had a way of keeping it in check during the day—but at night fear enveloped her. She reached for her phone, poked her mother's number, then remembered it was still night and cut the call short before it rang.

This was the first time she had ever lived away from her parents. Many of her classmates had spent weeks away from home at overnight summer camps or on backpacking trips with friends; a few she knew had been on month-long bike trips to Europe. She had spent the occasional, very occasional, night at Evan's house, and once she spent two nights alone in Redding with her grandmother Linda and helped out with her restaurant, but she had never been comfortable with even those brief separations from her parents and her home. She thrived on knowing Lu and George were in bed together at the end of the hallway, and that her mother would rouse her in the morning and drive her to school and they would talk. She had tried to make a good show of being a rebel, but in reality, she was a coward.

For at least a year she had been working hard to move beyond the shelter her mother provided—the comfort, the acceptance, the encouragement and love—but that shelter was hard to escape. It persisted like an expansive and ever-broadening umbrella, and each time she thought she was stepping beyond the perimeter of its reach, its reach widened, infuriatingly, to encompass her. Angry at herself for being so dependent, she'd thought that making a big break like this, moving hundreds of miles from home, would finally help her sever the cord, but she hadn't imagined how terrified it would make her. That was clearly what she felt now in the glaring morning light after only two nights into her new adventure: abject terror.

She forced herself from bed, and by 6:30 A.M. she was out the door, toeing Alice out of her way, promising she would return in a couple of hours.

Underfoot: the crackle of palm fronds, fallen, dead; lumps of black asphalt split by the muscular roots of a tree. An unruly stalk bearing giant red blossoms reached out from one yard, fondling her leg like a rude hand. Bad signs, even sinister, all arrows suggesting an imminent downward spiral. She walked fast. A bird with a broad wingspan tracked her, casting its shadow in her path.

It took her fifteen minutes to reach the campus. It was mostly deserted at this early hour, a week before the term would begin. The scale was vast. Building after redbrick building. Imposing façades. Romanesque arches. Grand steps leading to entrances. She followed winding concrete paths through grassy quads, into court-yards with benches and shade-giving trees. Ficus, sycamore, ca-talpa, magnolia, jacaranda, palm. Everything was pruned and weeded and, despite the statewide drought, the grass was a satu-rated emerald that appeared fake. She reached down to see if it was real—it was. She sat for a while on a bench under a sycamore enjoy-ing the cool, briny air, closing her eyes. A flock of blackbirds smashed the tranquility, squawking at her from the sycamore's canopy, where they'd concealed themselves. Another bad sign.

She moved on. The relative quiet was welcome, but it also made her uneasy; by next week these same pathways would be swarming with students and faculty, all purposeful, driven to get what was theirs.

What a mistake. She had come here on a hunch, and the hunch had turned out to be wrong. She should have done more research about this school and this city. She should have visited back in the spring when her mother offered to bring her, but by then she was deep into shunning the offers, trying to expel her mother's influence from her life. If she'd visited back then, she would have sensed what she was sensing now—that the size of this place was too much for her. Her father was right—she was going to be lonely and lost. A smaller school closer to home would have been a better choice. Then she could have occasionally returned home on the weekends. She wished her mother had been more forceful, as she had probably known this college and city wouldn't be right, but she had remained quiet. She wondered if any of her schoolmates had also made college decisions they now regretted. Not Evan—he was already ensconced at MIT, clam-happy.

The bear took her by surprise. Mascot for the school teams, the Bruins. He blocked her path, huge and unfriendly looking, his mouth agape, his teeth sharp, his eyes staring ahead directly at her as if he was sighting her as his next prey.

She snapped a photo and texted it to her mother without comment. Lu sent back a thumbs-up emoji. Philippa waited for more, but nothing came. She resumed walking, heading back in the direction of her apartment, overcome with nostalgia, remembering how it had felt to have her mother nearby, a best friend always game for anything. She knew she was much too old to be wishing for such protection. When she was beginning her senior year Evan had said something she couldn't forget: "Your relationship with your mother is sick, you know?" It startled her. She and her mother had always been close, closer than her classmates were with their mothers, but to call it *sick*?

"It's like you're lovers," Evan said.

"We're not lovers!"

"I didn't say you were. You're *like* lovers. The way you look at each other like you have secrets."

Philippa had no retort. How were they *supposed* to look at each other? After that she couldn't stop thinking maybe Evan was right, and she began pulling back from her mother, just a little at first, experimentally, then more forcefully. And she discovered she was angry at her mother for always being there and for being *too damn nice*. She realized she couldn't stand watching her mother deferring to her father as if he mattered more than she did. Philippa certainly didn't intend to become that kind of woman. Retreating and discovering the power of *no* had the benefit of strengthening some nugget inside herself. She stopped reporting to her mother about her days and about every trivial thought or feeling. And she refused the visit to LA.

From halfway down the block she heard Alice howling. As she began to ascend the outdoor staircase to the apartment, Mrs. Marvel emerged from her side door in a flowered robe and slippers.

"You have to do something about your cat. Every time you leave he screams nonstop. I've never heard a cat make so much noise. If this continues you'll have to get rid of him."

Every time? This was only the second time Philippa had left Alice alone. She stared at Mrs. Marvel, who had stepped off her stoop and traversed the driveway, stopping directly beneath Philippa. Philippa, keeping her expression blank, tried to think of something placating to say. Some of her teachers in high school used to call her blank face "troubling," thinking it was a sign of noncompliance or hostility. Philippa had never meant it that way, not back then, but now she could see it might be useful. Her height on the steps gave her an advantage, as did her silence, but still Mrs. Marvel's rage made her panicky.

Alice's distress was audible, yes, but the sound could hardly be called annoying. Not like a siren, or even a rowdy person. It wasn't even as loud as the traffic.

"Say something. Did you hear me?"

Philippa nodded and resumed her ascent. There was no way to react rationally to a person as unhinged as Mrs. Marvel was now.

"I'll take action, you know. Don't think I won't take action."

As soon as Philippa stepped inside the apartment, Alice's anguished howls subsided, and she meowed in ordinary cat parlance. Philippa scooped Alice into her arms and ferried her to the bed. "I'm home. It's okay. She's not gonna do anything. We're fine."

Lying down, she corralled Alice into her armpit, stroking her back hard. Alice stretched and writhed—the joy of being reunited and touched and loved. How easy it was to satisfy Alice, so much easier than satisfying herself. Philippa was sure Alice was more adorable than most cats. She knew her name and responded to commands, which often made her seem like a dog. Her face was marked on one side with a blotch of white shaped like Africa. It was an asymmetry that mirrored Philippa's half-shaven head, and Philippa liked to think this asymmetry was part of what connected them. It spoke to their strong, off-kilter personalities. She had never met such a devoted and emotionally expressive cat. She chuckled and mirrored back Alice's joy.

I'll take action. What exactly did Mrs. Marvel mean? The police? Eviction? Alice wasn't an old cat, but nor was she young, and she'd been an indoor/outdoor cat for her entire life. Philippa worried she might not adjust to being indoors full-time. Then what? She could send Alice back to her parents. But that would leave Philippa alone in this garage apartment, the witchy landlady keeping constant track of her comings and goings.

She could drop out of school altogether, admit to her father he'd been right about this being the wrong choice, swallow her pride and return home, try to make amends with her mother, work for a while and reapply elsewhere for next year. Her father might find her a job at the winery, not working with customers like her mother did—Philippa didn't have the pleasing temperament for that—but there were dozens of other jobs behind the scenes she could do. There was an appeal in that. Her father would be delighted to hear she'd changed her mind. But what would her mother think? She wouldn't object, Philippa was certain of that, but would she disrespect Philippa for not toughing it out? No, that was unlikely—her mother had never before shown any sign of disapproval.

She chewed on thoughts of her mother, as she often did, puzzling over how different she had always been from the other mothers, though it had taken Philippa until seventh or eighth grade to see this. Before that she had been too young to be thinking about the nuanced differences among mothers, the variety of ways they presented themselves to the world. Before that Lu existed for Philippa as simply her main go-to person, her anchor in the world, the body that cuddled her, the voice that sang to her and consoled her and raved about her accomplishments. Everything about Lu— her soft, accepting personality; her long, shiny black hair; her radiant smile; the side of the bed she slept in; all her sweaters and jackets and the handmade mug from which she drank coffee and tea; the beads and Day of the Dead skeletons in her sewing room— all those things Philippa had thought of as her own. Everything about her mother was an extension of herself—or maybe the other way around, that she, Philippa, was an extension of Lu. She'd once read about certain animals who, when climate conditions could not support the healthy growth of a fetus, absorbed the blighted progeny back into their bodies.

But as Philippa matured and racked up enough years in school in the presence of other kids and their mothers—observing interactions at playdates and birthday parties and school assemblies and concerts and bake sales—she evaluated the other mothers and came to understand that her own mother was substantially different from those women.

Lu was nicer than the other mothers, but the difference amounted to more than that. She was a person who inhabited the world as if surviving on some nutritive gas whose properties were different from oxygen. She was looser than the other women, all of whom carried themselves with a slight rigidity, a brittleness, as if they'd constructed bamboo huts around themselves and knew a stiff wind might easily break them. The other mothers talked down to you, even when the kids became teenagers, some of them using ultra-high, chirpy, disingenuous voices as if speaking to two-year-olds with scant comprehension. By contrast, her mother spoke in a regular register that invited you in instead of pushing you away. She gave off the sense that you could ask her anything, and she would answer truthfully without taking offense, even if the answer was embarrassing. She didn't stand on ceremony and was a comedically indiscriminate hugger, sometimes flinging herself at relative strangers on a sudden wave of good feeling. Philippa thought it was funny, but George disapproved of the lack of reserve in his wife.

There was something else, too: While Lu loved talking to people one-on-one, sometimes a curious detachment surfaced in groups. If she had nothing specific to do, she often appeared dazed, as if she wasn't sure how she'd ended up where she was and what was expected of her. And sometimes, in conversation with George, Philippa watched Lu not only deferring, but vanishing into an interior world. When Philippa saw her mother in those drifty, aimless moments, she felt responsible and called upon to come to her rescue, worried Lu had been wounded by something she couldn't discuss. Philippa would sit down next to her or summon her to another room and try to make her laugh. She always wanted to ask Lu what was troubling her, but the few times she did, Lu always maintained things were fine. Maybe. Maybe not. Philippa had no way of knowing for sure.

Could she really give up and drop out now? No, probably not—she was too proud, especially when classes hadn't even begun yet. And Evan was right: It was time for her to strike out definitively, and that was impossible to do when your mother was right there in the house with you, more than willing to listen and help. She could endure here for one term at least. Then she'd know better if it was the right place to be. Meanwhile, she and Alice had each other, and they could adjust to these new digs. It would be fine. It really would be totally fine.

7

THE OTHER FIVE WOMEN were already assembled, sitting under an umbrella'd table on Lisa Blackwell's flagstone patio. It felt like a fortress out there, parapets along the perimeter giving out to an impressive valley view, perfect for sighting an advancing enemy. The women, all wearing oversize shades that lent them the air of mobsters' wives, turned their attention to Lu, clapping as if she were stepping onstage, their collective gaze so forceful it competed with the sun's glare. Their welcome seemed excessive, and it made her feel too visible, almost trapped. Usually she arrived at these monthly Saturday lunches on time, slipping in without fanfare, but with Pippa gone, her adherence to timetables had been loosening.

These women all lived in houses at one end of Sunset Loop, and though they'd been meeting for at least eight years, Lu still thought of them more as neighbors than as friends. Julie had initiated these lunches, wanting to create neighborhood cohesion. She owned the Nirvana Spa where Lu had worked years earlier, before she married George. Lu would never forget the look of surprise Julie couldn't conceal when she learned that Lu would be her neighbor. Lu had also been dismayed to see that her imperious former employer lived so close. Julie was a kind woman, but, a bit like Lu's mother, she had a habit of insisting she knew best. However, over the years both women had mostly adjusted to this reconfigured relationship, and Lu had felt flattered when Julie invited her to join the group. What kept the group together, other than the proximity of their houses, was the entrepreneurial spirit of the individual women and the fact that they were all, except for Janet, mothers. Their children were all grown, Lu the last to confront the empty nest. Now more than ever Lu marveled at how they'd all moved on from motherhood, establishing new identities.

The glass table around which they sat was spread with dishes of nuts, edamame, carrot sticks, cantaloupe slices, sushi rolls. Her hunk of Manchego was unnecessary and not something most of the women would partake of, watching their weight as they were. Lisa fussed to make room for the new plate. Lu took the empty seat and squinted against the harsh sunlight, which, only partially blocked by the umbrella, challenged her equilibrium. In her haste she'd forgotten sunglasses, which were useful for shielding so much.

"We're talking about the missing women," Alyssa said, wanting to make sure Lu felt included. She was the consummate therapist, who had returned to school after her kids left home and was close to finishing her PhD in psychology.

"Missing women?" Lu said.

"Where've you been, girl?" Gloria said, her face a mask of surprise, at once ludic and deriding. She was a businesswoman and former New Yorker with an outsize personality that took up considerable space. She, along with Julie, formed the group's power center. "Four women—young women, artists—went missing from a cabin near Mendocino. And then two more women went missing a week after that in the San Juan Islands when they went fishing."

"People think the disappearances are related," Julie said. "You know—maybe a kidnapping by the same guy. It's all over social media." Julie's signature patchouli scent was amplified by the day's heat.

"Oh," said Lu. She'd been avoiding social media for months now. She found it depressing. It made people stupid, she thought; played on their worst instincts. "Maybe I shouldn't say this, but don't women go missing all the time?"

"Well, not usually *groups* of women," said Gloria. "And usually they're able to find some evidence of wrongdoing even if they haven't found a body."

"Very strange," Lisa, the sixty-year-old hostess, said. It was clear she wanted to shift the focus of the conversation. The rough-and-tumble of raising four children had done nothing to make her less conflict aversive. Her gaze pivoted to the parapet, where a gray squirrel crouched, eyeing the food.

"It's made my female patients really anxious," Alyssa said. "They're constantly looking over their shoulders. I've been kind of skittish myself."

"I find it amazing that felons can still conceal themselves in this day and age," Gloria said.

"Felons?" Lu said. She was a step behind the others, playing catch-up. How widespread was this? Could Pippa be in danger?

"Well, I'm assuming there's some criminal behind this. Or several criminals. People don't just vanish."

"The fact that there aren't any bodies makes it worse somehow," Julie said.

Janet, always referred to as the one with a "formidable intellect," hadn't registered a reaction so far—it was unclear to Lu if Janet had known. She was a hospital administrator and a bit too serious for Lu's taste. It would have made Lu feel better about herself to know she wasn't the only one who'd been in the dark. She would have liked to ask when exactly the disappearances had happened, but she didn't want to underscore her ignorance. Had George heard about this? If he had, wouldn't he have said something?

The squirrel jumped off the wall onto the patio and skittered halfway to the table. Lisa stood. "Go! Get out!" she commanded, gesturing wildly. The squirrel stood his ground. In a snit, Lisa headed inside.

A second squirrel appeared on the wall, and the first one began making a run for the table. He leapt, landed on the table's lip. The women gasped. The squirrel couldn't maintain his grip and thudded back down to the patio. Julie and Gloria stomped toward him, and he retreated to the wall. Lisa came back out with a broom, which she jabbed toward the squirrels until they scurried over the wall and out of sight.

"I'm so sorry," Lisa said. "I can't tell you what a problem they've been since summer. They've been so bold, unnaturally bold. They come right up onto the table and steal the food. We've been putting out poison, but you can't kill an entire population of gray squirrels. If it bothers you, we can go inside."

"No, no, we're fine," the others murmured.

Lisa held up a hand. "Okay. I'm going to get our lunch. Maybe a couple of you could give me a hand? I guess someone needs to stay out here on squirrel watch. The menu is nothing fancy today—just cold poached salmon and salad. Good for our waistlines—and our hearts."

Julie laughed. "Sure. Now that we've all stuffed ourselves on nuts and cheese."

No one had sampled Lu's cheese, and the nut dish was still full.

"Save room for my chocolate almond cupcakes," Lisa called as she headed back into the house. "They're tiny, I promise. But I thought we deserved a little treat because—well, just because."

"I don't mind watching for squirrels," Lu said.

Julie and Gloria and Alyssa all rose and followed Lisa inside as if they were part of a regiment, carrying the barely touched plates of hors d'oeuvres. Lu suddenly regretted volunteering to stay out-side, as now she'd been left alone with ultra-serious Janet. Ordinar-ily Lu specialized in listening to people and drawing them out. George loved to have her at the tasting room for that purpose—putting people at ease was her great gift, he said. But there in the blinding sunlight, head filled with images of women disappearing and poisoned squirrels and concerns about Pippa, it was a challenge to generate conversation of any kind, meaningful or simply polite, particularly with Janet. Lu scanned the parapet, thinking the squir-rels might have lost interest now that the table was empty of food.

"I feel sorry for the squirrels," Lu said. "They must be starving if they're being so aggressive."

"It's an imbalance," Janet said. "One of many imbalances."

"Oh?"

"The whole human enterprise is on a collision course. Just look at the statistics. Shorter life expectancy. Lower job satisfaction. Greater income inequality. Higher rates of unemployment. Wide-spread environmental degradation. Rampant hate crimes. An over-all decline in mental health that leads to things like kidnapping, or rape, or whatever it was that happened to those women. You name it, the stats aren't good."

"I'm sure you're right." Lu fell silent. She had never been the kind of person who could talk about stats, the kind of person who would make a theoretical connection between the squirrels and dis-appearing women. These facts didn't assure her the way they seemed to assure Janet. "But, life—you know—isn't there some-thing sweet about it even when things are bad?"

Janet shrugged as if she was only stating the obvious, and the other women reappeared with plates of salmon and salad and two bottles of chilled white wine, which Lisa offered to them somewhat aggressively—*You deserve it, just a little won't hurt*—getting them all to relent except Janet, who placed a palm over her glass. "I need to be productive this afternoon."

"Any squirrels?" Lisa asked.

"No squirrels," Lu said.

"Hey, Lu," Julie said, "are you okay? You don't seem like yourself."

"I'm fine."

"How was your trip to LA last week? Did you get Pippa situated?"

"It was fine. I'm not fond of LA, but she'll probably adjust. She insisted on taking her cat."

"How unusual," Alyssa said.

Julie sighed. "They really come into their own when they go off to college—isn't it a kick to see they can actually survive without you? Maybe even thrive."

Lu imagined it was a requirement, in Julie's line of spa work, to believe in the invincibility of the human spirit and the rising arc of justice.

"Well," Gloria said, "my kids didn't always thrive, but at least they never came home. I don't know what I would have done with one of those failure-to-launch kids."

"Oh, Gloria." Julie swatted Gloria's shoulder. "Don't be so humble. Your kids are such success stories."

"Remind me what they do." Lu was sure she had learned this once, but she'd forgotten.

"A lawyer and a cancer researcher," Julie told them.

Gloria shrugged, feigning indifference.

"*Award-winning* cancer researcher! He's on Wikipedia, for Pete's sake! Hey there, girl, don't give up your bragging rights. We women need to put it out there." Julie again swatted Gloria, who mugged and pretended to cower.

Lisa bustled around the table, refilling wineglasses and wiping crumbs. Lu wondered what it would be like to tell these women the truth about dropping Pippa at school, to describe the sense of despair that had claimed her since they drove away from LA. Surely they had felt similar things themselves when their children left home—but perhaps not. Since she'd known them she hadn't borne witness to their yearning—the group had never been a place for self-disclosure.

"It's too hot for this time of year," observed Gloria. "I don't do well in the heat. I guarantee it's only going to be a matter of days before a wildfire breaks out here. They're already being hammered east of San Diego and up in Oregon."

"Come to the studio," Julie urged. "You should all come and learn to do some deep breathing. It helps you get through the heat. Or fire. Or the doldrums. Anything, for that matter. Lu? All of you. I'll give you all vouchers."

"How many times do I have to tell you—that's not my bag." Gloria unleashed another in her repertoire of pessimist's faces.

When the plates were mostly empty and second glasses of wine had been drained, Lisa went inside for the tiny chocolate cupcakes she had promised, and Janet, oblivious to niceties, took advantage of the transition to excuse herself. Lu had been hoping to join Janet in departing early—Janet always left early—but she couldn't organize herself before Janet had already made her way through the gate, and now Lisa was outside again, fluttering around the table and urging them to take cupcakes.

Lu's brain floated. The wine. The debilitating, dehydrating sun. The news about the missing women and the poisoned squirrels, the thought of imminent wildfires, the black hole of Pippa's absence. A prickling ran along the skin of her legs and arms. The fishy smell of the poached salmon had stuck in her nostrils. It occurred to her she might have been, all along, a rescue project for these ambitious women, for her former boss Julie in particular, just as she knew she'd been for George, who, in marrying his uneducated tasting room employee, had imagined he was doing something for humanity. He hadn't said so directly, but he had certainly implied it. She had always liked these women well enough, but today a touch of resentment for their wealth had crept in. She was seeing them through Pippa's eyes—she was starting to see so much through Pippa's eyes since she'd left—and Pippa would mock their privilege. But how could she resent them when she, too, was wealthy, at least by her nearly twenty-year association with George? She swallowed the cupcake whole and washed it down with wine. She thought of the yoga classes she had attended during her lunch breaks at Nirvana Spa. They had been pleasant, but not satisfying in the way gymnastics or Zumba used to be, or as invigorating as her long walks were now.

"Squirrel patrol," she said, rising from the table and going to the wall, where she sat and peered down to the other side. A squirrel was, indeed, hovering in the dry grass, waiting for his moment. Lu said nothing, briefly engaged the squirrel's startled black eye and felt his fear shivering throughout her own body, a creature chased and reviled by everyone, maligned as an inferior species. She could be that squirrel. She was him. Shivering. Unsettled.

Something Lu missed in the conversation had prompted the other women to bring out their phones, which they now passed around the circle, displaying pictures of their children. So yes, of course they were proud of their children, but that wasn't the same as missing them, and needing them as she needed Pippa as a predicate for survival. Lu tried to pay attention. She was struck by how similar the children appeared. Caucasians ranging in age from twenty-two to forty years old, heads and legs and arms all attached to torsos in the same configuration, all with upturned mouths, white teeth, some kind of head hair. She could not distinguish one from another, just as she would have had trouble picking out an individual cow, or buffalo, or shark from an in-kind grouping.

She had left her own phone back at the house, and the other women were surprised she would leave without it. They looked at her quizzically, as if she'd abandoned a limb, or worse, a part of her brain. She felt the bothersome prick of their pity. *Don't pity me*, she wanted to say. She wondered if Pippa, in a photograph, would stand out to these women, or if she, too, special as she was, would simply appear as another unidentifiable member of the human herd.

8

IT WAS ALL OVER the West Coast news. Four young women had gone missing from a cabin they'd rented on the California coast near Mendocino. They were artists in their twenties who had booked the cabin for a long weekend of artmaking.

On Monday afternoon at 2:00 P.M. the cleaner for the rental outfit arrived and found a car in the driveway. The contract stipulated that clients were supposed to vacate the premises by 11:00 A.M. The cleaning woman was annoyed; it wasn't the first time she'd had to chase out lollygaggers. She knocked loudly, but no one came to the door. Finally she entered, using her key before realizing the door was already unlocked. Inside it was a strange scene. There were small piles of clothes scattered around the living room. A family of raccoons had gotten inside. Two on the kitchen counter were ransacking the shelves; two more on the floor were scuffling and hissing. She called out to the women. No one answered. Outraged, as well as terrified by the brawling raccoons, she fled. She wasn't paid, she said later to reporters, to wrangle animals.

The police arrived by late afternoon. After trapping the raccoons, they searched the premises. They found the women's personal effects, their suitcases and backpacks and laptops and phones and art supplies, along with some of their drawings and paintings. The officers looked for signs of malign activity—evidence of violence, struggle, blood, semen—but beyond the mess made by the raccoons, there was nothing indicating malfeasance. The raccoons, they concluded, must have slipped in unnoticed when a door was left ajar. But where were the women?

Many people started to follow this story closely, amateur sleuths excited by a mystery and happy for the distraction it offered. Little intrigued the populace more than the unexplained disappearance of young women.

It was a time when so much was coming apart that, when another story emerged about more missing women, people found it unsurprising but still intriguing. They devoured the details.

A week after the artists had disappeared, two more women went missing off an island in the Pacific Northwest. Their neighbors had seen them taking a boat out to fish one warm autumn evening when the sky was clear and the water was calm and the fish were jumping. They were outdoorsy women in their mid-forties, experienced with boats and fishing. They were described by their friends as tough and beloved.

No one noticed they had not returned home until their boat, a fifteen-foot Boston Whaler, was spotted bobbing unattended in an inlet the next morning. Some seals swimming energetically around the boat aroused the attention of a person onshore and led him to investigate.

It appeared the women might have gone swimming and drowned, as pieces of their clothing had washed up on the rocks. They were experienced swimmers, but the water was cold, and it was not hard to imagine, in a place where tides and currents moved in mysterious ways, that the water had defeated them. Over the course of several days, divers were unable to locate their bodies.

There was no evidence of malintent on anyone's part. No bodies. No sign of murder or rape. An accident, it was assumed, and yet people still had the impulse to affix blame on someone. They couldn't help thinking a person might have abducted and abused these women, left them for dead. If only those seals around the boat could speak to what they'd seen.

People searched for patterns, as the press was doing, even though it was understood that no clear pattern could be found in only two events. Women going missing was a paradigm everyone already understood; such disappearances had been happening for decades, even centuries, probably since humans first evolved. People craved to know if and how these disappearances were connected. Had they been perpetrated by the same person or persons? The women were in different states, and they were of different ages, which seemed important, but it wasn't unusual for a malicious person to travel to a new state looking for victims and choosing different kinds of victims to keep law enforcement confused. The information was incomplete, and many cautioned themselves not to speculate, but they speculated anyway. As always, a few conspiracy-minded types began to put forth ideas about alien abductions. If people had known then what was known now . . .

They were limited by *umwelt*, a German word that referred to what animals perceived about their circumstances. Their perception was always limited by their sensory equipment, which was designed to favor the apprehension of certain stimuli over others. Sharks perceived smells. Bats perceived sound waves. Ticks perceived heat. And so on. In other words, people weren't equipped to notice everything. And, as it turned out, no one noticed the most important things, or considered the wilderness of possibilities.

9

GEORGE BRACED HIMSELF before he went into the house, taking a moment to admire how the many windows mirrored the setting sun, allowing himself to be infused with the feeling he'd done well for himself. Inside, she stood at the kitchen's island scrolling through her phone, glancing up as if surprised to see him. As he bent to kiss her forehead, his eyes swept the countertop and dining room table for evidence of that night's menu. He would know she was back on track when she once again began producing her trademark gourmet meals.

Not tonight. The plates held hot dogs in squishy white buns, a side dish of potato chips. A new low. Was it really too much to expect your unemployed wife to put a wholesome meal on the table? By now he'd endured over two weeks of these boxed and canned meals. Mac-and-cheese, ramen, takeout pizza. It was faux food, bad for their health and worse for his mood. The last time he'd eaten a hot dog was at a Fourth of July picnic when he was ten. It had made him sick, and he still remembered vividly the humiliation of retching into the hydrangeas while the party continued behind him. Had he never told Lu about this? In their nearly nineteen years of marriage, he realized, it hadn't come up.

He took his seat at the table and pushed his plate aside, grunting involuntarily. Even the sight of a hot dog could roil his stomach.

One of their wines, a Cabernet, had won a silver at the San Francisco International Wine Competition, a huge honor, but he didn't feel like telling her.

Lu took her seat gingerly, her scant weight perched on the edge of the chair as if she was about to leave. "You're mad?"

"No."

"I can tell you're mad."

"Okay, yes, I'm a little miffed. Are you ever going to cook again?"

"I cooked. See?" Grinning, she pointed to her hot dog, which was sliced down the middle and drowned in cheese.

"You know what I mean, Lu. This isn't cooking. This isn't even real food. A diet like this will kill us. You're such a talented cook."

"Some people eat food like this every day."

"Some people, not us. We don't."

"When I was growing up, I ate tons of food like this, and I'm perfectly healthy."

He was bereft of words. She knew exactly what he was saying, but she refused to acknowledge it.

"And by the way, I'm allergic to hot dogs."

"You never told me that."

"It never came up."

She shrugged and began to eat, posture still tentative, her face so placid he could only see it as passive-aggressive. His irritation opened him to a frank appraisal of her. It had been weeks since they'd had sex, since before Pippa left, and at this moment she was too distant and checked out for him to imagine touching her.

He got up and scraped his hot dog into the trash, returned to the table, and poured himself more wine. "Look, Lu, something has to change."

"It's just food."

"I'm not talking about food; I'm talking about *you*. You need to start doing something. If not school—I don't know—I can't—you used to love Zumba. You could do that again now that you have more time."

She raised her eyebrows, masticating her hot dog with a zeal that disgusted him.

"Okay, maybe not Zumba, but something. Maybe you should see a therapist."

Mouth still full, she exhaled loudly. For a moment he thought she was choking.

"No. Really. It might help to talk to someone. If I hadn't gone into therapy I might never have had the confidence to start the winery."

She laid down her hot dog. "Don't you see? Zumba, therapy—why do men always want quick solutions to problems that—"

"That what? Go on."

"It's all of it—the whole thing." She cradled a mass of air in both hands as if trying to shape it. "Why don't you get it? There's no instant solution for the whole grabby thing. Everyone wants things so badly—I don't get what everyone wants."

"You're not making any sense."

"How can I make sense when nothing else does?"

Hands suddenly limp, they fell audibly into her lap. Her large brown eyes appeared to shrink into dense balls about to be swallowed by quicksand.

10

HER DAYS WERE FILLED with the rush of school, but during her in-
somniac hours after midnight Philippa sat at her computer poring
over the sketches of the six women who had disappeared, the four
young ones and the two who were middle-aged, trying to see if
there was anything similar about them, something a rapist or an
abductor would have been drawn to. There was nothing obvious.
They were all people with ordinary lives as far as she could see. The
younger women, the artists, were only two or three years out of
college and were working hourly jobs to make time for their art.
One was a barista, one a receptionist in a dental office, one a phle-
botomist going through EMT training. Nina Goldstein, the youngest, was unemployed and living with her parents.

Something about the picture of Nina, the one that all the websites featured, interested Philippa almost to the point of obsession.
Nina stared into the camera as if someone had chained her there. It
would have looked like a mug shot had there not been a refrigerator in the background. She was an exceptionally pale woman, Cau-
casian, her dark brown hair flat as if painted on her head, her
mouth a severe slit, hyphen-straight and determined to stay closed,
reminding Philippa of a snake with the potential to yawn wide and
swallow a rat. She looked scary and unapproachable, venomous
really, but also like someone who knew her mind and didn't suffer

fools, a quality Philippa admired. Nina had allegedly been raped, the internet said, not once but four or five times over a period of nine months when she was attending college at Berkeley. (*You've got to stay alert and take care of yourself*, Grandma Linda warned. *There are nasty people out there*.) No one—not the college administrators, or the police, or the DA—had believed Nina's stories. They thought she was fabricating them as a way of extorting money from the men she'd accused, and they cited her need for money as a scholarship student.

Philippa felt terrible for Nina. Why hadn't the authorities believed her? Hadn't they understood how bad one rape would be, let alone more than one? She had probably been the target of men who thought she'd be an easy lay. Philippa pictured a dank fraternity room full of drunk men mocking Nina and placing bets on what kind of a fuck she would be. Philippa herself had never been around such men, but she'd heard plenty of stories. Was it possible that one of the men Nina had accused had taken revenge and was responsible for the disappearance of all the artists? Philippa hoped the police were looking into the possibility.

The middle-aged fisherwomen both lived in Seattle and co-owned a small cabin in the San Juan Islands they visited as often as they could. One of them worked as a financial advisor; the other worked in the insurance industry. The photographs of them made them look like twins, both with long, narrow faces, close-cropped hair, a hint of defiance. It wasn't clear if they were a couple or just good friends. Philippa speculated that these women held something in common with Nina Goldstein—a *don't mess with me* quality. Was that why they'd been raped or abducted, because their defiance irked certain guys?

As she reread the stories of these women on different websites, she noticed something else. All of them, it seemed, were leading dual lives—they had day jobs that were at odds with their dream lives. They hadn't settled into a singular life that suited them. There had to be so many people like them. Maybe Philippa herself would end up in a life like that.

The more she thought of these things in the oneiric light of wee-hours LA, mainlining the dull thrum of traffic, the more strange ideas came to her. Maybe the disappearances had nothing to do with being abducted or raped. Maybe men had nothing to do with it at all. It was possible it was something else entirely.

11

THE PARKING LOT at Lupita's Place, Lu's mother's restaurant in Redding, was packed with cars and long-haul trucks, so it suddenly occurred to Lu she might have to wait for a table. How foolish to have driven three hours without telling Linda she was coming, but the need to talk had gotten the best of her. The hostess stand was unattended. Lu spotted Linda on the far side of the restaurant, talking to a family seated at one of the round tables.

A formidable woman. You wouldn't have known she was sixty-three. Her glossy, still-black hair fell below her shoulders; her complexion was remarkably unwrinkled; and she held herself with the confidence of an empress. At home she dressed in jeans and T-shirts, but at the restaurant she always wore what had become her uniform: a brightly colored full skirt and an embroidered blouse. She wanted her role as proprietress with Mexican ancestry to be unmistakable. A couple of the longtime employees, Tomás and Adriana, waved their greetings at Lu, then Sofia swung by for a hug.

"Three people out sick today," she told Lu. "Your mother—she do it all. Look at her go." They both laughed and watched the whirlwind of Linda, a quality that was especially on exhibit today. "I tell your mother you're here."

A moment later, Linda surged through the double doors from the kitchen, skirt swishing, ponytail swinging, eyes on Lu. Their embrace unleashed a potpourri of Linda's scents: red sauce, sweat, aloe vera lotion.

"You should have told me you're coming. We're crazy today. Three people out sick. And Carlos came in late because his car broke down. I've been busting my butt since sunrise. You drive three hours without telling me?"

"Good to see you too, Mom."

"I'm sorry, honey. I'm glad to see you—you know I always love to see you. I've just been stressed recently because of the heat—and those goddamn fires just north of the border. As if California doesn't have enough fire of its own—we don't need it creeping down from Oregon. Take a seat and I'll join you when I get a minute. You want the special—chicken burrito?"

"Sure, whatever." Linda returned to the kitchen, and Lu, feeling chided and sheepish and overly dependent, took a small table for two, one of the few remaining. Adriana brought water, and they chitchatted about their kids. Every time Lu spoke to the employees she felt bad that she'd never learned Spanish. When she was growing up, Linda had tried to speak Spanish at home, but Lu had been resistant, wanting to fit in with her American classmates. By now, she'd even forgotten the few years of high school Spanish she eventually took.

When Adriana left, Lu scanned the clientele for people she knew. No one. This was no longer the home it had been throughout her childhood, first as a taco truck, then in the more intimate space on Delmore Road, where it became well known for serving simple, wholesome dishes enhanced by Linda's unflagging hospitality. From fifth grade through high school, Lu used to hang out there after her gymnastics classes, logging more hours at the restaurant than at the Nest. She missed that old location on Delmore Road, but if her mother did, she didn't show it.

What Lu didn't like about the "new" place—Linda had

relocated twelve years ago, so it wasn't really new, but Lu still thought of it that way—was that it was too cavernous; the Mexican décor Linda had collected over the years—the Day of the Dead drawings, the tin ornaments, the carved wooden animals, the retablos—all faded into insignificance in the shadows. Today Linda had the AC cranked much too high, and as Lu sat there shivering, she couldn't stop thinking about the missing women. She'd done some internet research to get up to speed. It was true what the luncheon ladies had said; speculation was rampant. People assumed the women had been raped and murdered since no ransom notes had appeared. Apparently George had heard about them too, but he didn't seem disturbed by the news.

"It's gone viral on social media," Lu had told him.

"Short news cycles. People will forget soon enough."

She doubted it was something most women would forget when it exacerbated an already lively sense of danger. "Don't mention it to Pippa," she cautioned George. "I don't want her to worry."

"Why would I tell Pippa? But I'm sure she knows anyway— she's on the internet all the time. Wait—you're not suggesting we should try to protect her from bad news, are you? She's an adult now, on her own. Give her more credit."

"But something like this. I just—"

"Pippa's fine."

But how could he say that? They'd heard so little from Pippa.

Linda made her way back across the floor to Lu's table, hips swaying and skirt eddying as if she was solo ballroom dancing, aware of the eyes following her. Broad-faced and beaming, she was a handsome woman, made more so by confidence.

Linda sat. "What's up, Lulu?"

Lu blinked. Her mother hadn't called her Lulu in years. Lu's palate swelled as she tried to fend off tears. Her mother saw in an instant: Lu had come here to be coddled and told all would be fine. But at forty-five, she was much too old for coddling, and what could Linda say that would really help her? Linda probably had no idea what Lu was feeling—the restaurant had kept her busy so she'd never had to face the endless, empty, ill-defined hours of the day Lu now faced.

Lu shrugged. "I thought it was time to visit."

Linda squinted. "Something is up."

"We took Pippa to school a few weeks ago."

"Ah, so you're lonely?"

"I'm fine."

"Girl, don't bullshit me."

Linda's expressive black eyebrows, given to motion like speaking lips, remained raised as Lu narrated how Pippa had insisted on taking the cat, and how addled George had been during the drive, and how Mrs. Marvel had turned out not to be who they'd expected her to be. Linda laughed, but she wasn't deceived by the diversion.

Adriana laid down Lu's chicken burrito. "Enjoy!" she said, waving as she disappeared, not wanting to interpose herself between mother and daughter. Lu turned to the food, not particularly hungry but grateful for the focus it provided. Linda filched a chip.

"New chef," Linda said. "I hope it's okay. Let me know."

Lu ate, and Linda watched her eat, periodically stealing a chip.

"Go on, have them all. It's too much food for me," Lu said. She ate with a keen awareness of her mother's assessing gaze.

"So, now's your moment, right?" Linda said. "Now you get to be Lu. You finish school. You build something great."

"Oh, Mom, what is it with you and George—you both place so much importance on school."

"Because school is important! I wish I'd had the good sense to go, but after your father died I had to keep us afloat. I didn't have the time or money to go to school. But you, girl, have both."

Lu sighed. "You and George are ganging up on me. You did fine and you never finished school."

"You have no idea. I had to bust my butt. Getting a loan for this restaurant without a college degree wasn't easy, let me tell you." Linda brushed chip crumbs from the table and laid down her forearms. "Okay, so maybe school isn't the right thing for you, but you have to make something to be proud."

"I made Pippa. I'm proud of her."

"But you're done with that now. It's time to move on and focus on yourself."

"You act like it's so easy. There it is, ta-da, the new me. It doesn't just happen instantly."

"Oh, Lulu. You could do so much."

She didn't get it, why everyone wanted things for her that she didn't want for herself. Why did they keep urging her to make and build things? Things, things, things. Wasn't it enough to just *be*? She'd find the right life eventually, but she needed time. She didn't need everyone telling her what to do. This was one difference between herself and Linda as mothers: Lu had never pressed Pippa to do something she didn't want to do. She'd made it a matter of principle not to judge Pippa's choices. She wondered now if that approach had been wrong. If she had weighed in on the college choice, Pippa might not have gone so far away.

"George thinks I should go into therapy."

"Maybe he's right. You want to be a hippo for the rest of your life?" Linda said. "Wallow around? Eat my burritos? Drink George's wine? You need to get your own thing going. What if George leaves you? You never know."

Lu laid down the remaining third of her burrito, already sick with the deadweight of refried beans and meat. Perhaps Pippa was onto something with her preference for vegetables. Lu missed the empty space in her gut. "He's not going to leave me," she said.

She had always felt secure with George, even through the recent tension. She had fallen in love with his steadfast paternal aura, his eagerness to protect her. He had always been all-in with the project of family. It had never, ever crossed her mind that he might leave her, despite their occasional impasses. But Linda's words carried weight. It suddenly seemed credible that George might leave her now that Pippa was gone, their family blasted apart. The thought was chilling. Marrying George had catapulted her into a life of privilege. Without him it would be hard to support herself. All her job experience, with the exception of the winery gig, had happened years ago. And they loved each other, of course, didn't they? You could have fights and still love each other.

"Why are you always so suspicious of George?"

"You know I think the world of George." This wasn't entirely true. Linda and George got along perfectly well, even admired each other as fellow business owners, but Linda had never fully trusted him, being wary of all men with large bank accounts. "*You* might even leave *him*."

"Why would I leave him—that would be idiotic." Of course she'd thought of that, but as an outlandish idea. She'd been with him far too long for any other life to feel possible, despite the fact that they didn't always see eye to eye.

"Okay. You know best. But you're gonna get to be an old lady and have regret. I'm telling you."

"The burrito isn't very good, by the way."

Linda recoiled.

"You asked," Lu said.

Minutes later Linda was summoned to the kitchen, and Lu left without saying goodbye. She would text her apologies later.

It was late afternoon by the time she got home. She collapsed on the chaise in the solarium, one of her favorite locations in the house, its southern exposure offering a cascade of warmth all day. She stretched her bare legs in front of her so her toes, through the fringe of her half-closed lids, appeared distant as stars.

Linda's strong opinions had colonized Lu's brain. She should have known that would happen—it happened whenever they talked. It was almost as if Linda had been an invisible witness at the dinner table and heard her conversations with George, seen their perfunctory togetherness. Pippa, it was now clear, had been central in stitching them together as a threesome, centering their attention and making them laugh and cry together. Now they had been reduced to being only a couple, and a couple was not a family. In George's company Lu missed Pippa more than when she was alone.

She stared at the phone resting on her belly, dying to text Pippa, dying to beg her to come home. Exerting great self-control, she laid the phone on the floor and shoved it out of reach. She couldn't risk alienating Pippa. She wished Pippa was more in touch, but maybe her infrequent texts indicated she was happy—and what more could a mother wish?

Meeting George had been so exciting. He was even-keeled and took an interest in her right away, courting her in an old-fashioned way with roses and chocolates and candlelit dinners at expensive restaurants. She had seen he would be an excellent father. Beyond his steadiness—and financial stability—he was a lover of life, knowledgeable about so much, and an excellent teacher. Her sense of him was right—he had turned out to be a good father, introducing Pippa to music and art, taking her to plays and concerts and drumming clinics in San Francisco, exposing her to all sorts of things Lu was unacquainted with.

Would George really want to leave now, as Linda had suggested? She wondered if things would be different if she'd had more than one child. They had tried for a few months, and it hadn't happened right away. In that time she began thinking about the reality of another child, a baby who would demand attention and create a rift between her and Pippa. She couldn't imagine she would love another child as much as she loved Pippa. Finally she said to George, "I don't need another. I'm happy with just Pippa."

She hated feeling so lacking in energy—energy had always been a defining element of her personality. She thought nostalgically of the years she'd spent immersed in gymnastics. Her love for the sport had begun when she was five years old and her mother enrolled her in a class at the local community center in hopes of channeling some of Lu's superfluous energy. Throughout elementary and middle school and early high school, gymnastics had been her greatest source of pleasure. She was good at it—everyone told her so.

In her mind she was still that nimble gymnast. She still remembered the delicious otherworldly feeling of jettisoning her body aloft, muscles calibrating just so to execute a flip, the hush that would overtake her brain, the annihilating focus, the pell-mell rush of the world ceasing. As soon as she landed, the world would claim her again, and then she lived like an addict waiting for the opportunity to do it again. There was nothing she had found since then that matched that sense of all the rhythms of body, earth, and air locking into place, perfectly synchronized. She closed her eyes, trying to ignore the intransigent lump of burrito in her digestive tract, picturing a younger version of herself cartwheeling across the lawn.

Could she still do a cartwheel? It had been years since she'd tried. She dragged herself from the chaise and opened the door to the adjacent lawn. The scents out there were surprisingly strong. A trace of eucalyptus wafted up the hillside, though those trees, a fire hazard, had been chopped down the previous spring; another scent of rich loam drifted up from the watered grass, which glowed an impudent green in the lengthening afternoon sunlight. They shouldn't have been irrigating the lawn, and they paid a huge water-usage premium to do so, but George argued that watering helped keep the house safe from fire, and he shelled out the high fines without remorse or shame.

She took a few running steps and launched herself, stretching her hands above her head then down to the moist lawn, sucking in her stomach and whirling upside-down, legs sketching a circle in the air around a pivot point in her belly, so she spun as precisely as a human Ferris wheel. As she landed, she took an extra step, a few points' deduction, but she didn't fall. She looked around at the trembling landscape, amazed she'd pulled it off, proud. Maybe she could get back in shape again and be a credible middle-aged gymnast. A slight twinge bothered her left shoulder, but nothing serious.

She headed back inside and fell asleep on the chaise.

12

THE DAY'S SUBJECT in Philippa's zoology class was sponges, *phylum Porifera*, sessile creatures without hearts, or brains, or mouths, or muscles, or nervous systems, or circulatory systems, but still very much alive, animals that routinely repaired damage done to their bodies and that could reproduce either sexually or asexually. They were the first animals to appear in the fossil record, Professor Mulligan said, and unlikely candidates for extinction.

Professor Mulligan was a gauntly athletic man in his mid-thirties with narrow shoulders and a pointy face that suggested a difficult passage through the birth canal. His neck and forearms were spattered with patches of white, and he was given to a series of nervous tics—ear-pulling and knuckle-cracking—that made him seem like a species unto himself. For all his oddities, Philippa found him compelling. His energy burbled like a Yellowstone paint pot, and his gaze was unusually directional. In his passion for the subject, he danced around the podium, arms circling like conductors' batons, locks of his silky hair flopping. Philippa tried to guess, if Mulligan were really dancing, what the soundtrack would have been. Something syncopated. His rambunctiousness reminded her a little of her ferret Emilio, whom she still missed. It would have been Philippa's preference to sit closer, in the front row if possible, so she could get a better view of Mulligan, and it would be easier to ask questions, but she had to adjust to sitting in the corner at the back of the large raked hall, Alice tucked as inconspicuously as possible on her lap, wearing collar and leash. The leash was a temporary solution until Alice got used to being left alone. Meanwhile, Philippa had been bringing her to all her classes. At first Alice flopped over and refused to move when the leash went on, but more recently, true to her dog-like tendencies, she trotted alongside Philippa on the sidewalks and campus walkways. In zoology class and in 20th Century History, both large lectures, it was easy to conceal Alice. Philippa made sure to arrive early, situating herself at the back before the professor arrived. So far, the professors hadn't noticed. But Introduction to Music Theory had only forty students, and the required writing class only twenty-five, so Alice's presence would be obvious. Philippa had had to explain the situation to those professors on the first day, asking permission to bring Alice. She assured them she was making "alternative arrangements," and they reluctantly acquiesced.

The lights dimmed for a film. Philippa stroked Alice's back aggressively, afraid the sudden darkness would alarm her—she'd been more skittish than usual since arriving in LA. The screen at the front of the hall exploded with a parade of sponges in every imaginable color—lurid purple, fire-engine red, neon yellow, pink, royal blue, celadon. A candy-land of color, pure child fantasy material. The shapes were familiar and unfamiliar, half-resembling shapes from the terrestrial world: honeycomb, gingerroot, baskets, tubes waiting to be assembled into something, choruses with gaping mouths, worms, clusters of carrots and turnips. Bound to their rocks, they swayed slightly with the ocean currents, remarkably synced to the film's soundtrack of cellos, horns, piccolos, a harp, each instrument allotted a solo moment in a symphonic composition that defied easy labeling, though it seemed to have its roots in the soundtrack to *Fantasia*. It almost seemed as if the instruments were a form of speech, ventriloquizing the sponges themselves.

She loved these sponges. She loved their sessile nature. She loved saying the word *sessile*—Professor Mulligan's word—over and over in her head. She imagined that sponges, attached to their rocks without brains or nervous systems, were worry-free. It occurred to her that the life of a sponge was almost ideal.

A raucous sound erupted in the row in front of her, a heavy metal notification tune coming from someone's phone. A guy fumbled in his backpack to silence it, but too late—startled, Alice had leapt to the floor and dashed beneath the seats, releasing her trademark howl. She reappeared on the steps and, leash dragging, skittered down toward the front of the hall, her meows morphing into an impressive aria. One girl screamed; most of the students laughed. "It's a cat!" rippled from person to person. "It's a cat!"

Philippa pushed past the people in her row and ran down the steps in quick pursuit, though she was no match for Alice.

The film paused. The lights came on. Alice had reached the bottom of the steps and was prancing back and forth behind the podium, in search of an exit. Professor Mulligan stepped on Alice's leash, grabbed it, and held it taut, looking down at Alice. "Well, hello there," he said. "Welcome to Animal Behavior 101."

The class laughed. Philippa stood a few feet from Mulligan in a fervid swamp of humiliation.

"This would be your cat?" Mulligan said.

Philippa nodded and lifted Alice.

"She?" Mulligan asked.

Philippa nodded.

"Is she enrolled?"

Snickers and hoots. What could she say?

"This is zoology—all animals, no matter what phyla, are

welcome. But I hate to share the limelight when I'm teaching, so if you bring her—no more interruptions."

"Right. Yes. I promise."

"What's her name?"

"Alice."

"Welcome, Alice. Maybe Alice can learn something from this class about her fellow critters. Now, take a seat, you two, and let's get back to sponges."

Philippa collapsed into the empty seat Mulligan pointed to in the front row. She clutched Alice, weak with embarrassment, glad when the lights went down again and the film resumed. She prayed Alice would stay quiet and was relieved when Alice's slumbering bulk grew heavy in her lap.

13

THE NAMEPLATE ON his office door read: DAR MULLIGAN, Assistant Professor, Office Hours: T/Th 3–5. She knocked lightly, twice, and there he was, opening the door, appearing not the least bit surprised to see her. He'd been acting friendly in class—which was why she had dared to come. He brought treats for Alice, and he sometimes turned to them in the front row to ask: *What is the feline point of view on this?* Once, he lifted Alice from Philippa's lap and brought her to the table beside his podium, stroking her for a full fifteen minutes while he lectured.

Blinding sunlight streamed through the dusty widow, so bright it seemed to bleach everything in the room, including Mulligan himself. It was a small office on the second floor of one of the science buildings; the large window giving out to a courtyard somewhat compensated for its small size. Inside, the room was a total hodgepodge, his computer surrounded by stacks of file folders and papers, two bookshelves curiously empty, framed posters leaning against the walls waiting to be hung, featuring pictures of large game animals. Zebras. Lions. Elephants. Next to Mulligan's desk was a child's plastic blue-and-orange basketball hoop no taller than four feet.

"Welcome to my world," he said, guiding her inside and taking a seat in a noisy chair on casters. "Always on its way to becoming. Never arriving."

She looked around for a place to sit. There was only one other chair in the room, and it was occupied by a tattered gray backpack and a cracked mug.

"Oh, sorry." He rose to clear the chair. "Housekeeping isn't my strong suit."

He sat back down, crossing an ankle over his knee, then recrossing the other way, cracking his knuckles, his chair in creaking syncopation with each of his movements. He seemed more nervous than she. No, she decided, he was hyperactive, a bit like her mom, who could never sit still. She tried not to stare at the large patch of white skin on his neck. It almost gleamed there in the sunlight, becoming so much more prominent than it was in the dark lecture hall.

"Feel free to let Alice off her leash."

Philippa unhooked it, and Alice began her sniffing routine, checking the room's perimeter with her nose like a methodical forensic investigator.

"She's probably going to embarrass me by unearthing old sandwiches." He opened one of the drawers of his file cabinet and brought out a miniature basketball that he cradled in both hands. "Try to ignore me—restless hands, you know? So, what brings you here?"

She should have planned for this and brought some kind of question relevant to the class, but she had come here on such a sudden impulse it had never occurred to her. For several weeks she'd been walking around the campus taking note of how different she was from the other girls. They were all vacuum-packed into spandex and Lycra and thought nothing of revealing great swaths of

thigh and belly cleavage; they shrieked and squealed at the smallest
of surprises; they talked nonstop. She wasn't about to trade in her
jeans and work shirt for spandex, or develop a gabby, histrionic
interpersonal style, and she had to believe there were some people
out there who could appreciate her choices, but they were proving
hard to find. She had certainly "met" plenty of people since coming
to school, and she'd followed up with a few of them. There was
another drummer in her music theory class named Joel, and they'd
made plans to practice together, but he kept rescheduling. There
was a girl in her writing class, a dancer named Alix, whom she'd
had coffee with once, but Philippa could see that wasn't going anywhere because Alix was weirdly obsessed with spotting movie stars.
And there was a riveting guy who always sat at the edge of the history lecture hall, clearly an iconoclast, and she'd been eyeing him
until she noticed he was concealing a phone behind his notebook to
watch movies during class. Professor Mulligan was the only person
she had met so far who gave her a positive gut feeling.

"I've been thinking, wondering . . . I don't know, about, like,
what made you want to study animals? I mean . . ."

When he grinned he looked like a kid, and his silky hair underscored that impression. He tossed the mini basketball into the hoop
and let it bounce lightly across the floor. "Have a go, if you want."
He nodded to the ball, which had rolled—*ba-ba-ba-b-b-b-b*—to
her feet.

"I'm good."

"Okay, so if you're like me, the real question is, what else would
you study? I've loved animals since I was a young boy. When I was
in high school I wanted to be David Attenborough, you know, the
guy who made all those movies?"

"I *loved* those movies." She had seen them with her father when
she was in middle school and had particularly enjoyed the one

about gorillas. She loved the way Attenborough couched himself in the bushes so the gorillas wouldn't see him and whispered to the microphone and camera in his low, gentle voice. "Do you think the animals really didn't know he was there?"

"I think they knew—they'd just adjusted to him being there. It takes a lot of getting them acclimated before you make a movie like that. At some point I realized I could never be as still and patient as Attenborough was."

"He was brave too—you know, getting so close."

"That too. But I got lucky. Halfway through college a friend invited me on a trip to New Zealand and we went diving and I fell in love with cephalopods. You know, octopuses. I've been obsessed ever since. They look you in the eye as if they're really sizing you up. It conveys such a sense of sophisticated awareness that I couldn't stop thinking about what they might be thinking. And then I began extrapolating to other animals, wondering what they were thinking too. That's what I've been doing ever since, thinking about animal consciousness."

"I didn't know that was something you could actually study. You know, scientifically."

"It's not the most employable choice a zoologist could make. Lots of scientists think studying animal consciousness is a bunch of malarkey. Impossible to verify and all. But some philosophers are all in."

"Like whales, maybe? When I was a kid I was really into whales and their songs. Well, I still am."

"There you go—they're haunting, aren't they? You can't hear those songs without believing they're coming from a fairly developed level of consciousness."

Shouts were coming from the courtyard. A maintenance cart rumbled by. Alice's too-long claws ticked across the floor. Philippa loved being there in that light-flooded sanctuary of a room, talking to this geeky professor. Nervous as he was, he soothed her. She tapped her thigh reflexively. *Dum-dum-da-dum.* He made her feel like talking.

"I've always liked animals I can hold and talk to. Cats and dogs and mice and snakes. I used to have a ferret, Emilio, until my dad made me get rid of him. He thought Emilio was too rambunctious."

"Stealing keys and stuff?"

"Yeah. And messing things up. How did you know?"

Mulligan nodded. "I had a ferret once too. Same story." He went silent and cracked his knuckles again—*krk-krk*—and passed a thumb over the white patch on his forearm.

Alice had come to inspect the ball. Philippa picked it up, tossed it toward the hoop, missed. The prick of humiliation passed quickly. "I've never been a big sports person."

"Well, this isn't exactly sport—it's more like a way of assuaging my hyperactivity."

She floated, light-headed and beginning to sweat in the surfeit of sunlight. How could it be that she was in her professor's office listening to him casually discuss his hyperactivity? She felt as if she'd arrived in some occult alternative world she had never known existed. New, but not unsafe. Emboldening.

"I wanted a dog, 'cause, well, dogs—but my dad said no to a dog too—that's when I got Alice."

"You think you might want to be a zoologist?"

She hesitated, feeling the smart probe of his gaze. "Maybe. Yeah. But I like music too—I play drums, and I'm kind of interested in composing. Cindy Blackman—you know, the drummer?—I always kind of wanted to be like her. I saw her give a drumming clinic in San Francisco once and, well, she was awesome." She laughed—he probably thought music was trivial. "I know music isn't, like, going to save the world or anything."

He watched her. "You're a freshman, right?"

She nodded.

"You've got plenty of time."

She only now could name the unusual thing about him: the way he veered from serious to playful and back without warning. It caught her by surprise but also gave her permission to be as she was.

"I'm trying to be open-minded, but every class I go into it seems like the professors—not you, but the others—want you to think like they do. As if their way of thinking is the only way to understand the world. Like they're proselytizing. In history they want you to think about wars and treaties and all the great leaders and isms. In my writing class the teacher goes on and on about how important it is to know how to argue persuasively, as if we're supposed to spend our lives convincing people of things. She acts as if there are only two sides of every question, never anything in between. I don't want to spend my entire life arguing."

"Of course you don't. What a nightmare." He laughed. "We're a sorry species, we humans. I'm not plugging zoology—it's not for everyone by a long shot—but I will say that you don't have to look too far to see that most humans are greedy and dishonest and vain, in a way that animals aren't. Animals are just themselves, going about the business of surviving. And in the process, they're noticing a heck of a lot about the world around them. More than most humans."

He reached down to pick up Alice, who recognized his scent and liked him and didn't resist. She situated herself in his lap, and he stroked her back in the emphatic way that was his habit.

"Am I right, Alice?"

Alice's purr roared the affirmative.

~

She texted her mother three lines of happiness emojis—which seemed less needy than words—and Lu texted back a series of stars and balloons and fireworks, an odd but reasonable response. Then Philippa walked home in a froth of happiness, unworried about her difference from the other female students she passed, immersed in layers of city sound, which were usually cacophonous but now blended with one another into a sonorous, rhythmic symphony— *shoo-woo, shoo-woo, whah-whah-whah, ticketa-ticketa-ticketa-thwat, ga-ga-ga, boo-boo, schwoo-woo-woo, tsk-tskkk.* Triplets. Four-four. Sirens and car alarms and backhoes and barking dogs, all fitting together as if Cindy Blackman herself was conducting from on high.

14

HE HAD ACCEPTED the invitation—why wouldn't he—and they nailed down a date and time. He didn't mention the visit to Lu, except to say he wouldn't be home for dinner. She took it in stride, didn't ask why, didn't seem to care what he was up to these days.

It was dark when he drove up the unlit dirt driveway, so he couldn't see much of the five acres of former pastureland, only the shadowy suggestion of trees to one side. The building itself, a classic rust-red barn that reminded him of those he knew from New England, stood in an island of pulsing light, stepping up his heart.

He parked next to her Honda Fit—a car that seemed much too small for a woman of her stature—and stepped out with the bottle of wine he'd brought, his top-of-the-line Cabernet, the one that had just won a distinguished prize. He knew nothing and everything. He was innocent as a baby. Marley was much too smart for him, much too tall, much too independent and opinionated. Though attractive, she wasn't his type. But they could be friends, couldn't they? As fellow aficionados of art they were perfectly matched as friends.

They greeted each other with a hug, something they'd never done at the winery, but it seemed justified by the months of conversation they'd shared. She wore flat ballet-type slippers, but still the height difference between them made him feel short. He wasn't a short man, but she was still taller than he. He laughed a bit to elide the awkwardness.

He took in the studio: one area for living, another for painting; the flickering candlelight; the vaulted ceiling; the wood floors; the white walls; circulating scents of wax and lavender. An elegance born of simplicity. When he spotted the table laid out with bread, cheese, and wine, an audible click went off in his head.

He thought guiltily of Lu—her compact, athletic body, which was so familiar to him, too familiar, recently slightly off-putting—even as he tried to imagine the fuller body beneath Marley's layers of loose fabric. She wore purple tonight, a dazzling color, a departure from her usual red and orange palette. The idea of removing his own clothes was nothing short of horrifying—he'd been developing an unsightly paunch, and it had been years since anyone other than Lu had seen him naked.

They sat around the small table, and she held up a bottle of Petite Syrah from another winery, showing him the label. An esteemed winery, much bigger than his own. "I wouldn't presume to serve you your own wine."

"Save this for later," he said, laying down the bottle he'd brought. "I think you'll like it."

She uncorked her bottle, waving off his offer of help. It was stupid to feel repudiated by her refusal of assistance, but he did; she seemed to be telling him he was old-fashioned. She was perhaps a decade younger than he, a little older than Lu. Unlike Lu, Marley had been living on her own for years, supporting herself. He had no idea if she'd ever been married. Few men, he speculated, would be able to endure being paired with a woman who exuded such power, the very power that intrigued him.

They sipped the wine—impressive body and structure, but perhaps a tad too fruity for his taste. She handed him a slice of warm baguette spread with cheese, their fingers touching ever so briefly. In the silence that followed he could hear her breathing. She raised her glass to sip, casting a furtive glance at him as if peering at him from under a table. He felt himself getting hard.

She started to speak, gesturing to canvasses she'd laid against the wall, most of them six to ten feet tall.

"Some people do encaustic work on wood, but I prefer the texture of a canvas. Beeswax is the essential element. Some people use other concoctions, but beeswax is the best . . ."

She rose and went to a long rectangular table displaying her tools. The vat and burner where she melted the wax. Brushes and various metal tools for applying and shaping the wax. She held them up one by one. A heat gun to keep the wax soft and extend her working time. Powdered pigments and oil paint for color. Gold leaf, which, she said, when applied judiciously, could make a painting pop.

He sat in stunned silence, sipping too quickly. It was like a gallery talk. He'd wanted to know more about her work but wasn't prepared for this.

"As for inspiration—that's a hard one. I often begin with something as simple as a color or a shape, and that takes me down a certain path. It's almost like being hypnotized—I'm led by some force I can't explain. Only later, when I'm closing in on the completion of a painting, do I begin to sense what it is I'm aiming for.

"In my earlier work I felt I had to know exactly what I was doing at the outset—you know, that beginner's curse—and that constrained me. Would you be interested in seeing some of those early pieces, to see the difference?"

"Of course," he lied. What else could he say?

She disappeared to a storage area behind a partition. He poured himself more wine. Despite the candles and the wine, this was not a seduction. It was a sales pitch. Sex appeared to be far from her mind; seeing that, he realized he had not been ambivalent after all. If she had been ready to have sex, he would have been right there with her, rising above the embarrassment of nakedness and guilt about Lu. How could his reading of the situation have been so off the mark? He'd never been rejected by a woman, ever. Technically this wasn't a rejection because he hadn't made a move, but . . . Humiliation overshadowed his shame.

She reappeared, guiding two smaller paintings in his direction with her foot. She stood in front of him, balancing the canvasses on either side of her. "You see how stiff these are? These were made during my Schnabel period. For a while I even tried to copy his broken plate pieces, but that turned out to be more challenging than you'd think."

He tried to evaluate what he was looking at, riots of color that might have been good or bad—he couldn't possibly judge in his current state of mind.

"They're so constipated compared to my recent work. You can see the difference, can't you?"

He couldn't summon a single comment. She wouldn't stop talking, and he felt like a prisoner, sentenced to listen until she released him. Her body morphed in front of his eyes, her bare upper arms sagging, her neck becoming elongated and stringy; beneath her loose trousers he saw she was knock-kneed. She wasn't fit, not like Lu.

"I have to go," he said suddenly, glancing at his watch without seeing the time. "Lu is expecting me." He feigned being in a terrible rush, laying down his still-full glass, standing. "It's such wonderful work, really original." His disingenuousness was obvious, but she was gracious, thank god, and made no attempt to stall him.

He practically ran to his car, scattering gravel underfoot, aware of being an unwelcome disturbance in the wild velvet night. She stood at the window waving. Did she not understand what had happened—or was she trying to smooth things over? He couldn't bring himself to return the wave. It was unlikely she could see him anyway.

15

IT WAS DARK, and she had fallen asleep in bed fully clothed, and George was shaking her awake. She must have been sleeping for hours. His face looked unusually pale, alarmed. "What's wrong?" she said. "Is everything okay?"

Remaining silent, he nudged her to one side, making room for himself, his body hot. He lifted her shirt, popping one of its buttons, impatient, cupping both her small breasts, digging beneath her bra without bothering to unhook it, tonguing one nipple, squeezing the other one hard with his fingers.

"Wait," she said. She wasn't in the mood, but his determination was clear. She raised herself to unhook her bra, tossing it to the floor along with her shirt.

It was like teenage sex—his sudden urgency, so little regard for her clothing—but after twenty years he knew what she liked and, though her mind said no, her nipples thrilled to his touch.

"Not so hard," she whispered, and he shifted a hand to her trousers, unzipped, wormed his hand in to discover she was already gushing. Now he clawed, desperate to remove her pants and his. "Slow down. It's not a race," but for him it appeared to be. She helped him out with the pants. Then he was on top and entering, not waiting for her to come first as he usually did.

Done in a flash, his entire body went limp. He laid his head on her chest, pressing his forehead down to her sternum. "Amen."

"What about me?" Though did she really want to come? She wasn't sure. The need, weak to begin with, was fading quickly.

He lifted his head to look at her, a helix of alarm in his gray eyes. Nodding, he rolled off and nestled by her side, curling around her as if she was the rock to his barnacle. He moved his hand around the exposed folds of her crotch in halfhearted circles, his head throbbing against her rib cage. He gulped air. She didn't need to see his eyes to know he was crying. Confusion displaced her arousal.

"What?" she said.

It took a minute or so before he gained control of his breath. "I need to tell you . . ."

She couldn't possibly have known what those words meant, but the context made it clear. He wouldn't look at her. She pushed it away, this thing her mother had suggested might happen.

"I'm sorry I've been so hard on you. I need your help," he said, and the tears flowed again.

Pain radiated through her shoulder as she rose. Doing the cartwheel had been stupid—she would never be a gymnast again, who was she kidding. She left him and moved through the dark bowels of the house to Pippa's room. How unusual for him not to have turned on the lights.

She lay on Pippa's wrinkled, unmade bed, door ajar, light off, ambient light from the hallway illuminating the Dragon Lady's smile. It wasn't long before he came to find her. "Come back to bed," he said quietly from the doorway.

It sickened her to think of what he would say, his justifications, his apologies. She didn't care to know who the other woman was.

"Please," he said.

How forlorn he looked. How undone. He disappeared down the hallway and entered their bedroom again. A succession of fraught minutes passed, the swarm of his need careering between the two rooms. Okay. Okay.

By the time she arrived in their bedroom his mood had shifted. Desperation still leaked from his eyes, but he was making a credible effort to conceal it. He beckoned her into bed, and she relented, situating herself on her back to protect her shoulder.

"We never had sex, I promise—I love you, you know that, right? We're going to be fine without Pippa. It's going to be better than ever for us. Let's push reset and start again."

His palm circled her bare belly, an irritant. She seized his wrist.

16

ON WEDNESDAY, the day after visiting Professor Mulligan's office hours, and after a long phone call with Grandma Linda, in which she'd told her about the class and about how great Mulligan was, and Grandma Linda, opinionated as always, advised her to be a scientist, not an artist, Philippa went to zoology class with more enthusiasm than usual, a lightness in her step and a glittery feeling in her chest. Still, she wasn't prepared for Mulligan's hearty welcome: "Hey there!" She ducked into her seat in the front row, hoping none of the other students had noticed. "He likes you," her regular seatmate, a pink-haired Asian American woman, whispered.

"I think he just likes Alice," Philippa said.

But the girl was right, Professor Mulligan definitely did seem to like her, and it was surprising and wonderful to have someone like him single her out. She hadn't noticed him paying special attention to any of the other students.

"Okay, let's do a little thought experiment," he began. He perched on the edge of the table beside his podium, his long legs swinging, an appealing geek in a plaid, short-sleeved polyester shirt, his nod to professional attire. It was his custom to start the class by throwing out a question or an observation that allowed him to riff on some little-known aspect of animal behavior. "Let's say I blindfold you and take you on a helicopter ride for a couple of hours, and then drop you down in the desert, or maybe the forest somewhere, far from any city or town. You have no compass, no map, no cell, and you're not allowed to speak to anyone you might encounter. Your task is to get yourself home. How do you do it?"

"Call an Uber!" someone shouted.

"No phone," Mulligan said.

"Read the road signs."

"You're in the wilderness—there are no road signs."

"Maybe you could look at the sun and figure out north and south," someone ventured.

"Yes, that's a start, but how do you know if your home is located north or south or east or west of where you are now?"

"I'm fucked!"

Mulligan laughed. "That's honest—and true. Most of us would be fucked. But if you were a lobster, or a mole rat, or a salmon, or almost any bird, you might navigate by Earth's magnetic field. Certain birds would employ quantum entanglement to guide themselves. If you were a marbled newt, you would wait until night and then calculate your bearings from the stars. If you were a red-bellied salamander, or of course a dog, olfaction would play an important role in centering you. All these different species would eventually find their way home. Most humans, however, would probably die before getting home."

"I think a salmon would die on dry land," said a guy at the back of the hall.

"Imagination, buddy," Mulligan said. "We're talking hypothetical here. This is a *thought* experiment."

Philippa watched these exchanges, feeling nervous for Mulligan, almost protective. She worried that some of the students might want to mock him for his oddity. But so far he had maintained the upper hand. Sometimes his opening gambit was a simple question: *Do fish feel pain? Can dogs feel love? It's often said animals act out of instinct—do humans do anything instinctual?* Philippa was often surprised by the conventional, anthropocentric answers her classmates offered—*Of course animals can't think or feel!*—when they knew Mulligan was always ready to refute such orthodoxy. After these riffs he initiated his PowerPoint, which always included a thirty-second musical lead-in—a pop tune, or some hip-hop, or a few measures of classic rock—and during that transition he danced a little, looking gangly and awkward, in truth, embarrassing. Then, too, Philippa cringed, worrying about the possibility of ridicule.

The next day she found herself walking to Mulligan's office with the will-lessness of a zombie, or like one of those animals he'd talked about drawn by a magnetic field—a salmon, a mole rat, some kind of bird—as if a homing instinct had launched her forth.

He greeted her as if he'd been expecting her. "I'm making tea," he said. The electric kettle had already reached a noisy boil, and he fetched a second mug from the top of his file cabinet and poured water on top of lemon-ginger bags. From inside his file cabinet he pulled a package of Oreos, which he extended to her. She took one, fumbling past the plastic.

"Gotta have more than one," he said, handing her a second. "Next time I'll have a plate. Not good on the formalities."

She unhooked Alice's leash, and Mulligan laid down his tea to scoop Alice into his lap.

"I thought you'd come back," he said.

"Really? Why?"

"No, let me amend that—I *hoped* you'd come back. You're the first and only one who's come to office hours this term. No one ever came last term. No one sees the point. But you—well, I think you understand your animal nature more than most. I don't mean that as an insult."

"It's okay. I'm not insulted." She watched him lick the cream from the inside of his Oreo, keeping it beyond the reach of Alice's paw. So many things he did—licking his Oreos, petting Alice— had the effect of loosening and relaxing her, making her feel okay about being herself. "Have you ever wanted to *be* an animal?" she said.

He laughed. "You mean because I'm acting like an animal now?" He placed the entire Oreo onto his tongue, mashed it, then swallowed it whole.

"No, no, I didn't mean that."

"No worries." Then he turned from kid to dead-serious grown-up in a matter of seconds, leaning in and directing all his considerable energy onto her. "Yes and no. I've thought of this question *a lot.* It would be hard to give up language and human cognition. But that would also be the wonderful thing—to experience some other kind of awareness, as well as different sensory capabilities. Imagine being able to smell and hear as well as a dog. Or see as well as a hawk. It's a hard call."

"That day you showed the film about sponges—the day Alice got loose—I thought how awesome it would be to be a sponge, just floating there attached to a rock, you know, not having to make any decisions. What was that word you used—*sessile?*"

"Decisions, gah!" He threw back his head, and his arms flew into the air. "You know there's a proud tradition of humans attempting to live like animals. There was a guy somewhere in the British Isles who made himself a costume and lived among goats for months. He even developed a close bond with one of the females. You can read about it in *The New Yorker.* Another guy tried to live as a badger. You probably can't get all the way to full animal consciousness, but even partway could be instructive."

He touched the white patch on his neck as if it were a talisman, guiding him to truth, the same thoughtful way her mother fondled her necklace. She wondered if he could feel the whiteness internally.

"Would you ever try something like that?" she said.

"I might—who knows?" He grinned and meowed loudly, causing Alice's head to turn. "Problem is, a cephalopod would be my animal of choice, and that wouldn't be an easy simulation."

"Once, when I was a kid, I was sent home from school for pretending to be a dog. Every time my teacher spoke to me I barked at her. She wasn't very happy with me." Recounting the story to Professor Mulligan made Philippa suddenly embarrassed but, to her relief, he was laughing.

"Someday the people who remain alive here on Earth," he said, "the last survivors of everything—fires and floods and wars and viruses—they'll find themselves wishing they were animals. I have no doubt." He grinned again. "You and I, we're already thinking about this, so we're in the vanguard."

17

LU HAD BEGUN SLEEPING in Pippa's room regularly. George was driving her crazy trying to justify himself about a situation he hadn't even fully described, not realizing that the more he said, the foggier and more insulting things became. There was a woman named Marley who had come to the winery and he claimed not to have had sex with her; but maybe he'd almost had sex with her but only because she'd seduced him; but then in the end they didn't have sex, neither of them wanted it; yes, he liked her, but he really only liked the fact that she was a wonderful artist, and they had had intense conversations, which had maybe confused them both into thinking they were attracted to each other; but in the end he really wasn't attracted; she was much too big for him, too tall, and not very fit, not nearly as attractive as Lu, her manner too flamboyant; though come to think of it she and Lu had some physical traits in common; but really it was her active brain that had gotten him entangled, her appreciation of the life of the mind that had stimulated him and made him think differently about the possibilities for his own life; but now, whatever had happened was over, and he didn't want to see her again. Above all, Lu shouldn't personalize any of this. He loved Lu more than ever. Did she understand that?

The first few times they'd had these conversations at the dinner table, or getting ready for bed at adjacent sinks in their shared bathroom, their bodies repelling magnetic poles. Lu had genuinely tried to understand what George was trying to explain, but there were so many contradictions. He'd had fantasies about this woman, but he hadn't been attracted to her. She was a person who had stimulated the artist in him, but he never wanted to see her again. He sounded deranged—or at the very least deluded. But the worst part was that he hadn't stopped to consider the effect this was having on her. *She's out of my league*, he'd said of Marley. What was Lu to conclude? That she, Lu, was accessible but inferior? Didn't he hear how diminishing that was? Lu's brain did not, apparently, begin to compare to Marley's.

She'd confronted him with questions.

So, I'm not good enough for you?

No, no, you're putting words in my mouth.

But you've lost some interest in me?

You're hearing me wrong.

But you wanted to fuck her brain?

I was interested *in the way she* thinks. *That doesn't mean I wanted to sleep with her. Stop sexualizing this.*

She stopped responding, went mute, only half hearing him, spent her days walking long distances then dozing in some hazy liminal zone that disincluded him.

After a week he dropped the subject, as if he'd made a private decision. She'd never seen such a radical about-face in him—or anyone. Maybe he'd exhausted himself. Or perhaps he was embarrassed at having seemed so needy. Or maybe Marley had rejected him and he couldn't handle it—he'd once told her he'd never been rejected by a woman, something he seemed to take great pride in. She'd laughed when he told her this, amused that it was so important to him. An occasional rejection wasn't so bad. It toughened you up and taught you that you weren't the center of the universe. Whatever had happened, whatever he'd once felt in relationship to this Marley, he had tucked it away and moved on. In the evenings he talked about his days, details about running the winery that had always bored her, addressing her as if she, too, had erased all memory of the Marley incident.

When they were at the winery together, on the nights of her shifts, he was different—formal and pointedly cordial—but this difference was so subtle it was doubtful anyone but her noticed. He appeared to be assuring the world that everything was normal even if the world had never noticed anything amiss in the first place.

She watched him, both at home and at the winery, as if residing in a distant state. It was amazing to her she could live with someone and find so little need for conversation. The only conversation she initiated was about Pippa, whose texts were more obtuse than usual.

> P: *Do fish feel pain?*
>
> P: *What if humans could navigate by quantum entanglement?*
>
> P: *Do you do anything from pure instinct?*

Lu had no idea how to respond. These questions seemed to encode something, and her answers felt insufficient.

> L: *Interesting question.*
>
> L: *I know nothing about quantum entanglement.*
>
> L: *Isn't love instinctual?*

What did these inquiries say about Pippa's state of mind?

"What can she possibly mean?" she asked George. "Do you think she's okay?"

"She's growing up," George said. "Everyone does it differently."

"But what if she's drowning? Maybe this is her way of asking for help. Maybe I should go down there."

"Don't take it personally, Lu."

"What is that supposed to mean?" It was exactly what he'd said about Marley. What a useless thing to say. Everything was personal. You were a particular body, a particular mind, and everything that came to you was filtered through that body and mind. There was nothing but personal.

George, however, had sealed off the personal, becoming a public person even at home. The only personal thing he said was that he wanted her to sleep in their bed again, as if that would guarantee that balance would be restored.

It occurred to her that she had no public persona, no one else to be but herself.

18

LU WOULD NEVER FORGET her first days working at the winery. It had seemed to her like a magical place, full of sconce-lit alcoves and easy chairs and tables arranged for privacy. The bar and its shelves were constructed of cherry and maple and eucalyptus that were all dusted and polished regularly so they shone under the light, and each of the pieces of artwork on the walls had been given its own spot. Classical music—Mozart, Haydn, Vivaldi, and their aesthetic cousins—seeped from speakers mounted on either side of the bar. George maintained that listening to this kind of orderly music elevated a person's IQ, and she had no idea what it did to her IQ, but she knew it prompted her to move with the grace of a ballerina as she executed her duties, sweeping up and down the length of the bar, pouring wine and pausing to chat with the customers, feeling elegant and beautiful, black hair swirling behind her. She had the feeling when she was hired that she'd arrived at the happy ending of a fairy tale, all the troubling parts of her story finally laid to rest. It was here that George had begun courting her, singling her out from all the other young women he employed.

It was an elite group that patronized the Barnes Winery. Titans of business she wouldn't have recognized but for George pointing them out, eminent writers, occasionally a minor movie star. She eavesdropped on their conversations about business and travel and children and learned to spot signs of wealth, like the shabby-chic clothing many of the men favored and the scent of Aveda products worn by the women.

George had left her a note on the counter. *We're short-staffed, so come early please. (Maybe tonight you'll come back to bed?) Xoxoxoxoxo.* As if the extra letters might convince her of his unflagging love. As if he hadn't noticed anything about her recent distraction, her absence, the weakening leash of their bond. It was true, she was still his wife, his employee; she still lived in his house and ate food purchased with his money, but what of the rest—the personal, the raw guts of their lives, their hearts and souls? She tried to remember what their intimate connection had felt like. It wasn't something you could see or measure, but she knew it had existed. Had Pippa been the essential ingredient?

His words continued to hold sway even when she didn't want them to. She dragged herself to her shift, arriving only five minutes early, which prompted a chiding look from him. The place was mobbed with the fall wine-tasting crowd, all the tables full, only a couple of remaining seats at the bar. A new hire, a gorgeous young woman named Leticia whom Lu had not yet met, was working the tables, but Lu was the only person behind the bar, taking over for Isabel, who worked the afternoon shift. George was buzzing from the storage room to the tables, to the bar, multitasking as he always did, greeting the patrons warmly and exuding the noblesse oblige of successful proprietorship. She dove into work. Each time she'd been here since George's dalliance, she had found herself imagining this brilliant Marley person appearing at the bar, her eye on George.

A forty-something couple in matching ivory shirts claimed the last seats at the bar. Busy as she was, it took her a few minutes to approach them, and the man was already annoyed. He refused to establish eye contact, regarding his menu with obliterating focus. The undulant placid pink of his cheeks spoke to her of a lifetime of privilege. Trying to resist an embolism of hostility forming in her gut, she couldn't recall the spiel about the day's special wines. She had to let it go. The woman, more cordial, clearly accustomed to covering for her partner's rudeness, placed their order. The fig-and-goat-cheese bruschetta, she said, they would have that too. In the early days of working in the tasting room she had written down the orders, but now memory served her. She poked her head into the kitchen where José, their chef, made up small plates. No meals, only small gourmet hors d'oeuvres to absorb some of the alcohol. "Yup," he said when she placed the order, nodding amicably though his hands were flying, clearly harried.

A Vivaldi piece was playing—"The Four Seasons." Why was it so abrasive? Maybe because it was playing the summer section when they were already weeks into autumn. She moved down the bar refilling glasses, smiling, wishing she hadn't come. They were terribly understaffed—how had George let this happen? *The Caymans next week and Italy in early November. Yes, from Harvard, in June of this year. No, the younger one is at Stanford. Deplorable, all of them. Highway robbery. No, no, I've never seen such good returns.*

"Excuse me, ma'am, are you open over the holidays?"

"Yes, we are," she said, amazed by her ability to speak, to smile, to answer coherently. "It's delightful here over the holidays—really magical."

She laid down two glasses of Cabernet in front of the couple in ivory shirts.

The man frowned. "She ordered Chardonnay."

"Oh, I'm so sorry. I remember now. The 2018, right? I'll bring it right away. Apologies—we're quite busy tonight."

The man was appraising her, without any attempt to conceal it, his gaze more judgmental than appreciative. "Are you new here?"

"No."

"I don't recognize you."

She shrugged. "I'll bring you that Chardonnay."

A woman in a bright pink shirt and shimmery gold hair leaned across the bar, balancing on her belly amid a forest of wine-filled glassware as if she was at home. "Miss, miss, something's wrong with the music. It's repeating the same bars over and over. It's driving me nuts."

"Of course."

The glassware shivered as the woman withdrew her torso back across the bar. Lu placed the fresh glass of Chardonnay in front of the ivory-shirt woman, avoiding the man's gaze.

"I'm assuming we won't be paying for that," he said. "George would give it to us for free."

She nodded and walked away. Whatever, sure, if George said so. He sometimes curried favor with regular patrons this way. He probably let Marley drink for free. She paused the music, leaving a new choice to someone else, and went to the restroom. She splashed her face with cool water and studied her expression. She hardly recognized herself, the sourness and dissatisfaction lodged there, indicating she had the potential to be a person as objectionable as the man in the ivory shirt.

George, emerging from the men's room, stood in front of her. "You're supposed to be at the bar."

"I'm not allowed to pee?"

"When it's this crowded you need to get someone to cover for you. You know that."

"No one was around. This is crazy, George. Some woman is pissed about the music, and some guy wanted to shame me for getting his order wrong."

"You can handle these people. You've managed far worse."

"Well, I can't now. They're all so petty."

"They're our patrons, honey."

"I don't care. I'm not doing this anymore. You'll have to find someone else." She almost suggested Marley but stopped herself.

"Don't, Lu. Please. Don't be impulsive like this. You're self-destructing."

She left George in the hallway and returned to the bar for her purse. Without fanfare, she escaped into the night.

The next morning she got up early, thinking she was avoiding him. She couldn't bear the way he acted as if Pippa and Marley, both out of sight, had no ongoing effect on him. She was in the kitchen pouring coffee, still in her robe, when he came in dressed in one of his drapey rayon shirts, man-bag over his shoulder, set to go. Seeing her, he lingered.

"What you did last night was—unacceptable." He paused, lowered his voice. "Why are you punishing me so much?" His voice was almost plaintive. She poured milk into her coffee, stirred it. So he had noticed a difference in her after all.

"As you're always saying, it's not personal." She restored the milk to the fridge, turned her back on him, and ascended the first two steps of the staircase, heading for Pippa's room. Scalding coffee sloshed on her quaking hand.

"Wait, please. Can you just promise me one thing?"

She stopped, back still to him, licked coffee from her hand.

"That you won't leave? It would be insane to end our marriage for such a tiny transgression. I know I did a bad thing—or thought about it—but we can work it out, I promise you. But don't leave." He waited.

Was it a tiny transgression? It seemed to her to reveal so much about his way of thinking, the hierarchy he held in his mind in which she came up short.

"We're a family, you and I," he said. "You and me and Pippa."

"How can you say that? Pippa isn't here. We're not a real family when she isn't here."

She laid her coffee mug a few steps above where she stood and examined her seared hand, already puffy and red.

"But you and I are still here. And we need each other."

She turned to search his face. Did she need him, this man who was unaffected by the absence of his own daughter, who didn't feel the difference between a real relationship and mere cohabitation? And what about him—were the formal outlines of a marriage all he wanted? A voice she had never used before came from deep in her throat.

"Stop pressuring me."

She willed him to leave, but he remained where he was, his posture growing more rigid, suggesting something terrifying. Would he lay hands on her to extract this promise? A promise coerced would be an empty one.

He had to leave. He headed through the door that led to the garage, emitting a cyclone of sighs, closing the door behind him with a distinctive snap. His BMW started up and shot out of the driveway at faster-than-usual speed. She didn't move until the sound dwindled to nothing, only the relentless whir of her own consciousness.

19

HER COFFEE WAS cold now, but she drank it anyway, propped semi-upright among Pippa's pillows, which still smelled of the vetiver soap Pippa favored. Her smarting hand pulsed like a second heart. Making a fist, she admired its solidity. If she'd been an artist, she would have drawn this fist—its shape and color evinced such power and refusal. She ignored a text from her mother, inquiring about her well-being. There was nothing she could say to her mother that wouldn't prove her mother had been right. She texted Pippa instead, trying to sound upbeat.

> L: *Dad says the harvest is going well, but replanting might be necessary. The drought gets worse and worse, as you know. But for now we're good. Love, Lu-Mom.*

> P: *Zoology professor says a guy in England tried to live as a goat. Ha!*

> L: *Interesting.*

Silence. Pippa's non sequiturs often caught Lu off guard, but she was trying not to overinterpret them. Pippa had always been that way, combing the world for odd or surprising tidbits of information she brought up randomly in conversation.

With a second cup of coffee, Lu wandered into the living room, trying to remember where she usually perched. The couch, the chair, the window seat, nothing seemed right. Something was fomenting. The house smelled bad, despite the expensive filtration system George had installed. She couldn't quite identify the source of the smell. It wasn't the usual suspects: rotten food, Alice's litter box, toxic sanitizing products. It was something more subtle. Maybe a few amalgamated smells. She walked around sniffing the curtains, the couch. She got down on hands and knees to sniff the Gabbeh carpet. She lingered on all fours, nose roving, inhaling the molecules embedded in the fibers. They traveled up through her nasal passages and suffused her brain. Skin secretions from George and Pippa, herself too. Cracker crumbs, and drops of spilled wine, and dead spider carcasses, and tiny flakes of garden grass, and George's shoe polish.

She stood up, altered. This room, this entire house, suddenly enraged her, jam-packed with so many beautiful useless things. The mantel piece with its parade of framed happy-family photos, and the sensuous blue glass vase whose provenance she couldn't remember.

And the artwork! Why was there so much artwork?! George had been assembling this stuff for years. Before she met him, he had traveled abroad regularly, partly for business, and now he still traveled for business to Europe, Africa, Australia, South America, and on those trips he prowled through the shops and galleries of foreign cities acquiring more with the fervid drive of a dope addict. Everywhere he went he saw artifacts he had to possess, and now they were displayed everywhere in this house, beautifully lit on walls and shelves, in bookcases, on pedestals, objects and paintings he had probably admired for no more than a month or so before they faded into the background. Now she was quite sure he rarely noticed them at all, except when a guest complimented him on his taste, and he treated the person to a guided art tour.

The artwork fell into two main categories. There were paintings from the Western tradition: many abstract expressionist paintings from the mid-to-late twentieth century, along with some Picasso look-alikes, some Modigliani look-alikes, some Matisse look-alikes. There were two genuinely valuable works, according to George, that had come to him from his parents when they moved from Connecticut to Florida. One was by Mark Rothko, whose name Lu would not have recognized were it not for George. It was a painting made of horizontal blocks of color in shades of muddy yellow and blue, and it took up a huge section of wall in the hallway, which was designed to be wide enough that George could make it into a gallery. Lu took her nose to its surface and sniffed. An acrid, desperate odor. She'd never been fond of that painting. It depressed her. She wasn't surprised to learn that Rothko had killed himself. The other was by Frankenthaler, Helen Frankenthaler, a *woman*, George noted when guests came and he guided them through the artwork like a docent. As if women hadn't been making art for centuries. That piece Lu liked; it was composed of pale coral and blue shapes superimposed with the suggestion of a thoughtful woman's face. It had a dreamy quality that appealed to Lu. Sometimes she liked to pretend Frankenthaler had made it with her in mind, a dreamy woman who floated through the world. George liked the Rothko better, because, while the Frankenthaler might have been worth several hundred thousand dollars, the Rothko was worth millions. He seemed to regard the painting as a score more than as a piece of artwork.

The other category on display was folk art: textile wall hangings from Uzbekistan and Romania, soapstone sculptures made by Inuits in Alaska, Australian Aboriginal carvings of owls and a dingo, a Navajo headdress, a Chinese dragon kite, tribal masks from

Zimbabwe and Kenya and Rwanda. He even had several folk paintings in the style of Grandma Moses, made by African Americans from Alabama and Mississippi.

Some of these things he had obtained from their countries of origin; others had been purchased in folk-art markets in New York and San Francisco. Every item from both categories was displayed to optimal advantage, in a sconce-lit corner, or on a pedestal, or on a wall with adequate surrounding space to highlight its attributes. He had designed the whole house—and the winery's tasting room—with art displays in mind. She had always accepted that George's artistic vision was beyond reproach. When she met him, she had known nothing about art; she still only knew what she'd learned from him. While she liked some of the pieces more than others, she'd always respected him for paying attention to art from all over the world.

But now, the sight of this artwork made her livid. How had she failed to see the pure braggadocio at work here? *Look at my open-minded, eclectic taste. See how I am part of the cognoscenti. See how I value the artistic contributions of poor, abused, colonized people.* George had no relationship to the Inuit of Alaska, or the Aboriginal culture in Australia, or the Navajos of the Southwest, all of whom had been deprived of land and sustenance by white men like himself. He'd never met any members of the African tribes whose masks and beadwork he displayed, or the Chinese people who had made the exquisite dragon kite.

In her sewing room she dumped several boxes of stalled craft projects onto the floor. Their contents flew across the room—tiles, beads, fabric. Cameras thunked to the floor. She fled with the boxes, leaving the room in furious disarray.

She began her attack downstairs, ripping the folk artwork from shelves and walls and pedestals, hurling them into the open boxes without regard for what damage she might have been inflicting on them. She paused momentarily to stare at one of the Inuit sandstone sculptures: half-woman, half-seal. The in-betweenness of a mermaid. She was amazed she'd never fully appreciated this sculpture before. She stroked the seal-woman's smooth black back, inhaled deeply, and was rewarded with the faintest trace of seawater. She set it aside for herself and continued with her mission.

Moving through all the floors of the house, including George's study, she filled ten boxes. Objects jutted from the tops so the box flaps wouldn't close, and hefting them to the garage was a challenge. She deposited them along the wall at the back.

Inside the house after multiple trips she stared at what remained. The Western artwork, including the two "valuable" paintings by Rothko and Frankenthaler. Alone now, without their folk brethren, they seemed as hubristic as George. Some of the paintings were large, and it required pulling and pushing and humping to get them off the walls, across the floor—in some cases down the stairs—and into the garage.

It took almost three hours to clear the walls entirely. Done, she stood in the kitchen, which gave her a panoramic view of the entry-way alcove, where several pieces had hung, the living room with its two high, gapingly blank walls, and the long, wide hallway-cum-gallery that led to the study and the solarium. The entire house was now a study in vacancy. She breathed in the emptiness and felt it enlarging her, lending her energy that had too long been absent. George would be furious, but he wouldn't do anything beyond yelling, and that she'd heard before. For now, she had the upper hand.

Past Petaluma the road to the coast was narrow, cutting through hills and around sharp corners. She drove the powder-blue Lexus that George had insisted on buying for her like a fugitive, desperate for the cleansing salt air of the ocean and an uncluttered horizon. The Lexus took the curves nimbly, bringing forth its bells and whistles of comfort and maneuverability.

On the beach the wind whipped her shoulder-length hair. It was mid-afternoon, mid-week, past the summer season, and the beach was mostly deserted but for a few dog walkers and some twenty-somethings tossing a Frisbee. The tide was going out and, with energy to burn, she trotted along the water's edge, dodging the occasional wave that rose higher than the rest. One of the dogs captured her interest, a lean, long-legged bounding hound with hair so short he wore his musculature like a pair of skinny jeans. He waded into the water, high-stepping through the waves, impervious to the cold, then he dashed back out, positioning himself on the sand and barking as if the waves were alive and might answer back. She loved watching his playful energy.

She had no idea what time George would get home that night, probably late, as had been his habit recently, diving into work to clear his head of whatever Marley had done to him. He would drive his BMW into the garage between her Lexus and the Odyssey. The bright beams of his headlights would illuminate the boxes and artwork lining the garage's back wall. It would be impossible not to notice, especially for George, with his keen eye for disorder. He would step from his car already infuriated, and when he went inside and saw the empty walls, he was likely, she now saw from that distant beach vantage point, to become apoplectic. He'd made a noisy entrance when returning home at midnight last night, and she was glad she was sleeping in Pippa's room. For so many years of their marriage she had never done anything intentionally that would annoy him. Occasionally she would forget to do an errand she'd promised to do, or she gave Pippa permission to do something he didn't approve of, but she had never done anything consciously, willfully, with clear foresight, that she had known would infuriate him—until recently.

She would be at home by then, ensconced in Pippa's room with the light out, pretending to be asleep. But she would hear the car drive up, and the garage door opening and closing, the door to the house opening and closing. She would hear him tossing his keys onto the kitchen counter, the aggressive flipping of light switches. Her eyes would be closed, but she would feel the light waves oscillating through the house, scouring evidence of her wrongdoing, and she would hear him stalking from room to room, the soles of his feet inebriated with anger, his eyes imploding as he regarded each empty wall, still stippled with picture hangers. The volume of his anger would crescendo with each step he took.

Would he retreat to his room, waiting until daylight to confront her, or would he roust her from bed, unable to contain himself?

The skinny hound ran to her and buried his nose in her crotch. She laughed and stepped away, and he dashed back to his master then back to her. The man shouted, "So sorry!"

"No worries," she shouted back. "I love dogs!" She crouched and held the dog's muzzle in both hands, and they sniffed each other, sharing a moment of communion, until the man whistled for the dog's return.

The wind and waves and salt air scent had blunted her anger. As she walked back down the beach, her mind turned to Marley, as it had been doing of late. The Other Woman. The tall artist with the alluring, fuckable brain. She had rented a ghost-room in Lu's brain, where she whispered to Lu of her deficiencies. George had said he'd seen her around town occasionally, but Lu couldn't recall having seen anyone who fit her description. She envied such a woman, a person everyone noticed and admired, someone who had intimidated George. Lu couldn't imagine intimidating anyone. And she was sure she, too, would find Marley intimidating. What had an acclaimed, successful woman like Marley wanted from George? From what George had said, it was hard to know.

Lu pressed these thoughts away as well as she could. It did no good to wonder about things so far beyond her control.

The trip home was less salubrious. The setting sun cast shadows of leaves and tree branches across the road and windshield, confusing her perspective. With the light playing tricks, distances were hard to gauge. She couldn't even tell how far away her hands were, and their grip on the steering wheel was weak. Oncoming cars appeared out of nowhere, threatening to cross the center line. She tried to open the window, hoping wind on her face would soothe, but her hands were clunky, almost paralyzed, and she only managed to crack the window a slit. With equal difficulty she turned on the radio, but as soon as she heard voices discussing some new tragedy in Michigan, she swatted it off, desperate for silence. Why was the whole world so desperate to hear about other people's misery?

20

IT DID NOT take long for the missing women to fade from public consciousness. Nothing sustained interest for long. Occasionally people thought of those women, wondering if they were dead or alive, but even those thoughts were fleeting. It was the norm to reel from crisis to crisis. There were so many disasters vying for attention, sending minds into overload.

Then a report came out of Michigan's Upper Peninsula. A group of nine people had fled there from Chicago to live off the land. They were people in their thirties, women and men, who had become disaffected with the challenge of trying to piece together lives in an urban center in a decimated economy. There had to be something better, they thought. They decided to pool their resources to buy some land on which they would plant crops and raise chickens and cows and sheep, to become as self-sustaining as possible. Their aspirations became grandiose. They hoped to create a utopian community such as was seen more commonly in the nineteenth and twentieth centuries.

Fifty-five-year-old Randy Walters became a central source of information about these people. He was a neighbor and a lifelong Michigander, and he'd come to know this group over the five years they'd been in the area. He worked a small farm of his own and was a firefighter. After meeting him at the feedstore, they sought his advice. Some of the local residents regarded the group with skepticism, but Randy was touched by them, sometimes amused. His own sons and daughters had fled the area, seeing no future in farming and having no interest in leading a "life in the sticks." So Randy took a paternal interest in these young people and was happy to help them out.

It was a steep learning curve, Randy reported. The young commune members had been city dwellers all their lives and knew next to nothing about farming. The first couple of years were a real struggle. The Upper Peninsula was a challenging place to farm, due to its short growing season and less-than-optimal soil. But after five years they were still at it. "They were tougher than I thought," Randy told reporters. Still, every year they confronted new problems—infections, infestations, equipment breakdown—and he worried about their sagging spirits.

They were always talking about how rotten the world was and how soon it was likely to end. Given their bleak view of the future, Randy was surprised when they went ahead and had kids: four-year-old Zoe, three-year-old Henry, and a baby named Clara. There were four men and five women in the group, and Randy confessed he never knew exactly who was coupled and which of the adults were the parents of those kids.

"Some people around here suspected they were all doing it with each other—you know, free love and all that—but I never asked. If that's what they wanted, have at it. But lots of folks disagreed with me."

Randy had gotten into the habit of stopping by to check on them at least once a week. He enjoyed chatting with them, and they appeared to enjoy him too. He felt responsible for them, and his visits, he felt, lifted their spirits. His own too. Sometimes he saw them more frequently if they sought his advice on a problem.

"So, I go by one morning—a Wednesday—for a friendly chat. They'd recently taken to raising pigs, just a few, you know, and I don't know a damn thing about raising pigs, but they loved to ask my advice anyway. They would tell me about those pigs, how smart they were and how much the kids loved them. It's true, by the way—pigs are damn smart animals. They named all their animals, and they'd named one of their pigs Wilbur after that kids' book. The little girl, Zoe, she just loved that pig. She would walk around the property with the pig on a leash as if it was a dog.

"So I drive up to the farmhouse, a big house, not in great repair. All nine of them lived there, along with the kids. A bit crowded, but they made it work. Right away I could see something was cock-eyed. Usually there would be a bunch of them outside doing chores, but that day I didn't see anyone. I go looking for them out back behind the house where the barn was and there was a yard there too, and I see some of the animals had gotten out of their pens and they were laying there in the grass. A couple of cows and some sheep and a couple of pigs. Just laying there, not the least bit interested in straying. And then I see the two kids, Zoe and Henry, they were there too. Zoe had her body draped over one of the pigs, maybe Wilbur, maybe not—I couldn't tell those pigs apart. She was sobbing. *Mommy! Mommy!* I kept asking her what had happened, but she wouldn't say. And Henry, he was sitting in the grass holding one of the chickens, his face right down in the chicken's feathers and the chicken not doing anything to try to get away. I've never seen anything so strange in all my life.

"*Where are your parents?* I kept asking, and both children looked at me as if they had no idea who I was or what I was asking. Shell-shocked, you know? Like they'd been through something pretty bad.

"So much goes through your mind at a time like that.

Corralling the animals. Finding the adults. I tried to get the kids to come with me into the house, but Zoe wouldn't leave her pig, and then I thought maybe some intruder might be in there and it would be dangerous to go in with them. You know, my mind was going crazy with thoughts. At any rate, I left the children in the backyard and I went inside by myself. I wouldn't normally just enter someone's house without being invited, but I knew something was really wrong. I went in with my hand on my weapon. I was ready for anything, you know, bodies, bad guys, whatever. I walk around in there, real careful. It was eerie quiet and a terrible mess. There was laundry everywhere—you know, jeans and T-shirts and overalls and work boots and caps. Scattered everywhere in the living room and kitchen. Underwear too. Who leaves underwear in the kitchen?

"Then I go upstairs and I hear something coming from the end of the hallway. I go down there, real cautious, and, for the love of mike, there was the baby, little Clara, six months old, lying in her crib, whimpering. It'd been so long since I'd held a baby—but she was reaching up to me, so I picked her up. Poor critter. She had a dirty diaper, and she reeked something awful. I felt so bad for her. Such a lightweight innocent little thing.

"I go back outside with the baby to the backyard, where I'd left the other two kids. By then I knew we had a major problem underway, so I called the police."

Randy's story captivated large numbers of people, not just those in the Midwest, but people across the country. No one could find those nine commune members—the Michigan Nine, the press had started to call them—not after a week, not after two weeks. People wondered if maybe a hostile community member had done something to them. Remembering the abandoned clothes, people speculated that the nine commune members might have been forced to disrobe at gunpoint then were marched into a van stark naked, exposed and helpless. Some wondered if the disappearances of the Michigan Nine had anything to do with the women who'd gone missing in Mendocino and the Pacific Northwest. The big difference was that men had disappeared with the Michigan Nine, though much of the media focused on the event as if it had only included women. Women disappearing excited the media, but missing men seemed more ho-hum. It was hard to come up with any meaningful motive for a perpetrator except sex. Everyone seemed certain that sex was involved, though the people putting forth this certainty weren't experts in forensics or sex crimes. They had no real idea how to explain any of those events. People kept expecting law enforcement to tell them what had happened, and then they felt naïve for believing that such disappearances could always be explained. Systems were breaking down all around—everyone should have known better.

The children had been taken into protective services, where they were under psychiatric observation. The baby seemed to be okay, but the three- and four-year-old were not doing well. They wouldn't respond to questions about what had happened. They sobbed when they were separated from their favorite animals.

After a month passed no one still had any idea what had happened to the Michigan Nine. It made people think existential thoughts. It made them wonder if someday they, too, might disappear.

21

SOME NIGHTS PHILIPPA DREAMED of Dar, vague images of them in a car, or walking along a ridge with a view out over the ocean, resembling a place in Mendocino she once went with her parents. In one dream they were walking along a beach strewn with dozens of resting elephant seals, still and imposing as the monuments of Stonehenge, animals so big they could easily crush a person, but he wasn't afraid and neither was she. Weaving among them, they placed their hands on the leathery skin of the creatures' backs, brushing off flies and parasitic creatures that appeared to be making homes there. They never talked in those dreams, and they never had sex, but she woke feeling aroused and furtive, as if she was harboring a terrible secret she must never divulge.

Everything around her began to look different. While the city was still chaotic, it no longer felt as if every passerby and every car was out to get her. She walked to campus feeling bold, determined to thwart whatever appeared. As little as a year earlier she would have confided all this to her mother, but now she felt stronger for telling no one.

He told her to call him Dar. Not in class, he said, but when she came to office hours. He couldn't stand the formality of titles, and he said his identity as a professor was tenuous. She told him about her nicknames—how her parents called her Pippa, but she preferred Phipps. After that, she had a dream in which she was walking around campus repeating loudly: *Dar. Dar. Dar.* The force of his name spoken aloud made people jump out of her way.

Confident as she'd become, each time she made her way to his office she worried a little she was making a fool of herself. She thought of the mime she and her parents had seen on one of their trips to San Francisco, a guy in white face and a fedora on the corner of a downtown street pretending to be stuck in some room from which he couldn't escape. They watched for a while—she was seven or eight and had never seen a mime before and wondered why his face was white—until her father rolled his eyes and urged them to move on. "My god," he said when they'd passed out of earshot, "didn't he get the memo that we're done with mimes? You gotta feel sorry for the guy." This had surprised Philippa. She'd liked the mime, but apparently the rest of the world thought he was pathetic. She wondered if people would roll their eyes at her now. How pathetic she was to be obsessed with her professor.

Their meetings had become almost ritualized: tea, Oreos, a little tossing of the baby basketball, which she was getting better at, his taking Alice onto his lap and indulging her with attention. They played a game in which each of them suggested an animal they might like to become. Dar often mentioned animals she'd never heard of. Tarsiers he liked because they had huge eyes that allowed them to see in the dark. Sea cucumbers did a kind of shape-shifting by turning themselves to liquid in order to slip into a crack before solidifying again. He liked the albatross too—of course she knew about albatrosses, but she had no idea they could fly up to ten thousand miles without having to rest. Even in this so-called game, he was teaching her.

To rise to his level, she did some research. Wouldn't it be fun to be a lyrebird, who could mimic almost any sound, including chainsaws, lawn mowers, car alarms, barking dogs? Or maybe the mimic octopus, who could impersonate its predators? Or what about the self-healing axolotl?

Dar suggested the scarlet jellyfish, an animal with the talent for immortality. At the end of its adult life cycle it reverted to a polyp and started its life cycle again. "Well," he said, "it's really only *theoretical* immortality because the polyps can't move and are fair game for predators. Still, it's not a bad gig if you can get it."

Philippa considered immortality. "I'm still figuring out this lifetime. I don't know if I need more than one."

"When you get to my advanced age you begin thinking another life would be pretty sweet."

"You're not so old."

"Another four years and I'll be looking forty straight in the eye. Funny how you can get so old and still feel like a kid." He separated his Oreo and licked the cream with extra exuberance to underscore his point.

She watched herself beginning to flirt with him, collecting tidbits of information and observations she thought would please him. She used to think flirting was something you learned and decided to do. Now she saw it was a behavior that lived inside you like an instinct, waiting to be activated.

He told her chickens had thirty different alarm calls.

"I don't think I'd like to be a chicken," she said. "Not if they need thirty alarm calls. They must be scared all the time."

Sometimes she was sure he had a crush on her too, but then, just as she was settling into the delicious possibility of reciprocity, some tiny thing would shift, something as small as the way he repositioned his body, and she felt herself becoming the pathetic mime again, the guy who imagined his audience was interested when they were really only humoring him.

One day Dar said he'd like to be an animal that moved gracefully. He brought up several YouTube videos: gazelles bounding over an African plain; a murmuration of starlings circling a church steeple; a school of bright blue angelfish gliding through a reef, changing direction in perfect unison. "Imagine moving like these guys," he said wistfully. His aspiration touched her.

Another day he answered the door with his phone at his ear. "Gotta go. A student is here." She hesitated, but he beckoned her inside. "Don't forget. I'm still a working stiff," he said into the phone as she passed through the doorway. The person on the other end of the line said something inaudible that prompted a gruff belly laugh from Dar before he hung up.

He told her it was his friend Ivan. Throughout their meeting she felt unbearably self-conscious again, and after ten minutes she made up an excuse to leave. She couldn't stop thinking about the way he'd said *working stiff*, italicizing it with his voice, as if her arrival was a burden to him, an unpleasant reminder of his obligation. She'd thought he liked talking to her; it had seemed to her they were becoming friends. Now she saw it was possible he'd only been indulging her.

22

FOR TWO FULL DAYS after Lu had removed the artwork George didn't speak to her. Not a word. She had crossed a line she'd never crossed before. He was furious about a hole that had been poked in the Rothko. She overheard him on the phone talking to people who might fix it. The walls remained empty. On the third day a call came in from his mother, Abigail, in Florida. His father had had a stroke, and she needed his help. George had a brother in Maine and a sister in Vermont, but George was the go-to son, the youngest and last to launch himself. Because his parents had helped him out so much, he felt he owed them. Furthermore, Abigail was a forceful woman, impossible to refuse.

"Do you want to come with me?" he asked, knowing Lu would say no. How could they travel together when he wouldn't even talk to her? Visits to George's family were never easy to begin with, and to bring their current discord into a visit would be foolhardy.

"I doubt your mother wants me there at a time like this. I bet she wants you all to herself."

He conceded she was probably right.

"And I should stay closer to Pippa, just in case."

"Pippa is fine. You worry too much about her."

"We have no idea, do we?"

"We need this break. It will be good for us. When I get back, a long talk is in order." She turned her face so his kiss fell on her cheek. George drove himself to the San Francisco airport and flew to Florida, an irritated husband but an obedient son.

In his absence, Lu became a wanderer. A domestic nomad. She swam from room to room, a fish incapable of stopping. A hummingbird allergic to stillness. Insubstantial, lonely, missing Pippa with a poignancy she wouldn't have thought possible.

Channeling young Pippa, she went outside and lay belly down in the grass, ear to the ground, listening. She didn't hear anything special, only a distant chainsaw and some blackbirds in the trees, but it was pleasantly cool. A car approached, slowed, stopped. Lu remained still, eyes closed.

"Lu! Are you okay?" It was Julie, the spa owner from the ladies' lunches, her former boss. "We missed you at Alyssa's the other day. I've been meaning to email you. Gloria is doing the next one."

Lu remained silent.

"Lu?" The car door opened.

"I'm fine!" Lu called. "Just napping. Sorry about the lunch—I just forgot."

"No worries. Go back to your nap. Sorry to interrupt."

Julie drove off. It occurred to Lu she should be embarrassed, but she wasn't. She texted Pippa: *Hey honey.* That was all she could think of to say. She should tell Pippa about George's father, but she didn't have the energy. Fifteen minutes passed then a cat emoji appeared. Lu sent back a dog emoji. Pippa sent a fish. Lu sent a snake. Pippa sent something Lu didn't recognize.

L: *What was that?*

P: *Ferret.*

L: *I miss Emilio.*

P: *No, you don't.*

Lu closed her phone, proud of herself for knowing when to stop.

It suddenly occurred to her that Marley's painting might be somewhere in the house, the painting George had bought for himself. She found it in his study closet. A three-by-five-foot encaustic painting featuring a bright red human heart against a pale orange background, a few nonsensical words carved here and there in the wax. She dragged her fingertips over the textured surface, noticing the *M* embedded discreetly in the lower left corner. To her surprise, Lu liked this piece—it wasn't often that she and George shared the same taste in art.

She began another text to Pippa—*Something has happened here*—then deleted it. Since Pippa reached high school Lu had been on the verge of confiding in her, but at the last minute, she always decided against it. Why open floodgates best kept closed?

George called, and she answered out of habit. His mother sent her love; she was sorry Lu couldn't be there too.

"Hello back to her," Lu said. Abigail didn't want her there. She had always condescended to Lu, believing George had married beneath his station: a woman with working-class origins who'd eschewed education. George's parents had not traveled west for George and Lu's wedding, a beautiful occasion held at the winery with two hundred guests in attendance, including Lu's mother, but not George's parents, who said it was too far for them to travel, though they routinely traveled to Europe. On their visits east Lu had tried to be cordial, to help Abigail around the house, and

Abigail had always been overtly cordial back, but Lu could feel the underlying restraint and hauteur.

"It's a shit show here," George said. "My father can't speak. He's like some kind of an animal now—he eats and sleeps and shits. He can't walk without a lot of help. There seems to be something going on in his brain, but it's impossible to tell."

"What does the doctor say?"

"It's wait-and-see. At least he recognizes me. That's something."

"Yes."

"How're things there?"

"Fine."

"I'm a little concerned because I haven't been able to get hold of Tom. I'm sure things are okay, but as you know, he's not the greatest communicator, and he still hasn't told me if the *bois noir* will be a problem. Maybe you'd stop by the winery to check things out?"

He sounded as he used to sound, as if nothing had ever come between them, as if Florida had whitewashed his memory; he almost seemed personal again.

"I'll try." She knew she wouldn't. She hadn't been to the winery since her last disastrous shift.

"Good. See, the thing is, I have no idea how long I'll be here. It might be a while. Dad's a wreck, and Mother's another kind of wreck. God, I hate Florida. Hurricane warnings every other day. Disaster season. And I can't sleep in this goddamn mugginess."

"It's disaster season everywhere."

"I spoke to Pippa and told her what's going on. She seems okay, all things considered. She's taking Alice with her to class, if you can believe it. On a leash."

This was news to Lu, and it wounded her that Pippa was telling George such things instead of Lu herself. "Yes, she mentioned that."

Was Pippa's primary allegiance shifting from Lu to George? God, she hoped not.

"Hey, are you alright? You don't sound like yourself."

How could she respond? He was right, she wasn't herself, but then what was she? She decided against telling him she'd found Marley's painting and had sequestered it in the closet of her sewing room along with the Inuit sculpture of the half-seal woman. She was beginning to understand that her ennui was only partially about George. Every night she'd been taking the seal-woman sculpture to bed. The sensuous shape of the cool black soapstone held an idea she was trying to understand. She cradled it in both hands as she drifted into sleep, thinking about the person who'd made it—a woman?—and the world she lived in. It had to have been a culture that understood animals and respected them, Lu thought, a kinder culture than the one she herself lived in.

"I understand you're still angry, but I think you're making too much of what happened."

"No, actually, I'm not angry." And as she said this she realized it was true—the anger had fractured, like a shattered bead of mercury, then dissipated. "I'm just—tired."

"You haven't done any more house-wrecking, have you?"

She poked back with silence, letting him imagine the worst.

23

AWAKE AT 4:00 A.M., Lu forgot where she was. On the count of three it came to her—Pippa's room. There was an unmistakable smell of smoke. She hurried downstairs, opened the front door. A hazy orange glow pulsed behind the silhouetted trees at the end of the block. How reliable her nose was. Back inside she checked her phone. It screamed out notifications. A wildfire had erupted thirty miles away; it was moving rapidly. A Level One evacuation alert had been posted, but there was no order to leave yet.

She knew what to do, had done this countless times before. She unearthed the prepared bag of documents in the safe. She filled a backpack with a few changes of clothing and toiletries, laptop, chargers, baggies of nonperishable food she kept on hand. If George had been there, he would have been stuffing the car with large items: the Rothko and Frankenthaler paintings, perhaps a carpet or two, a box of his most valuable old books, his portfolio of drawings. But George was not there.

She settled in the dark living room with coffee, the evacuation website open beside her. She considered calling hotels where they'd gone in the past when they'd had to evacuate, but she decided to wait until business hours. Then she sat still, a frog on a lily pad, quietly absorbing information from the world, ready to leap when necessary.

At 6:00 A.M., Mo Blackwell, Lisa's husband, knocked on the door. Plumes of black smoke etched with orange billowed into the gray dawn behind Mo's head. Miles away, but still menacing.

"You heard?" he said. "It's Level Two now, so we should be ready to go. Let us know if you need help."

How sweet of him to drop by. How neighborly. She knew him only as Lisa's husband, but before she could stop herself she was hugging him, squeezing his beefy torso, feeling him recoil momentarily until he returned the squeeze. Drawing back from the hug, she thanked him, assured him she was fine. Only after he left did she realize she should have asked them where they were planning to go if the order came.

She knew she should call George, but she didn't. Worrywart that he was, he would be calling her soon enough. She thought of texting Pippa, too, but why wake her early and alarm her unnecessarily? Maybe the fire would amount to nothing—it sometimes happened.

She filled several gallon jugs with water and stashed them in the car along with her backpack filled with essentials. Then she returned to the house, repositioned herself on the living room couch. At 10:30 A.M. she began to call hotels. The Best Western was full. The Red Lion was full. The Motel 6 was full. Already? How had that happened so quickly? She checked her laptop. Still Level Two.

She closed her laptop, which was already shooting out sensationalized fire stories that were sidelining news of the missing commune members. She hated all the information that came at her uninvited—a cultural tyranny she couldn't escape, all of it negative and nerve-wracking. It was her best guess that those commune members had wanted to disappear—why couldn't everyone leave them alone? She waited, alert even as she drifted. If she couldn't find a hotel she could always go to the evacuation center at the high school. They had gone there once for two nights when all the hotels were full. George had hated it—the indignity of so many people thrown together in a gymnasium—but she had found it interesting, not comfortable, but a good place for observing people. She tried several more hotels. No luck. She realized she should have made a move as soon as she heard about the fire.

Linda called. *I know you're avoiding me*, she said into voicemail. It was true. Linda didn't even know that George had gone to Florida. Now Lu picked up.

"Come up here and stay with me," Linda urged. "There aren't any fires here—not yet, at least."

It had been years since Lu had spent a night with her mother. Now, much as she adored Linda and depended on her, she couldn't imagine it—Linda would intuit her distress instantly and offer nonstop unsolicited advice. Linda always thought she knew best.

"I need to stay. George is in Florida—his father had a stroke—so someone needs to stay and keep an eye on things."

"I'm sorry to hear that—I hope he's okay. But still, it does no one any good for you to be putting yourself in harm's way."

"I need to stay."

Her mother was right, as usual, but so was she—she had to stand her ground. She soothed herself by stroking the soapstone seal and fingering the embossed initials on her necklace. Both objects held secret caches of meaning. The necklace was a kind of memory bank. Now it released an image of her and her mother bedding down in the Nest. *Good night, Lulu*, her mother would call out from the bed next to her. *Sleep well, my little birdie*. How safe she'd felt in that house, falling asleep beside her mother. She'd loved the tiny size of the house, which made it extra cozy. Why was it that, until now, she had never felt the need to push her mother away as Pippa was pushing her away, especially having grown up in such a small space? She'd tried to re-create that same cozy, nest-like atmosphere for Pippa, but maybe it was impossible in a house as large as theirs. *Pippa. Pippa. Pippa. Forgive me for the ways I've failed you.*

She pictured Linda and Pippa side by side in the kitchen of Lupita's Place, Linda teaching Pippa how to make tortillas, Pippa's little fingers pulling at the elastic dough, then pinching off a piece to sculpt a dog.

She remembered how Pippa, just after starting kindergarten, had become obsessed with war. How she had learned about war was never clear—they hadn't discussed it in school or at home—but there it was in the air, part of the zeitgeist, available even to a five-year-old. At bedtime, over and over, Lu had had to assure Pippa she was safe, that a war was not about to break out. A lie, of course, as war was always a possibility, and she could see the suspicion in Pippa's wary gray eyes.

Boom-chicka-boom-chicka-boom-boom-boom. Clack-da-da-clack. Boom-clack-boom. Pippa in her room late at night throughout high school, too late to be making noise with her drum set or her homemade instruments, but still practicing rhythms quietly with her sticks and the practice box. Evan was often in there with her; occasionally he'd spend the night. George had always worried about them having sex, but Lu was sure Evan and Pippa weren't interested in sex. Pippa wasn't fully mature back then, not in the way that made a person hunger for sex, and Lu believed Evan was gay, even if he didn't know it yet himself.

Once the family had gone on a whale-watching expedition out of Half Moon Bay. It was a harsh March day, too cold and windy for most people, the sea a choppy gun-metal gray. There was only one other family of four on the boat. Eight-year-old Pippa spent the entire boat ride standing close to the railing of the boat's bow, lifting her face to the wind and salt spray, so eager to spot a breaching whale she barely let herself blink.

The gray whales, heading north to their feeding grounds, were on full display that day. Every fifteen or twenty minutes a new pod swam by, blowing and breaching not far from their boat, undeterred by human presence, their impressive size—seventy-two thousand pounds, the tour guide said—a guarantee of their invincibility.

They had certainly looked invincible, gigantic but still sliding through the water with the sensuousness of snakes, then propelling their bodies into the air with such Herculean thrust they made their breaching appear effortless. Pippa was thrilled and couldn't be convinced to leave her perch for cocoa or sandwiches, despite her shivering. Lu brought the cocoa to her, and she drank it dutifully. *See! If I'd gone inside, I would have missed it!* she crowed. And sure enough, there it was, the Holy Grail of whale watching: a humpback shooting out of the water, back arched, fins extended, pausing briefly at the apex of his leap to show off his mammalian triumph of strength and size.

Pippa was beside herself with joy, and it seemed as if the joy she exuded summoned more humpbacks—they kept coming and coming and breaching photogenically. Even the guide was impressed. *You're our good luck girl*, he told Pippa.

As they headed back to the harbor, seals surrounded the boat, heralding their return, sensuous as the seal-woman she was now stroking. Pippa, as she watched them dive and surface, arched her own back, mirroring the seals' movements as if she was practicing to be a seal herself. After that trip she was insistent on learning to swim better. She had discovered there were places you could go to swim alongside dolphins, and she wanted to do that, and maybe, eventually, graduate to swimming with the seals and the whales.

They know who they are, she kept saying in the car on the way home. *They love their bodies.*

Lu grounded herself in memories like these, even on the verge of imminent evacuation. Maybe the possibility of evacuation made these memories more comforting. How else did one make the world seem habitable? *They know who they are. They love their bodies.*

Smoke crept through the vents, past the well-sealed windows, around the minuscule spaces between the doors and their frames. Slithering, invisible, insidious. It roused Lu from her reverie just as her phone began to scream. *Out now! Out now!*

24

NEWS OF THE FIRES in Sonoma commandeered the internet, stealing attention from the Michigan Nine, at least for the time being. The photos were terrifying: firefighters with smudged, blistering faces and clenched jaws wielding hoses like AR15s, houses crumbling like toppled LEGO creations, aerial shots revealing acres of destruction. It took no imagination at all for Philippa to picture the flames spreading throughout the valley, leaping up hills and over roads, consuming their house. Terrifying as the images were, she couldn't look away; fire demanded unswerving vigilance if you expected to survive it. Fire or ice? She would always have chosen ice.

She was five years old. Her parents awakened her in the dark. It was cold, and she was not done sleeping. *Come on now. Wake up.* Her father was gruff and moving more quickly than usual. He swaddled her in a quilt and ferried her to the car, where, still in pajamas, she huddled against her mother in the back seat, trying to warm up. Lu covered them both with a blanket. *It's okay. We're going to be okay.* She repeated this over and over, like the refrain of a song or a poem, but Philippa could feel her mother's body trembling, and it did not feel as if things were okay. Still, she liked having all three of them together in the dark car.

The back of the car was filled with stuff. *Where're we going?*

Shush, her parents said, both at the same time.

She wriggled out from under her mother's arm to sit up straight. Through the front window she saw flashing red lights and a long caravan of cars. Behind the hill that rose on the right side of the road an orange glow oozed, finger-painting the sky, making the trees into black skeletons. Philippa did not cry. She nestled into her mother's belly.

Are we going to die? she asked.

Shh, said her mother.

No one is going to die, her father said.

When she woke again, they were getting out of the car at the winery and it was still dark. Smoke bothered her nose. The orange glow was still present, but it was in a different part of the sky. Her father disappeared into the darkness. She waved at the two friendly lions on either side of the wide entrance, trailing her fingers over their granite backs as they passed inside to the big room where tourists came to drink wine. She had only been there a few times on quick visits. It was dark, and the ceiling was so high it was eaten by space. Their mother turned on a couple of lights, which spilled down on them, making a dim yellow pool as if a huge egg had plopped down its yolk. She brought sleeping bags and pillows from the car and made a nest in one corner of the huge room, encircling them with easy chairs to make it cozier.

We're safe, her mother kept saying.

Where's Daddy? Will we go to school tomorrow? She had just started kindergarten. *Is this a war?*

Daddy's checking on things. Don't worry—it's not a war. Hush. Go to sleep. It will be fine.

Her mother lay down with her on the sleeping bags under the blankets. Her body was no longer trembling. It smelled calm, like the clear water of a stream. She sang songs in her raspy voice. "Hush, Little Baby." "Swing Low, Sweet Chariot." "Amazing

Grace." "Cielito Lindo." "La Cucaracha." Philippa loved those songs. She loved hearing her mother sing even though her father thought she had a bad voice. *My ears hurt*, he would say when their mother started to sing. *You're making my ears bleed.* But Philippa liked it, and her father's ears weren't really bleeding.

Her mother had super-long hair then, and Philippa grabbed a lock of it and held it tight like a leash, so she'd know if her mother tried to leave.

There was a lot she didn't remember about what had happened the next day and the days after that. How long had they stayed at the winery? What had the fire burned? She had vague memories of driving by forests of blackened stumps, but beyond that, the whole experience now seemed like a dream.

In the years following that fire, when she was six and seven and eight and awakened occasionally in the middle of the night without knowing why, she would go to her parents' room. *I think there's a fire*, she would say, and they would say, *No, go back to bed.*

When she was ten there was another unforgettable fire. That one began in daylight—or it was daylight when people noticed. It was September, a hot, dry day when the earth made a clicking sound, like cicadas, like the popping sound that comes when you try to talk through a dry mouth. *Clickety-clickety-pop.* She tapped the rhythms on her thighs. *Clickety-clickety-pop.* She and her mother were driving home from Santa Rosa, where they'd been shopping for school clothes, which was never a fun thing to do. Her mother wanted her to branch out from her usual jeans and T-shirts and make some more feminine choices, but Philippa wanted to dress as she'd always dressed. The salesclerk kept telling her how pretty she was, and she wished the woman would shut up. She didn't care about being pretty. She knew it wasn't her destiny. She had her father's stocky body, his gray eyes, his artistic and musical talent. She was glad her mother never insisted; she was lucky to have such a mother.

There were wineries along the road, and thirsty brown fields, and hillsides with just a few trees, and some more humble houses. Even worn down by a long hot summer, it was beautiful. They rounded a bend and there was the fire, not just smoke or glowing sky, but daredevil flames shimmying over the crest of the hill.

Fire! Philippa yelled. *Mom, it's a fire!*

Through the window, from a distance, the fire was mute, but in her head she heard the crackling soundtrack it appeared to be dancing to. *Swa-wah. Swa-wah. Kltl-da-da. Kltl-kltl. Scrl-scrl-kltl. Clssss-clssss.*

Shit, said her mother quietly. *Close your window, Pippa.*

She did as her mother instructed. The traffic ahead of them had slowed with people rubbernecking. The fire shot skyward and lobbed off separate squads that somersaulted down the hillside in an orange avalanche. You could hear it now, a muffled roar rising in volume like an approaching train. Smoke ballooned around the blaze, turning the daylight to dusk. Ash rained down on the hood of the car. How could fire move so quickly? Where was help?

Drive faster, Mom, Philippa pleaded.

I can't.

The road curved again, and on the other side of the bend was a house with flames shooting through its windows like long arms outgrowing their sleeves. It taunted the people driving by. *Ha-ha, you can't stop me.*

Her mother's hand snaked past the gearshift and took hold of Philippa's hand. *It's okay, Pippa*, she whispered, and Philippa nodded and scooted her butt to the left to be closer to her mother.

That was the day Philippa's fear of fire took root. Fire was no longer an abstraction, an eerie glow in the distance, but a real thing that ate up houses and the people inside them, and it couldn't be stopped. In the years since then she and her family had been evacuated more times than she could count on one hand. Each time it got scarier, the fires bigger and hotter, with lunatic minds of their own. And now her mother was up north, facing such a fire alone.

25

LU ARRIVED AT the high school parking lot at dusk but couldn't bring herself to go inside. She was thinking about how George had hated being there. He despised the knots of worried people, the gloppy cafeteria meals, the nights on a cot in a gymnasium side by side with strangers, kept awake by snoring and coughing and crying children, people traipsing back and forth to the bathroom, sirens and helicopters blaring in the distance, only partly muffled by the school's brick walls. The smells disturbed him too, the institutional cleansers trying to mask the odor of overused toilets, the collective stew of body odor, the stratiform layers of past meals that never entirely disappeared. He had no ability to ignore these discomforts and find satisfaction in the communal aspect of the situation, strangers and neighbors gathered to face down a danger that threatened them all.

Procrastinating, she hung out in her car for a while listening to some music Pippa had recommended, then she took a walk around the playing fields and down the road in the grim, smoke-darkened light until fire officials stopped her. Back in her car she nibbled trail mix and watched others arriving, toting bags and backpacks, their faces twisted into expressions of anguish and disbelief. The volunteers greeted everyone with exaggerated good cheer without realizing their insistently upbeat manner underscored how bad things were.

Just before 10:00 P.M., when they were about to lock the doors for the night, she roused herself from a light sleep and went inside with backpack and sleeping bag. A volunteer pointed her to the dim gymnasium, where cots had been arranged in rows a few feet apart. They'd been made up with sheets and blankets—who knew where from—but Lu preferred to use her own sleeping bag. It could have been an army barracks or a refugee camp—it *was* a refugee camp, she realized. She was directed to one of the few empty cots in the far corner. To reach it she had to navigate a path over the lacquered gym floor past dozens of people, some sleeping, some still awake, all surrounded by moats of their personal belongings. Some had changed into pajamas or nightgowns, but most wore street clothes; a few had pulled blankets over their heads, caving themselves into dark mounds; some lay curled in fetal shapes, sleeping or not, it was hard to tell; still others lay on their backs, staring into the porous half-light, made listless by dread.

She tiptoed past them all, trying to keep her gaze from piercing the membranes of imagined privacy people had constructed around themselves. The cots on both sides of her, separated by four feet, held blanketed people who appeared to be sleeping. She stuffed her backpack under the designated cot, laid out her sleeping bag, and crawled into it, fully clothed.

Tired as she was, she was much too wired for sleep. She had never evacuated without other family members, and though she was lonely, she was glad George and Pippa were safely elsewhere, even as she hated to think of how far-flung they were from one another. She thought about the fire wending its way up and down the dry hills in the dark, irreverent and unpredictable, challenging and demolishing illusions of human control, emboldened by the human need to sleep. Maybe the movement of fire didn't seem so random to the scientists, to people who studied wind and air currents, temperature and humidity and topography, the condition of the trees and grasslands, how all those elements interacted with one another to govern a fire's path, but if you were a civilian, fire looked like a trickster, changing direction suddenly, for no apparent reason. Even the meteorologists sometimes shrugged in an admission of helplessness.

Lu and George had been lucky so far. The vineyards had seen some smoke damage four years earlier, but they had recovered, and the fires had never reached the neighborhood where they lived, though if conditions had been slightly different they easily could have.

Her eyes adjusted to the dark, which had morphed to blue-gray. Three red exit signs pulsed like pilot lights. She wondered if any of her neighbors were there—probably most of them had had the foresight to secure hotel rooms early. She thought of her mother up in Redding. She had claimed to be safe, but there were fires just over the border in Oregon. No one was safe for long.

The Mexicans who worked the vineyards had settled with their families on one side of the gym. Many of them were undocumented and spoke minimal English. Some of their employers might have been there too. She liked to think of this leveling, owners and workers eating and sleeping side by side, facing the same threat, having to acknowledge their shared humanity. The Mexican families kept their children snuggled beside them, two or three to a cot, reminding Lu of the intimacy she and her mother had shared at the Nest. Except when she was at her mother's restaurant, she rarely thought about her Mexican ancestry. She'd always felt a part of mainstream Anglo-California culture. But seeing the Mexican workers there she felt sad for having ignored that side of her heritage, for never having learned much Spanish. She hadn't consciously severed the connection, but it had floated into insignificance. Could she ever reclaim that part of herself, as her mother had done so actively?

A restlessness prevailed, people rustling, whispering, turning over, sitting up, uncapping plastic water bottles, lying back down, giving sleep another try, everyone doing their best to stay sane amid the uncertainty, but after a while the timbre of the room shifted, and a new rhythm took over. A long legato, a slow release, each body in the room synchronizing itself with the bodies beside it, until they were all inhaling and exhaling in unison, a single, many-parted breathing organism.

At some point Lu slept too, though it was a light sleep skating just below consciousness. When she woke, the sense of a coordinated group had shattered. A gray-haired woman on one of the adjacent cots fumbled with her cache of belongings; seeing Lu awaken, she nodded then turned respectfully away. One of the Mexican men was wiping the nose of his young daughter, whispering to her in Spanish. An elderly white woman, face dotted with warts the size of small mushrooms, wheeled her walker slowly toward the exit. Many of the cots were empty, but the air was still imbrued with collective distress.

Multiple panicky texts had come in from Pippa while Lu was sleeping. She texted back. *In high school evacuation center. I'll keep you posted. Don't worry. Love, Mom.*

It was almost 8:00 A.M., later than she usually slept. She had sweated into her street clothes. If she were to be here for more than a few days, which was probable, cleaning only with sponge baths, she would soon reek like a barnyard animal. She rolled up her sleeping bag and left it on her cot.

People milled around the lobby, immersed in their phones or

conversing in small groups. Outside, a few teenage boys, the scions of Sonoma's wine barons, hung in a loose circle, laughing uproariously. Small kids, channeling their parents' anxiety, jetted around the lobby. She made her way to the cafeteria, where people had set up laptops, catching what news they could. Lu hovered behind a man whose screen displayed an aerial shot of the fires. "Mind if I watch?" she asked.

"No problem. There's a second fire now, the Yulupa Creek Fire, a little farther north than the Hawk Fire. The wind is blowing them both east. They're concerned the two might merge, become another fire complex." He pointed to his screen but before she could recognize the topography the image was replaced by a newscaster. She walked away. She had wanted to see the fires for herself but hated listening to the speculation of newscasters, sensationalizing everything to raise their ratings, pretending to know what was happening when no one really knew.

Breakfast was being served by a group of cheerful women with hairnets. She couldn't tell if these were the usual school cafeteria workers or volunteers, but they were doing double duty, serving food while also, like social workers, attempting to bolster people. The fare was cold cereal and scrambled eggs, along with orange juice, coffee, and milk. Served from metal troughs, none of it was appetizing, but Lu had come to understand the imperative to eat in these situations. The relationship between food and survival clarified itself in emergencies, removed food from the realm of artful pleasure. Anorexia as a stress response did no one any good.

She stood with her tray, awkward as a teenager, surveying the tables, spotting no one she knew. It wasn't crowded, so she took a table by herself. Barely awake, she sipped the institutional coffee, hoping for quick results to offset her poor sleep.

"Hey there!" It was Gloria, Julie close behind. So they weren't in hotels after all. They took seats at the table as if she'd been expecting them.

"I'm surprised to see you," Lu said. "I thought you'd both be in hotels."

"We tried," Gloria said. "Believe me, we tried. Every damn place was booked."

"I tried too. Same thing. Where are your husbands?" Lu wasn't sure she could pick out either of their husbands from a crowd.

"Oh, they're out there somewhere pretending to be important." Gloria waved an arm in the direction of the lobby. "When they come back in here they'll be armed with 101 Facts About the Fire."

"We're supposed to get them breakfast, but they can get their own," Julie said. "How did you sleep?"

"Well, I might have slept for an hour," Lu said.

"Me too," Julie said. "But Gloria here, she slept like a baby. Or did you say a log?"

"Definitely not a baby. I have nothing in common with a baby. I love sleeping with the hoi polloi."

Hoi polloi. The term made Lu cringe—she'd never heard it until she met George. Lu herself, as Julie's former low-wage employee, would once have been considered the hoi polloi.

"Have you heard anything about the fire? How much is contained?" she asked, but only to make conversation—she knew it was much too early for containment.

"The news isn't good," Gloria said. "Unless the wind changes, our neighborhood is directly in its path. And you heard about the other one, right, the Yulupa Creek Fire? Apparently they're likely to merge."

Lu nodded.

"Where's George?" Julie asked.

"In Florida. His father had a stroke."

"So sorry to hear that. Crises always happen in multiples, don't they? Is he going crazy not being here?"

Lu shrugged. George had called minutes before she left the house. He was a predictable hotbed of worry and had made her promise to stay in close touch.

"He wants to come home, but what for? He can't fight the fires—he's much too old for that. And he'd be miserable here. He'd only be adding to the high level of anxiety already in the pot."

"From what I've seen his winery may be okay." Gloria shrugged. "But what do I know? Of course, it's much too early to tell."

"He'll be trying to orchestrate things from Florida," Lu said, laughing a little to obscure whatever truth she spoke.

A couple had entered the cafeteria with a herd of six children in tow. One of them, a toddler, was crying, an older child was calling out for a Band-Aid, but both bedraggled blond parents ignored them.

"Aren't you glad to be done with all that?" Gloria said.

The father's athletic shorts drooped to reveal his butt crack. It fascinated Lu to see how people let themselves go in a crisis like this, herself included. Her gaze strayed from the family and landed on a woman at another table who was staring unabashedly, downright rudely. The woman was a collage of hot colors—brassy copper hair, red lips, red fingernails, pink blouse, orange neck scarf—an elaborate getup that contrasted sharply with the general informality. Had she put herself together with those colors to embody the heat of the fire?

Lu's attention returned to the table, where Julie was narrating her mad scramble to gather things at the last minute. Business documents. Titles. Licenses. She had thought she had them all in the same place, but she turned out to be wrong. She thought she'd learned from the last fire, and she was a businesswoman so it was her job to be organized—how could she have been so stupid?

"But now I see the yogi in me predominates. At least my diamonds were where I expected them to be." She fluttered a hand, on which every finger, including the thumb, was covered with two or three diamond rings. "What did you save?"

Lu held up her backpack, then realized the question wasn't aimed at her.

"Not much," Gloria said. "I'm not going to be happy if everything burns, but it wasn't long after we moved here that I saw the writing on the wall—even ten years ago I could see that someday we'll lose it all. We'll be lucky if we don't die in a fire someday, that's what I think. Hey, if we were in Florida, water would be our big enemy, right? It's always going to be something—water and fires don't care if you have degrees and jobs and bank accounts. You just have to hope, when the time comes, that you have the cash—not to mention the will—to rebuild. Or maybe drive off a cliff, if you're so inclined." She laughed her big habitual laugh.

"You're a brave lady," Julie said.

"It has nothing to do with bravery." Gloria's voice was part growl. "It's reality, hon."

The brassy-haired woman stood and glanced again at Lu. She was tall and commanding. Her orange scarf quivered. Marley.

26

"MOM? MOM, are you there?"

"Pippa," Lu said, exhaling, enveloped in a microsecond of luxurious relief—her daughter there at the end of the line, calling voluntarily. "I was just about to call you. Are you okay?"

"The question is are *you* okay?"

"Then you've heard what's happening?"

"It's all over the internet. It sounds bad. I'd have to be an ostrich not to have heard."

How rattled Pippa sounded, almost combative. This tendency to overreact was exactly why Lu was always cautious about breaking bad news.

"So I'm here at the high school. You remember what that's like?"

"Is Dad coming home? Should I come up there?"

"No, there's nothing you can do. I told your dad the same thing. We just have to wait it out."

"You don't have to protect me, Mom. I can see on the internet it's heading in the direction of our house. Aren't you worried?"

"Yes, I'm worried. But there's no need for you to worry too. Worry never does any good."

"You know I'll worry. You can't just order me not to worry."

"Pippa—Phipps—is everything okay there?"

A long silence followed in which Alice meowed. A siren passed somewhere, maybe here, maybe there.

"It's fine."

"You like your classes?"

"I like zoology."

"That's good."

"Hey, how can you tell . . ." A long pause.

"Tell what?"

"If someone . . . Never mind."

"If someone what?"

"Forget it."

"Is this about a guy?"

"I said forget it."

An ambulance was driving up to the front of the school, its lights flashing. Lu closed her eyes for a moment of respite. She couldn't absorb another emergency.

"Talk to him. There's never any harm in talking."

A background crash. Pippa's phone seemed to have fallen. The cat's meowing grew louder. There was more rustling of objects.

"Phipps—are you okay?"

A muffled sob.

"Please say something, Philippa honey. Are you still there? What's wrong?" She waited.

A sniff. "Yeah, I'm here."

"Oh, honey, I wish—" How had it happened that she and Pippa were so far apart at a moment when they needed each other more than ever? So much to wish for, so much to fix. "I'm hugging you now. I'm hugging you with all my might. Can you feel it?"

More sniffing. "My zoology professor says if we were scarlet jellyfish we could live forever."

Another obscure reference thrumming with unknowable subtext? "That's interesting."

"For me, one regular life is more than enough."

"Are you okay?"

"I said I'm fine. Life sucks, but I'm fine."

"Pippa honey, it will get better. I promise." She hated herself for repeating what George had said almost verbatim. Sometimes things didn't get better.

"Maybe. Maybe not."

Fire engines, sirens blaring, were speeding into the parking lot; it was impossible to hear. "I'll call you soon, honey, okay? And you can call me. Anytime."

Pippa was gone with barely a sign-off. *One regular life is more than enough.* It sounded to Lu as if she'd found a guy she liked and was already heartbroken. It was impossible to tell from afar if Pippa's moodiness was merely a bout of transient unhappiness or if it spoke to serious depression. A child had to discover she could survive such setbacks, but Pippa was more sensitive than most children and possibly needed more protection. Maybe Lu should tell her to come home? Or she could drive down to LA right now and pick her up. What terrible timing though, to bring her home into the midst of this fire.

A stretcher bearing a body was being carried through the school's front door and loaded into the ambulance. A cardiac arrest? A stroke? A seizure? She hoped she didn't know whoever it was. It was still morning. So much more daylight remained. The days in evacuation, characterized by waiting, unspooled more slowly than ordinary days, making them ripe with opportunity for serial disasters.

Four-year-old Pippa appeared before her, naked, lying belly down on the grass, ear to the ground, her little pink bottom glowing in the air.

27

SHE SAT ON the top step of the outdoor staircase enumerating the ways the world was fucked. Fires burning close to their home. Her mother stuck in the evacuation center telling her to stay put. Her father in Florida trying to piece his father together like some Humpty-Dumpty project. And Dar being nice to her only out of obligation. She'd been trying to ignore her superstitions since coming to LA, but now there was no ignoring the fact that bad omens were piling up.

She'd inherited her superstitions from her father. It wasn't something they talked about, but she'd watched him making sure small things were in order, a clear form of disaster prevention. He aligned the items on his desk just so. He made sure the shoes they left just inside the front door were always in neat pairs. She often caught him sliding the living room chairs a few inches in one direction or another after a gathering, and he threw a hissy fit if someone put on a roll of toilet paper so it unspooled from beneath instead of from above. She never knew the specifics of what he feared, but it was obvious to her he was scared of something. When she commented on his behaviors, he laughed them off. *You never know*, he would say. *You never know what?* But he never answered, and she understood why. Admitting to his superstitions would make him appear irrational and foolish, and he prided himself on being in control, so he wasn't going to say to his daughter: *I fear an onslaught of irreversible mayhem.*

She wasn't as badly afflicted as he was, but she'd never been able to stop herself from noticing the signs that appeared suddenly before her indicating an imminent upward or downward swing. In the mornings she would sometimes see Alice biting her forepaw so ferociously it was hard not to take it as a warning of a difficult day ahead. A flattened garter snake in her path, a sudden siren, the lecherous smile of a politician on a billboard. When these things appeared at the wrong moment they could cast a shadow over her whole day. This habit of mind worked in the other direction too. She might hear a *klickety-clack-clack* in the floorboards, a perfect triplet; or see her cowlick in the mirror jutting up at the perfect pert angle; or a mourning dove, her favorite bird, would call out at just the right moment, and she would know her fortunes were turning upward.

Dar's comment to his friend about being a *working stiff* had made her rethink things—she was having to realize he didn't think she was special. She couldn't stand to think that she represented an obligation to him even though it made sense—she was his *student* after all. She wondered if she shouldn't visit him again until she had some positive sign he really wanted her to come.

The fires, however, now eclipsed her concern about Dar. She'd always been terrified of fires, but this year they were so much bigger than ever before. They were so massive they created their own weather systems, including tornados. She had already been feeling this might be the year her family's luck would run out, and now that a fire had ignited and was heading for her home her premonition felt right. She had no way of knowing if her mother was in imminent danger, but it was certainly possible. Shouldn't she go up there even though her mother had said not to? She wasn't old enough to rent a car, but she could take a train or maybe fly.

The night before Alice had been unusually agitated. She'd stalked around the apartment, leaping onto the bed, positioning herself on the pillow to knead Philippa's scalp, then jumping up again for more cruising. Of course Philippa hadn't been able to sleep either, and she couldn't witness that disturbed behavior without wondering what was bothering Alice. She must have sensed the fires. Now she had staked out the coolest place in the apartment, the bathroom rug. She was snoring loudly, leaving behind the day's events as animals do, fully embarked on the joyful voyage down the river of forgetfulness.

Philippa was scheduled again for a drumming session with Joel, the guy in her music theory class. He had reserved a practice room equipped with two drum sets for 11:00 in the music building. She was much too preoccupied to be meeting someone, let alone play drums, but their plan had been rescheduled so many times she hated to cancel. She headed to campus without Alice.

She waited for Joel at a table in a communal area surrounded by doors leading to soundproof practice rooms. Muffled sound reached her nonetheless. A trumpet, a piano, a string quartet. It was music that could have been occult messages from outer space. Every once in a while the phrases from all the rooms seemed to coordinate for a bar or two before veering into subdued cacophony again. Two women arrived with guitar cases and went to their assigned room. A flutist arrived. A cellist. No Joel.

After twenty minutes she texted him.

P: *What's up?*

J: *My bad. We have to reschedule.*

This was the fourth time their plans had fallen through. How many times should a person submit to being stood up?

She walked home again, wondering what was wrong with Joel. She was pleased not to hear Alice yowling as she mounted the apartment steps. Maybe she was finally accepting her inside-only status.

"A-lice!" She stood at the foot of the bed, waiting for Alice to pounce from her hiding place. "A-lice?" She peered behind the bathroom door. "Alice, come out."

She searched under the bed. "What the fuck?"

There was no other place to look—Alice was gone.

The certainty that Mrs. Marvel was responsible dawned on her slowly. It should have been obvious. Alice did not open the door herself. Mrs. Marvel was the only other person with a key. She must have come up here while Philippa was gone and let Alice out. So maybe Alice had been making a little noise, but that was no excuse—she was a cat, for god's sake, a small animal only capable of so much noise. What a hateful woman!

She texted her mother.

L: *Oh no honey, I'm so sorry. I was afraid of this.*

P: *But what should I do?*

L: *The police?*

P: *They won't care.*

She thought of contacting Dar but didn't.

She stood on the outside landing and glared down into Mrs.

Marvel's kitchen window. She would have liked to call the police and report Mrs. Marvel as her mother had suggested, but she doubted the law would support her, especially since she had no clear evidence that Mrs. Marvel was responsible, only a very strong suspicion. Still, she wasn't going to let Mrs. Marvel get away with this.

She combed the neighborhood on foot, a few blocks in every direction. Where would Alice seek refuge? Probably in someone's backyard. But Philippa couldn't just wander into people's yards.

Back home it took several rounds of knocking for Mrs. Marvel to answer her front door. She was wearing a royal blue jogging suit and looked at Philippa as if she was a stranger. The TV news blared in the background.

"Hello, dear. Can I help you?"

Philippa couldn't stand the fake sweetness. "My cat is gone. I got home late this morning and she wasn't there. I was only gone for maybe an hour."

"Oh no. How terrible."

"Did you let her out?"

"Heavens no. Why would I do that?" Her indignation was obviously feigned, which further burned Philippa.

"Because you don't like the noise she makes."

"Maybe you left the window open."

"I did not leave the window open."

Mrs. Marvel shook her head. "Well, she can't be far."

"I've been looking for her all day."

"Maybe you should check the animal shelters. Good luck." She closed her door abruptly.

The next day Philippa skipped her classes. She searched the neighborhood again, going farther afield this time, posting flyers on tree trunks with a picture of Alice on them, asking whomever she saw, "Have you seen a gray cat with white markings on her face?" No one had. Her rage at Mrs. Marvel crescendoed into an internal aria that was hard to suppress.

She located the closest animal shelter and took an Uber there. She couldn't believe how many lost cats there were. A large concrete block room had been devoted exclusively to cats, stacked in metal cages, each with a three-by-five card bearing a made-up name. The choral meowing made for a deafening clamor in which she could find no rhythm at all. How sad these cats must be to be keening like this—it made her soul hurt. One gray cat whose card read "Minnie" looked a bit like Alice—but wasn't.

Back at home she lay on the bed feeling the city churn around her. Such unending commotion. She might as well have been stuck in a cement mixer. When Alice was here with her, the city hadn't felt quite as intrusive. She rose to go on yet another walk, though her legs had begun to feel wobbly.

She thought about going home, despite what her mother had said, but she would have had to take multiple buses to get there, and once there, she'd be one more person for the evacuation center to house and feed. Also, if she were to leave LA, she would be abandoning the possibility of finding Alice.

The next day an email arrived from Dar. *You weren't in class yesterday. Just checking in.* She emailed back: *Alice is gone. I think my landlady let her loose.* His reply: *Come to my office.*

She stepped into his office. The overflowing shelves. The dust-filled sunlight. The perch of a man who appreciated Alice. "Still no Alice?" he said. The too-muchness of it all hit her, and she concealed her face beneath her hands and sobbed. He said nothing. She half expected him to wrap his arms around her, but he didn't. She was horribly aware of embarrassing herself in the presence of a man she might possibly love. She heard him opening the file cabinet drawer where he stored the Oreos. Then he sat in his musical office chair, and she sat too. Finally relaxing a little under the gentle prodding insistence of his attention, she dared to look up.

28

EVERYONE IN the evacuation center understood the capriciousness of fire and, knowing this, their minds turned readily toward disaster. Maybe if you were new to the area, you might have had faith the fires could be stopped or contained, but if you'd been living there for a while, you knew that what survived and what didn't was a crapshoot, which made the waiting torture.

Anxiety set up camp. An invisible but invasive presence, it threaded through every conversation, nibbled at tempers, disturbed sleep. Like a foul odor, it couldn't be dispelled. You would have had to be deficient not to sense its presence in some way, not to think about all the things you stood to lose and wonder how you would ever return from such losses.

For Marley, the nightmare was losing her artwork. She had dozens of paintings stored in her studio that she hadn't wanted to sell. They dated back to her first attempts at making art, when her days were spent as a software developer and she devoted her evenings to experimenting with paint. It had taken her almost a decade to make the leap into full-time art, a scary transition partly due to financial concerns, but also because she'd been one of the few women who wrote software back then and her reputation in the field was stellar. It was hard to say goodbye to that when there was no guarantee she'd achieve the same success as an artist. But she knew she'd never respect herself if she allowed the fear to hold her back. And now here she was, living the life she'd always fantasized about living. If her studio were to burn and all that work were lost, she'd be devastated. She'd never understood how most artists handed their work off to dealers or museums, never looking back. She herself was always looking back. *Look where I started. Look where I am now.*

Time moved differently in a crisis. A day ground through its minutes and felt like a month. Every hour a new mood blew in, took hold for a while, then dissipated. Everyone handled the anxiety of the unknown differently. Denial. Aggressive optimism. Information gathering. Building the communal spirit. Finding a specific task to do that you were better at than anyone else, like cleaning, or leading yoga classes, or running an ad hoc school.

Marley had joined the ranks of the helpers by convincing the supermarket to contribute what they had in the way of notebooks, colored pencils, crayons, so she could lead a group in making art. They'd been keeping fire journals, each day drawing and writing what they observed and their reactions to it. The results, crude but heartfelt, touched Marley.

Still, restlessness built. Marley was used to spending hours in solitude; here she was surrounded by people all day long inhabiting her extroverted public self. Over time it became exhausting. Marley could feel George's wife watching her, almost stalking her, a perpetual presence in her peripheral vision. She had recognized Lu immediately. George had shown her pictures. She was small and dark-eyed, with a smooth hazelnut complexion and long black hair, shiny as patent leather. She was much more attractive in person than she had appeared to be in the pictures, and it stirred up twinges of jealousy in Marley, who envied such petite women, small enough to be suitcase stowaways. Lu's response to being here,

Marley observed with amusement, seemed somewhat similar to her own. Lu was warm and enthusiastic most of the time, free with her hugs and notable for her animation in conversations, but she was also a loner, disappearing to her car for hours at a time as if the communal situation had become too much for her. Where was George? Marley was relieved he wasn't here, but where was he?

Being watched by Lu made Marley feel like a heel. By flirting so egregiously with another woman's man without ever intending to go through with the seduction, she had violated both Lu and George. She knew George had been expecting sex when he came to her studio and, while he was a perfectly nice man and a good conversationalist, he wasn't a person Marley wanted to have sex with. At fifty-two, having shed one brief, ill-fated marriage and endured another bad breakup just before leaving the Bay Area, she couldn't imagine partnering with anyone again. Even casual hookups had too many perils. What she'd hoped for in inviting him to the studio was simply to show him more of her paintings so he would talk her up among his high-rolling friends who might be interested in purchasing them. But if she was honest with herself, she had to admit she'd been leading him on, dangling sex as a reward in exchange for his connections. She felt bad about exploiting her femininity that way; she didn't approve of other women who did that, and she didn't sanction it in herself. After that evening, she'd stopped by the winery a couple of times, hoping to apologize and set things straight between them, but George had ignored her. She understood she'd wounded him. Men and their weak egos.

Marley had been sleeping terribly on her narrow cot in the gymnasium. They weren't built for tall people. She tried to stay still so as not to disturb those around her, but it was hard to get comfortable with her feet hanging off the cot's end. She put in earbuds and listened to music or audiobooks, lying on her back and thinking about the haplessness of humanity. So many insurmountable problems. She often chose Albinoni's *Adagio*, which never failed to make her weep. It seemed to encapsulate all the sadness of the human race. It was the folly of civilization (alongside her artistic aspirations) that had prompted her to leave the San Francisco rat race and her very well-paid job. She had cashed out her stock options and fled to Sonoma, needing to be somewhere remote, away from the tentacles of status-obsessed, consumerist culture. The world was a terrible place, run largely by grandiose idiots; nothing could ever entice her to return to the heart of such a world. Even Sonoma was turning out to be not remote enough. But it was hard to leave—you always needed some people in your life, and, though she hated to admit it, she needed access to the wealthy people who bought her art.

Movement in her peripheral vision. Lu was threading a path through the thicket of cots to the exit. She moved quickly, nimble, soundless, insubstantial as a hallucination. The sight of her aroused Marley's guilt again. She paused the music, removed her earbuds, sloughed the covers as quietly as she could, and tiptoed over the cold lacquered floor in bare feet. The lobby was empty, but the front door, always locked at night, was propped open with a brick. A figure scuttled beyond the reach of the outdoor light, into smoke-shrouded fog.

"Hey!"

Startled, Lu turned.

"Where're you going?" Marley's voice was a loud whisper, though there was no one else around.

Lu shrugged. "What do you want?"

"I couldn't sleep either. I thought we might talk."

Lu turned and walked away from Marley, toward the cars.

Marley, ignoring the gravel digging into her bare feet, followed, falling in beside Lu, towering over her. The night was cooler than the preceding nights had been, better for suppressing the fires maybe, but the smoke was still intransigent. Neither of them had protective masks. But Lu had shoes.

"You don't want to talk?" Marley said, already wondering what she herself sought in a conversation.

Lu stopped abruptly, staring ahead as if waiting for a command, reminding Marley of the Red Light/Green Light game she had played as a kid.

"What do you want to talk about?"

"George?"

Lu huffed, part laugh, part scoff.

"Where is he?"

"Florida. His father had a stroke."

"Oh no, I'm so sorry to hear that."

Lu shrugged again.

"For what it's worth," Marley said, "we didn't have sex."

"So I've been told."

"I never wanted sex."

"That's why you lit candles and served wine?"

"I know, I know. The optics were bad, but I always light candles, every night. I only invited him over to show him more of my work. That's all. I need patrons."

"I don't know if you've ever been married, but when your husband steps out it doesn't feel good. It makes a person question everything."

"I'm really sorry. I mishandled things. I get carried away sometimes."

"He thinks you're more interesting than I am. He said you were out of his league."

Did George really believe that she was out of his league—how could he really believe that, being married to an attractive woman like Lu? Still, the possibility thrilled her a little then shamed her. It had been a long time since she'd tried to please men, and she didn't want to return to those days.

"You might not believe me, but I don't have much interest in men these days. Any men. I'm not saying I'm into women, I'm just—I don't want to be attached, shall we say."

Lu turned to look at Marley, assessing her coldly. "You know what else he said? He said we look alike."

Marley stifled a laugh. Why would George have said that? Two women could not look more different than she and Lu. Their sizes alone put them in entirely different categories.

"What a strange thing to say."

Lu nodded.

"Maybe it wasn't our looks so much as—something else . . . I hope you can forgive me."

Lu crossed her arms over her chest as if to protect herself, her expression perplexed. "Why?"

"I don't know—I guess I just don't like being hated."

"*Hate* isn't the word."

Marley wanted to ask what the right word would be then realized there probably wasn't a single word to sum up what Lu felt.

"Okay. Point taken." She hesitated. "Okay then. Good night."

Marley left Lu alone and headed back to the school. Her feet were killing her. Before she passed through the front door she turned. Smoke had wanded Lu entirely out of sight.

Back on her cot, Marley checked the soles of her bare feet to see if they were bleeding. There was no broken skin, but they hurt like hell. She reinserted her earbuds, closed her eyes, and restarted the *Adagio*, feeling its crescendo going to work on heart and glands until tears came. She wished she understood this magic of sound waves, how they could press on internal body parts like massaging fingers. She wondered what Lu would think of this music. Marley hated being part of the problem, but there was no denying she was at fault.

29

LU WAS in the bathroom stall, done peeing but continuing to sit there, scrolling through her phone and savoring the rare moment of privacy. She was reading reports she had previously avoided about the Michigan Nine and the disappearance in West Virginia of yet another group. The reports were absurdly sensational as always, but a welcome distraction from speculation about the wildfires, Marley, her marriage. Reporters had been following the young children in Michigan who'd been abandoned and were exhibiting signs of deep distress. How laughable that this was newsworthy—*of course* the children were distressed, wasn't it obvious—*their parents were gone*, for god's sake. Didn't these reporters understand the most basic aspects of human nature?

Someone entered and went to the sink, and Lu could see through the door's slit that it was Marley. She'd been observing Marley for a full week now and experiencing a multitude of contradictory reactions. Marley had an undeniable charisma. In part due to her astonishing height—over six feet, Lu guessed—but also because of the way she sashayed around the evacuation center like a celebrity, known by many people and entering conversations with the expectation she would be welcomed, always well groomed and freshly made-up. George had described her as a hermit, but she wasn't behaving like a hermit. She was always dressed artfully in colorful fabrics that drew attention; it wasn't a style favored by Lu, who preferred utilitarian clothing in earth tones, but it was what one might expect from an artist. The clothes echoed Marley's emotionally forward style; she seemed ready to approach anyone. It looked exhausting to be Marley—in much the same way it was exhausting to be herself, she realized. But Marley was bolder, with fewer boundaries. When she had followed Lu outside in the middle of the night, she apparently didn't consider she might be intruding. Noticing these things, Lu understood why George had been taken with her. She was larger than life, and that was exactly what George had always aspired to be, though he was often disturbed to find himself falling short.

Lu's interest in Marley had ballooned into an obsession. She was partly transfixed by anger, yes, but her obsession involved something beyond the examination of a rival. There was something she needed to understand. The confidence of Marley. The magnetism. Things she wanted for herself.

Marley was washing her face with what looked like exfoliant, then drying it with a washcloth from her comically large red handbag. Digging into her handbag again, she drew out an array of makeup containers, which she lined up like toy soldiers along the sink.

Lu rose from the toilet and pulled up her pants, buttoning them with all the stealth and silence of a stalking cat. She brought her eye to the door's slit, widening her view.

Two colors of foundation. A compact of blush. Lip liner. Lipstick. Tweezers. Eyebrow pencil. Eyeshadow. Concealer. Brushes of various sizes. It was more makeup than Lu used for even the fanciest of occasions.

A complex and delicate operation ensued. A forefinger smoothed two colors of foundation over face and neck. A brush was used for texturizing, followed by tweezing of eyebrows and chin, errant hair by errant hair. Then the redrawing of the brows, and lip liner to exaggerate the Cupid's bow of the lips. The signature red lipstick was applied with a fine brush; a larger brush swept clouds of powder across brow and cheeks.

She examined herself from all angles, then closed her eyes and sprayed her entire face. Lu had never seen such an elaborate makeup ritual. Why do this for yet another day in the evacuation center, when everyone else was clad in jeans and hoodies, faces haggard, hair oily? Marley had said she wasn't interested in attracting men, so who was she doing this for? It was hard to imagine she was doing it only for herself. A wave of pity came over Lu. How terrible to be a woman who required such careful maintenance. Was this part of her persona as an artist? No, it wasn't that. It seemed to Lu that only a woman who doubted her value would spend so much time currying her appearance. Maybe Marley wasn't so confident after all.

She wasn't done yet. She drew a comb down the part in her hair, then hand-combed and fluffed the neon tresses that fell past her shoulder blades. Another appraisal. Left side, right side. Okay. She swept her equipment back into the red sack and strode out to the hallway. Lu sprang from her stall, washed her hands, and bent under the faucet to rinse her face. The cool water tumbled over her brows and cheeks, sweet relief.

30

PHILIPPA ADJUSTED HERSELF gingerly in the passenger's seat of Dar's Volvo and pinned her gaze out the windshield, ominously still except for one palm lightly drumming her thigh. The hair on the shaven hemisphere of her head had grown back as a light fuzz that reminded Dar of a newly hatched chick, belying the toughness conveyed by her jeans and denim shirt. He didn't regret offering to drive her to shelters in search of her cat—he had to give her *something* in the way of help with her life coming apart as it was—but getting into a car with her entailed an awkwardness he hadn't anticipated.

He hadn't made the offer lightly. Aware he might be transgressing professional boundaries, he had sought advice from Ivan, his best friend. The two had met in college, and Ivan, like Dar, was hanging on by a thread to his job teaching history at a small college in Iowa. They both knew their contracts as assistant professors were about to expire, and it didn't alarm them; they knew they could hustle up other jobs. They felt the nonsense of the academic enterprise, the futility of trying to transfer their passions to distracted adolescents, and they often riffed about the adventures they'd cook up together when they were finally, blessedly, cut loose: traveling to Africa and Southeast Asia, New Zealand and Australia.

"Not a good idea," Ivan advised him. "Not if you're wanting to fuck her."

"You've got the wrong idea. I have no desire to fuck her. I feel *responsible* for her. Paternal. Maybe avuncular. She's worried about her mom alone near the fires. And now her cat has gone missing—she's very attached to her cat. She's an odd duck and she interests me, but believe me, it's not sexual."

"If you say so."

"If you could meet her, you'd understand."

"What animal is she?"

It was a game they'd been playing for years, since they were college roommates and had a third roommate, Petey Spanbauer, whom Dar dubbed the Mole Rat, a moniker that had kept Ivan laughing for days.

"Well, there's something familiar about her—you know, in the way all dogs are familiar. But not a fawning dog, more like one that's a little wary at first and takes a while to get to know. Then there's a dove thing going on—she's got these gray eyes and she's a little mournful. Plus there's a strain of koala—she's cute and huggable like koalas are."

"Cute and huggable sounds dangerous."

"Get off it, Ivan. You're reading this wrong. I'm *worried* for her. She *cried* in my office. I might be the only person she talks to. And her family has had to evacuate because of the fires. She's understandably upset."

"Well, be careful with this dog-dove-koala girl. Let me know how it goes."

Dar would never have noticed Philippa had it not been for her cat going crazy in class and her subsequent visits to his office. The office visits alone were an anomaly. Students rarely came to his office hours, not seeing how it would benefit their grades. Over the seven years he'd been teaching he could count on two hands the number of students who had visited his office. In speaking with his colleagues he'd learned that empty office hours weren't unusual in this transactional, what-can-you-do-for-me school culture, but he couldn't help feeling that students ignored his office hours in part because they sensed his tenuous relationship to academia. They probably knew he was never going to become a full professor. After seven years he was still a lowly assistant professor, and when his eight-year assessment arrived it would certainly result in his termination. If he'd been committed to staying in academia, he should have been publishing papers regularly all along and currying favor with people in the field, but from almost the get-go he had realized he wasn't cut out for this life. He liked his research and the travel it entailed; he was born to think about animal consciousness. And he liked the teaching because it engaged the performer in him, but he wasn't interested at all in departmental politics and the politics of publishing in journals.

He had been pleased when Philippa started dropping by. He'd never had a student who seemed to enjoy his class as much as she did, and he had come to look forward to their talks. But he hadn't been prepared for her to cry in his presence. He wasn't trained to counsel anyone. He had offered the only help he could think of, which was how he found himself driving her north to a large animal shelter in his twenty-year-old kelly green Volvo.

He liked the sport of driving, and he drove as fast as his aging car would allow, weaving deftly around the slower cars. There was a sudden intake of breath from the passenger's seat.

"Am I scaring you with my driving?"

"Maybe a little," she admitted. "I'm a wuss about cars."

He slowed a little, but the slower speed was hard to maintain. Topics of conversation seemed more scarce here in his car than they were in his office. He floundered. "What do you think of the commune members that disappeared? Pretty wild, eh?"

"I've been reading about them—and about the women who disappeared. And I have a weird idea. I think maybe they wanted to disappear. You know what I mean? Maybe they're living somewhere even more remote, like off the grid, happier than they've ever been."

"Possibly."

"My dad works with a guy who lived off the grid for years."

"That's not easy to do."

"If you're motivated I think it would be . . . Hey, can I ask you something?" she said.

"Shoot."

"Am I your project? Like philanthropy or something—like, do you feel sorry for me?"

The question brought him up short with its hairy kernel of truth. "Of course not," he said, a beat too late.

They exited the freeway and headed up a canyon. The Gimme Shelter Animal Rescue Center was set on ten acres of a gently sloped hillside scattered with wild grasses, a Spartan beauty interspersed with occasional bright clumps of Indian paintbrush and lupine. An anomaly among shelters, it was part haven for lost domestic animals, mostly dogs and cats; part petting zoo with sheep and goats and a couple of deer; part aviary, housing dozens of parakeets along with raucous cockatoos and a couple of raunchy parrots. Built in the proud tradition of Southern California theme parks, the shelter's buildings and signage were painted in bright, kid-pleasing colors; there were dozens of short informational videos about the animals on display, and a gift shop sold various kinds of swag. It billed itself as a place that celebrated all animals and had become a destination for school groups and families looking for a wholesome weekend activity. Most of the visitors had no intention of adopting a pet.

Dar had never been there, and he immediately regretted his choice. He could see, even before they entered any of the buildings, that the place positioned animals as cutesy human adjuncts, an approach that always made him bristle. Philippa shared his reaction.

"I had no idea it would be like this," he said. "I'm sorry. Shall we forget it?"

"We might as well go in. I mean, if there's a chance Alice is in there . . ."

They wove past a classful of antsy schoolchildren on their way to the cat pavilion, past signage bearing pictures and factoids about cats. Just inside was an anteroom displaying a few cages of unusual cats: a long-haired Abyssinian, a giant Savannah cat, a nearly hairless Sphynx, a Japanese Bobtail that looked like a rabbit, a tiny white cat called a Teacup Persian.

"Cat sampler," Philippa quipped.

Inside the large cat room the sight was more typical of shelters, with long rows of metal cages stacked atop one another, each containing an animal made semi-psychotic by incarceration, everything suffused with a pungent cocktail of urine, dander, cleaning products.

Philippa, ignoring the chaos and pushing past the kids, had begun to stroll down the first row, bringing her nose close to the grillwork of each cage, investigating, her face alit with an expression he read as hope. She was doing more than looking for Alice, it seemed—a quick perusal would have revealed if Alice were there—she was lingering, making eye contact with the animals, offering them comfort. And the cats were responding, some reaching out with a paw, others beginning to purr. Watching her brought to mind his favorite memory, a memory that had also seemed to fascinate Philippa.

He had been diving in the waters off New Zealand with a friend who had guided him to a favorite spot for octopuses. So many octopuses in one place! Dar hung out with one of them for almost an hour, a creature so large and so entwined with the coral he could hardly locate all eight of its arms. At first he and this octopus merely watched each other, the retina of this cephalopod, so structurally similar to his own retina, considering him with uncanny sentience, swaying in the water currents, its undulant arms moving like a qigong master harvesting energy. There were no distractions, and neither of them looked away during this extended mutual investigation. After a while it felt as if the octopus was mirroring Dar's movements, the two engaged in a slow-motion duet. Then, the octopus reached out, looping one of its arms around Dar's gloved hand. Curious, unafraid, this animal seemed to be befriending him, and Dar had the sense it knew him in some intimate way he'd never been known before. He had certainly never spent an hour looking uninterruptedly at another human being in this way. The octopus was strong, and it seemed to be trying to pull Dar somewhere. Perhaps it wanted to eat Dar, but that wasn't the way it had felt. It felt as if the octopus wanted to show him something. He knew that sounded dopey and certainly unscientific, and he had never been tempted to tell anyone except Ivan about it, but he had learned something then that he'd never learned in all his years of studying zoology. Something to do with his own hubris and the hubris of most human beings. Ever since the world had looked different.

The experience was echoed when his grandmother was dying of ALS. Over the course of eighteen months she lost her ability to speak; the muscles throughout her body had weakened and finally given up, so she was confined to bed and reduced to communicating exclusively with her eyes. All her personhood was distilled in those sapient light brown eyes. They were like pieces of unearthed amber whose beauty could only have been formulated by time. She did not seem like less of a person to him, but like more of a person, more loving and more knowing, without a scintilla of pettiness or hatred (all past grudges rendered meaningless by the imminence of her death). One blink for yes, two for no. He talked to her about his life and hers, reading her responses not only in the blinking of her eyes but in the various patterns and atmospheres that passed through those eyes, some strong as stormy weather fronts, producing emotions that caused tears to leak. Inevitably he missed some of the nuances of what she was thinking and feeling, but the currents of her emotion were unmistakable, and they traveled to him and through him as if he was dialed directly into her gamma waves.

Those final days he had spent with her two weeks before she died were not unlike the hour he had spent with his New Zealand octopus. In both cases he was bathed in their focused attention and curiosity and high spirits, and it became an exploratory dance. Now Philippa seemed to be communicating with the cats in that same way.

It took almost a full hour for Philippa to explore all the cages. Alice wasn't there.

"I knew right away she wasn't here. I would have smelled her," she said. "But these cats are so sad I couldn't bear to leave without saying something to them."

They returned to the car, relieved to escape the circus-like atmosphere. The desperate animals. The unhinged kids. "It's a Small World After All" regaled them from a loudspeaker as they descended the walkway.

Philippa cocked her head. "'A Small World'? You've got to be kidding. Does Disney have to worm its way into everything?"

"I don't suppose you'd think of adopting one?" he said when they were ensconced in the car.

"I thought of it for a second. But it would be such a betrayal. Like going out and seeking another family member because someone in your own family was gone for a while. If Alice came back and found another cat in her place, what would she think?"

He nodded and started the car. He doubted if Alice would return after having been gone for five days. But it would be cruel to say that. Besides, Philippa was probably thinking the same herself.

They visited two other shelters, more conventional ones, without any sign of Alice, and on the drive back she was silent.

"Your mom is okay?"

She shrugged. "She's not telling me much. She's gone quiet on me."

"That sounds stressful. But they seem to be getting control of the fires, so that's good."

Why had he said that when he'd been on the internet and was fully aware the fires were still raging? He felt bad he was so bereft of skills to cheer her that he had to resort to lies.

"You'll be alright?" he asked as he dropped her off.

"Fine-ish."

He watched her plod up the steps to her garage apartment, touched again by some quality in her. A porousness that allowed her to understand the world more acutely than most. The responsibility he'd unwittingly assumed for her made him nervous. He didn't trust himself to live up to it. Back home, he called Ivan.

"Weird day."

"But no untoward behavior?"

"*Untoward behavior?*" Dar scoffed. Ivan's insinuation about his suspect motives was becoming annoying. "What the hell century are you from?"

31

INFORMATION BEGAN to come in from the cops and firefighters who stopped by for rest and refreshment. In certain limited areas the fire had been contained; elsewhere it was still raging out of control. Exhaustion spilled from the smudged, heat-ravaged faces of these men and women. They seemed to know things they were unlikely to divulge. What it was like to quell a fire and find human remains among the sodden ashes. How it felt to see deer and squirrels catching fire, becoming flameballs on legs, running maniacally away from the inferno then, confused, heading straight back into it, collapsing and dying in front of your eyes. The mordant smell of it all—a smell you could never adequately describe. The smell entered not only your nose but your mouth and eyes, ruining your ability to taste for days. Marley wondered if any of these men had read Dante's *Inferno* and thought of themselves as traveling through the circles of hell.

She loved these men—how could she not? Their willingness to damage their own bodies to help others, jeopardizing their own lives. Some of them were so young, boys really, who had traveled from other states seeking adventure, wanting to be heroes. She had never understood the appeal of heroism. She faulted herself for that. Going forward maybe she could focus less on herself and find a way to become more useful to others.

~

Marley's studio was still standing. The news came from the lips of a dazed, blue-eyed boy from Oregon who sat on a grassy area in front of the school eating his way through a box of jelly donuts. She knelt beside him, kissed the crown of his head, and sobbed.

"Thank you. Thank you," she whispered when she could push aside her sobs.

He extended the box of donuts to her, and she took one gladly. She had never loved a young man more. Her mouth was stuffed with donut when someone tapped her back. Lu.

"Your house?" Lu asked. "Did I hear it's okay?"

Marley nodded, swallowed her bite of donut quickly. "What a relief. Yours?"

"No news yet."

"The winery?"

"No news of that either."

Marley, fingers sticky with jelly, stared down at the remaining hunk of donut. "I shouldn't be eating this." She tossed it onto the grass.

Not far from where they stood a woman was crying, and one of the firefighters patted her back. People were rushing into the school, hot with purpose. Others rushed out. It was hard to say if something new had happened, something worse than all the bad that had already happened. Instinctively Marley and Lu both stepped back at the same time, as if they'd come to some agreement, and they watched the unfolding drama in silence. The awkwardness between them had been muted by the unfolding life-and-death crisis, as well as the days and nights—almost ten now—they'd spent under the same roof. Lu's cheeks gyrated in a rubbery expression of empathy, and heat simmered from her compact body, a barely contained conflagration of thought and feeling.

"I'm sorry I was so rude the other night," Lu said suddenly. "I'm in a fog these days."

"No worries."

"Whatever happened between you and George—it just, I don't know— It's not that important anymore. You look at the world— Something is happening to me—" She stopped speaking and clamped her palms to her temples.

"Are you okay?"

Lu, gaze on her feet, didn't respond. Marley kept as still and quiet as she could, feeling Lu to be on the doorstep of an important self-revelation. The young firefighter flung his empty donut box into the withered grass, a pink blot on the grayed landscape. Marley realized she was holding her breath.

"My head's on fire. Too many thoughts. Too much—everything."

Marley exhaled quietly so it didn't sound like a sigh. There was no way to guess what Lu was thinking.

"I'm sick of— This can't be— So much fire—inside and out." Lu's eyes had closed, and she shook her head back and forth, violent as a wet dog.

Reassuring words would seem condescending, so Marley held to her silence, aware of them as an island of two amid the hubbub of first responders. Several minutes went by. Lu's shaking head finally came to a standstill.

"I think I'm the one who should be apologizing for the other night," Marley ventured, her voice as soft as she could make it. "When I come out of my cave I can be overbearing. Many people have said that to me, including a therapist." She laughed to lighten the moment.

Then Lu was throttling Marley with a hug, her strong arms circling Marley's torso, her head resting on Marley's clavicle. The sudden ferocity of it was so startling that Marley could only return the embrace, pressing Lu's back so their bodies were glued tight, feeling the insistent thumping welcome of Lu's heart.

32

FIRE OFFICIALS HAD blocked off the main road up to Sunset Loop with orange cones and emergency vehicles. Lu evaded them easily, parking her car miles away and following the path she knew well that wound up the back of the hill through the pastures and woods. During the conversation with Marley something had been revealed. All along the crack in her life had been only tangentially related to George; now it had widened to a chasm that mirrored the world itself. The senselessness was not going to change. Ideas of improvement and healing were bunk. To figure things out she needed to see the devastation for herself.

Small and quick and dressed in brown, she kept her head down, willing herself not to be seen. If anyone had noticed her in the smoke-shrouded landscape they might have mistaken her for a deer.

The smoke was everywhere, thick and impossible not to inhale despite her mask, and it smelled terrible, nothing like the comforting smoke given off by a fireplace, more like the aftermath of a petrochemical explosion. She took shallow breaths, hoping to diminish the harm to her lungs and, though she was in good shape, her heart clattered and she found herself panting, in part because of the furtive nature of her expedition. No one knew she was here. Not the people at the evacuation center—Marley or Gloria or Julie—not George, not Pippa.

She hiked this trail frequently but, transformed by fire, nothing looked familiar. In most places the trees—juniper, walnut, live oak, cypress—had been reduced to charred posts. Occasionally there was a single survivor, a tree that seemed to have been untouched, jutting up like a steadfast warrior in the decimated landscape. What accounted for this? The aerial shots she had seen had shown some of the fire's random appetite, but when photographed from the ground the hellacious wall of fire appeared to spare nothing in its path.

The distance to the top of the hill seemed farther than usual today; the debris underfoot required caution, and the smoke fastened around her, disorienting. She had to force herself to keep moving. On and off she thought of George, of how much had changed in his absence, how she'd marinated in anger and seen it morph into an abstraction, disconnected from George. She was relieved he was far away in Florida. He didn't have the transgressive spirit or the stamina for this walk. *Stay where you are*, she'd told him each time he called. *Your father needs you.*

She turned to a faint sputtering, hoping it wasn't an ember springing back to life. After a moment of listening, she couldn't clarify what it was and decided it was the echo of organic matter gasping as it succumbed to death. It mingled with the sound of her own labored breath.

She pressed on. A short, steep rise then the trail followed the perimeter of the Blackwell property and delivered her to Sunset Loop Drive. Nothing bore anything in common with the place she had left ten days earlier. She'd heard from several firefighters that it was all gone, but she wasn't prepared for the annihilation she was seeing. The Blackwells' driveway and Sunset Loop Drive resembled roads in war-torn countries, their asphalt buckled and almost unwalkable. The Blackwell home had been razed, and in its place was a heap of ash and blackened debris. The foundation marking the building's original footprint was so much smaller and humbler than the three-story edifice it had once been. Amid the rubble lay scattered hunks of charred metal—household items, but what? She spotted a bathtub, then the husk of Mo Blackwell's prized white Mercedes, now black.

She negotiated the uneven turf slowly, stopping periodically to try to remember how each property she passed had once looked. The transformation was unlike anything she'd ever seen—complete erasure. Not only were the homes gone, but all the identifying markers of the landscape too. It could have been another planet altogether. Everyone at the evacuation center had said it was bad up here, judging from the drone photographs, but the face-to-face reality was so much worse. It was foolhardy to have come here, inhaling all this smoke, doing god-knows-what damage to her lungs. But she had been driven to sift through the rubble and see how it made her feel.

She could hardly wrap her mind around everything that had been lost, not just to her and George, but to all the residents. On some level none of it was important—they were only *things*, as Pippa would have said, and Lu had been making an effort to endorse this view herself—but she and George and all their neighbors had spent their entire lives building and acquiring things: families, companies, fortunes, professional reputations. A home had been the cornerstone of all that building. Your territory. Your empire. Your place, marked with a personal stamp, to settle and grow. Owning a house in this neighborhood had been a way of showing how hard you'd worked, not to mention how elegant your taste was. In losing it all, would you remain the same person? Could you ever feel safe again? She had said to herself that she hated being ruled by objects, but now she vacillated, the enormity of the loss before her calling everything into question.

Would she be able to accurately describe what she was seeing to Julie and Gloria and Marley, not to mention the emotion it evoked? Sadness and despair were inadequate descriptors—it was the sense of total obliteration, a reminder you'd never been important from the outset. George would be livid when he learned the house was gone. On the phone he had asked her countless times if she was sure she had gotten the insurance papers, the investment statements, the passports and birth certificates. She had all those things, and she'd tried to reassure him over and over. His worry had acted on her perversely, resulting in a refusal to allow herself to believe there was anything concrete she would miss. For millennia people lived fine without home furnishings and documents, she'd been telling herself. She had not entertained the possibility of her own denial—she felt only flattened, dull.

What would future archaeologists discover in this scorched and melted debris? she wondered. Would they piece together individual portraits of the families who had lived in each of these destroyed houses? Or would they all be grouped together as indistinguishable members of the human tribe, their artifacts testifying to a similar way of life at a particular time in history? Everyone, they would point out, possessed washing machines and TVs and toilets and cars.

She rounded the crook of the loop and blinked to clear the mirage that filled her smoke-irritated eyes. Before her, composed of smoke and ocular distress, was the palimpsest of their house. A hallucination that refused to resolve itself. Dizzy, she walked closer, arms sweeping at the smoke as if she might clear it.

The house, their house, was still standing.

It couldn't be.

But it was. The iron gate. The flagstone walkway. The front steps with blue ceramic urns on either side of the front door, their flowers long dead. The door itself, dark crimson with a brass handle.

She turned the handle and the heavy door opened without resistance. She remembered leaving it unlocked when she left. She stood at the center of the living room, scanning everything: the red leather couch, the brown-and-blue Gabbeh carpet George loved so much, the vaulted ceiling, the empty white walls. It was all ruined by smoke, but it was still here. She didn't budge for a long time. The only surviving house in the neighborhood—how was that possible?

She pressed her face against the floor-to-ceiling living room window and gazed out at the terraced garden that led down to a copse of half-burned live oaks. Smoke wandered among the extant tree trunks in ghostly swirls, looking so alive she had to turn away, exhausted, gut-punched. What had happened was something she had never bothered to imagine, never believed was possible.

She collapsed on the couch. It wasn't wet, nor was the carpet—if the indoor sprinkler system had been activated, certainly the carpet would still have been wet. The outdoor sprinklers might have gone on—was that what had saved the house? But all their neighbors had sprinklers too, and that hadn't helped them. Was it George's insistence on watering the lawn, racking up huge monthly fines? The sense-making part of her brain was overloaded.

She wandered from room to room, upstairs and down. It was like being in a museum, a window into a bygone culture that was preserved but altered, not just by smoke but by the overall context of the surrounding devastation. With the sun obscured it was hard to tell the time of day. Her Fitbit said it was just before 3:00 P.M., but outside it looked close to nightfall. She had walked over forty thousand steps.

She sat for a while in George's glass-domed study at the top of the house. His desktop computer was open on his desk, its screen ominously blank. Darkness bore down. The power was out. No water ran from the tap. She couldn't possibly make it back to her car in daylight. She was much too tired anyway. Would it be dangerous to stay the night? She couldn't imagine the fire returning to torch what it had already bypassed.

She opened the refrigerator door and unleashed the stench of spoiled food. She snagged a jar of almond butter and shut the door quickly to seal off the smell. Grabbing a spoon, she retreated to the library, the coziest room in the house with only a small high window to the outside. There, despite the warmth, she buried herself among pillows and throws to shield herself from the stench of smoke. She ate a few spoonfuls of almond butter until its dryness made her gag. Suddenly sleep was more important than food. After a week of sleeping among so many other people it was a relief to be alone, but then, to her surprise, she began to miss the chorus of other breathing bodies devoting themselves to sleep.

She was kept awake for a long time thinking of this swelling chasm in her life. Would it repair itself? If not, where would it lead? She dozed and woke, dozed and woke. On the fuzzy margins of sleep, she thought of the people who had disappeared so mysteriously. She thought of Marley, wondering if they'd become good friends. She stroked her necklace for comfort, thinking of Pippa, worrying about Pippa, missing Pippa with a yearning that ached throughout her body. Had Pippa ever felt such a chasm?

She woke in a panic in the early morning. Something hopped around in her chest, squirrel-like, making it hard to breathe. She couldn't remember ever feeling such overwhelming thirst, but her water bottle was empty and the faucets weren't giving up even the slightest drop. She thought of the water jugs in her car with longing. She had to leave. The smoke alone made it dangerous to stay. She added a gray cashmere sweater to her backpack and draped her favorite red-and-purple throw over her shoulders, both smoky but still tolerable.

She stepped outside and started to lock the front door, but for what? *Looters, have at it. Take the furniture and the multiple TVs. Take the dozens of specialized kitchen appliances and Henckels knives. Take the smoke-ruined leather furniture and the Persian carpets. Take the bags and boxes of craft materials, and the dozens of smoky dresses and skirts and pants and blouses and sweaters. Take the multiple pairs of diamond earrings, the pearl earrings, the diamond necklaces. Take the LPs and the antique books—hell, don't hold back, take all of George's precious collections, including the Rothko and Frankenthaler in the garage.*

Standing on the front stoop, shivering from lack of food and thirst and scant sleep, she drew the throw more tightly around her shoulders and knotted it at the waist. She sniffed, trying to assess if the smoke had abated since the day before. It was hard to tell. Threaded through the smoke, there were other smells she hadn't noticed yesterday. Fungal, musty, not unpleasant, but seemingly from some other place. They pierced straight to her limbic core. This phase of her life was over. The house was holding her back with all its beauty and solidity, its surfeit of things. It was over for all of them. George needed to change as much as she did, even if he didn't know that yet. Even Pippa needed to be sprung from this house and this fire-prone landscape. A purge was the only way for them all to move on.

A rhythm rolled through her gut, like a sign from Pippa. A summons. *Da-da. Swish. Da-da. Swish.* She would explain to Pippa. Pippa would understand.

She turned, went back inside, and out to the deck off the living room. She found the butane lighter on a shelf next to the gas barbecue. She began in George's third-floor study—the books, bookshelves, stacks of desk paper. A quick wanding touch, like a fairy godmother. On the second floor, a methodical visit to each room.

Surprisingly flammable bedding and closets full of clothes. On the ground floor, the study's books and love seat; in the solarium the chaise cushions. The long living room drapes succumbed with a great gulping *whoosh*.

Back outside, she ran. Fast. Retracing her steps to the trail. Following it down the hill. Stumbling a little on uneven ground, but mostly swift and nimble as a deer, breath a continuous purr filling her ears, spurring her on. She ran for ten minutes. At a bend in the path, she paused to glance back up the hill, where an arrow of flame shot skyward, gleaming through the smoke.

33

HER BABY BLUE LEXUS was wrecked. It looked as if someone had as-
saulted it with a baseball bat, pummeling the hood and the engine
and attacking all the windows so their shatterproof glass sagged
into the radial pattern of a spiderweb. The driver's-side door had
been wrenched open, the upholstery in front and back slashed, and
the lock on the glove box picked, though nothing of importance
had been in it except for the registration and insurance card, which
were still there. Kentucky Fried Chicken tubs spilled fries and
grease and hunks of chicken on the seats and floors, and someone
had taken a loose, foul-smelling shit just behind the driver's seat.
When she pushed the starter there wasn't a sound. Even if she had
been able to start the ignition, she wouldn't have been able to drive
far with the broken windshield, not to mention the intolerable
smell.

She perched on the edge of the driver's seat, door open, feet on
the ground, head in her hands. She could have asked why someone
would do such a thing, but she already knew. She hadn't been proud
of herself for driving an expensive car like this. It was pure excess.
She would have done fine with one of those tiny Hondas, even a
junker Ford, but George had always wanted her to drive a "safe"
car, which was his euphemism for a high-end car with all its array
of top-of-the-line performance utilities. As if a person, by owning

the right things, could be saved. George didn't understand how such a car inspired hatred. But she knew and had been remiss in ignoring it. She had sensed for a while that a pernicious anger was at large in the world, roving for targets wherever they could be found.

It was impossible not to try to connect this chain of recent events. Someone must have known about the thing she'd done at the top of the hill. As she was doing it she'd felt so righteous and clear—now she saw it as purely impulsive.

She refilled her water bottle from one of the jugs she'd stashed in the back, drank gulp after gulp until it was empty, refilled it again. Then she left the trashed car in her wake without a twinge of remorse, kicking the rear bumper as she departed, suddenly enraged at herself for driving a car that invited so much ire, enraged at the inanimate car itself, enraged such cars existed.

Her legs moved without commands from her brain. What else was there to do? She was now a fugitive, even if no one knew—yet—of her crime. Wouldn't everyone assume all the houses in the neighborhood had gone down together? No one but she had been there to bear witness to the survival of their house. George wouldn't know, nor would Pippa—unless she told them. The butane lighter in her backpack poked into her spine, a sensation that settled in the most primitive part of her brain stem. Material evidence.

After walking a few miles under the confining pall of smoke, she stepped off the road into a grassy area and dug a shallow hole with her hands, first pulling up grass, then digging furiously at the dense, dry soil until the tips of her fingers hurt and her fingernails filled with dirt. A blue jay stood a few feet away at the base of a live oak tree, watching her intently, curious about her frenzy. At some point he'd seen enough and returned to preening, lifting one wing then another. She laid the lighter, coffin-like, into the shallow declivity she'd dug and covered it with dirt and grass and leaves. Then she hurried back to the road, scaring the blue jay into flight.

Her scissoring legs took charge and overruled conscious thought, an involuntary bodily response like a centrifuge that would sift and stratify her thoughts into greater coherence. The current moil in her brain, the mash of fear and guilt and uncertainty and lingering traces of rage, was not a guide to anything good, nothing but shutdown and collapse, a capitulation to the sense that she wasn't made to inhabit this world as others did.

Her strides, long and decisive, chewed up the miles. First along the shoulder of a country road. Then a larger, busier road that passed through town centers with cafés and gift shops and wine bars, before giving way to agriculture again, endless neat rows of vineyards and their associated châteaus and tasting rooms. Everything looked weary from smoke. She didn't stop except for an occasional water break. Once she entered a café to have her water bottle refilled. As she waited for the young woman to fetch the water, her restless muscles twitched, eager to be on the road again, moving now her default state, as essential as breathing, the only thing that would keep her alive.

Back on the road she worked hard to close her ears against the pandemonium of traffic. Its appalling noise dominated the landscape, and some of the vehicles honked as they passed as if she was in their way. She plugged her ears with her fingers against the offense of it all, and when she removed her fingers she found her focus had moved inward, and she could proceed in some state of concentration and flow she hadn't experienced for quite a while, not since her gymnastics days, when she had been body-confident, all her muscles coordinating perfectly, even upside-down in the air. For brief intervals a kind of euphoria flooded her now as it had back then.

Every once in a while, a quick stabbing in a random nerve in her toe, her shoulder blade, her buttocks, brought on a flicker of memory. Flames consuming the gauzy living room curtains with that alarming *whoosh*, as if some ghost idling in the floorboards had come back to life. The violence embodied in the sight of her trashed car. Pippa with Alice in her arms outside the door of her apartment, listing forward, saying with her body, *Please don't leave.*

She took out her phone and texted Pippa, her fingers inflamed and clumsy, the screen obscured by the bright sunlight. *On my way.*

She pictured Pippa as a four-year-old, always clinging, looping her rubbery limbs around her mother's limbs, demanding piggybacks, wanting to hold hands, looking at her mother with those inquiring gray irises as if there was something she needed to understand.

So many shoulds. Too many shoulds.

The day had progressed into late afternoon, and she had logged countless miles, but how few faces she'd seen, only the faces half-hidden behind windshields, and a few downturned faces of passing pedestrians. Except for the young woman who gave her water no one had smiled. The birds and cows and horses she'd encountered, even the bees, had regarded her with more interest. She returned their interest, envying them. She wondered if anyone had noticed her absence at the evacuation center.

With the intensifying colors in the tainted western sky her fear and guilt ebbed, and the saturated colors of sunset brought with them a longing for something she couldn't express. To be with Pippa, yes, but to be with Pippa in a place that neither of them had ever been before, possibly never imagined.

34

THE SUMMONS TO FLORIDA had come to George as a relief, though he wouldn't have said this to Lu. The tension between them had become unbearable, and she'd become unhinged, so it was a relief to fly across the country, arriving alone in the balmy air of Florida. But after twenty-four hours, panic set in. He began to worry about what Lu might be doing in his absence—destroying more of the house and artwork—and now this fire had broken out. All the fires were epic this year, posing more of a threat to house and winery than ever before. He couldn't have chosen a worse time to be away—not that he'd had a choice in the matter.

On the phone Lu was inscrutable, answering his questions succinctly without elaborating, and now she'd gone completely silent, refusing to answer her phone at all so his pleading went straight to voicemail. She was clearly trying to punish him, but it seemed as if her punishment far exceeded his crime. He hadn't slept with Marley after all; he'd only *thought* of sleeping with her. And even that he'd only entertained briefly. He should have kept the whole incident to himself. But he'd been trying to honor their marriage. Their nineteenth anniversary was coming up in December, and he had been planning to throw her a surprise party at the winery. She would never suspect a surprise party on a nineteenth anniversary. Now a party wouldn't go over well.

At home he was occupied throughout the day, but here there were too many idle hours for thinking. During the day he helped his father get to the bathroom and back, he talked to doctors and potential caregivers, he listened to his mother's harangues, but after his parents retired to their bedroom at 8:00 P.M., he had hours to himself for ruminating. He had mismanaged things with Lu, telling her too much, wounding her. He should have used more restraint, but it was impossible to backtrack. His subsequent pronouncements of love were doing no good to reassure her. He *did* love her; he loved her dearly. He also understood that no one person could ever satisfy *all* of another person's needs—but that shouldn't make her feel like a lesser person. He was sure he didn't satisfy all her needs either. He certainly had never meant to suggest they should part ways. The thought of losing her filled his gut with foreboding. He wouldn't survive that. If only she were willing to discuss these things.

His problems were exacerbated by being in Florida. He couldn't stand anything about the state. For a nanosecond the warmth and sea air were welcome, but over time the humidity, the inescapable sun, and the sunbathing tourists gored him.

He wasn't fond of his parents' specific location either—a light-saturated, white-walled, twelfth-floor condo with an ocean view— a sun lover's wet dream, but an odd choice for his staunchly New England parents, who had sold their spacious Connecticut home on five acres and slogged down here with all their anachronistic antiques. All of the rooms reeked of medicine and illness, the plaque and decay of aging human bodies, and George's mother was refusing to see that a move to assisted living was inevitable.

George's life had become a perfect demonstration of Murphy's Law. His wife's refusal to speak, his father's stroke, the fires, now Pippa falling apart and calling obsessively several times a day. She was worried about her mother, and Alice had disappeared. She couldn't reach Lu, and she was delirious with anxiety. He couldn't seem to convince her that things were probably just fine. Cell and internet reception was always dicey during fire season. He didn't divulge that he, too, had been trying to contact Lu, repeatedly and without success.

"Your mother's okay," he said to Pippa over and over again, feeling wretched in his lies, necessary as they were. "You know how crazy the evacuation center is." As for the disappearance of Alice, which Pippa said was Mrs. Marvel's doing, he couldn't help with that. It confirmed his belief that it had been a bad idea to take the cat to college in the first place, though of course he wasn't dumb enough to say this. "I'm sorry, honey. Keep looking," he told her, knowing full well how lame he sounded.

It was only natural that a child of his would be a worrier, given that he himself was the Olympian of worriers. It was a birthright, not a sport one chose. But never, until now, had he been on the front lines of managing Pippa's worries. Throughout high school Pippa had never talked to him much. He took her to various cultural events, they'd shared the usual father-daughter pleasantries and snipes, and sometimes she would indulge him in her childhood game of tapping rhythms on his back or his thigh or his forearm, challenging him to replicate them, which he could rarely do, but she had confided only in her mother. The two had been bonded at the hip, the shoulder, the head—always in close touch, always texting and talking on the phone, always touching and grooming each other like chimps. It was, to be honest, a little strange, but who was he, a mere man, to weigh in on such things?

"But she promised she'd stay in touch," Pippa moaned. "Aren't you worried?"

Of course he was worried. He was worried sick—about his

marriage falling apart, about his home and winery being threatened by fire, about his aging parents. There was nothing he wasn't worried about, but he wasn't about to share his helplessness with his daughter.

"I'll find out what's going on and get back to you," he promised, hearing his habit of paternal reassurance sounding empty.

Late in the afternoon George noticed a voicemail from Tom. A message from laconic Tom did not bode well. There was no way George could return the call from the apartment without his mother eavesdropping and hounding him with questions, so he served his mother a stiff vodka and tonic and escaped to the beach, promising he would be back soon.

It was sunset and the beach was finally emptying out, the tourists heading off for bars and restaurants and nighttime entertainment. This was the only time of day George enjoyed the beach, when it mostly belonged to him. The sun was making its clarion descent over the bay, turning the blue water to a pearlescent silver and orange mingled with softer hues of pink and purple. He stood where the fine white sand met the water, small waves washing over his bare toes.

Tom spoke in such a low voice he was almost inaudible.

"Whose car?"

"Your wife's."

"And—?"

"Well—" Tom's sigh was louder than his voice. "I hate to say this, but it was trashed."

"It was what?"

"Destroyed. Everything. Windshield. Hood. Engine. Interior. Like someone had throttled it with a baseball bat or something."

"And Lu?"

"No one knows where she is."

Tom said some other things about where the car had been parked and where it had been towed, but George barely heard him. Why would someone do such a thing? Did this mean someone had done something to Lu herself?

Tom stopped talking, and for an incalculable period of time both men remained where they were on opposite sides of the country, breathing audibly into their phones, George trying to tame his soaring heartbeat and spiking adrenaline. Finally, George thanked Tom, because what else could he do and, though Tom was the bearer of bad news, it wasn't his fault. "I'll be home soon," he said.

Once George had signed off, he stepped farther into the water, closing his eyes. Had Lu been pummeled like her car? Had this been perpetrated by whoever had abducted all those other women? He thought of Pippa. He couldn't possibly let Pippa learn of this news. He waded up to his waist, soaking his shorts and shirt, imagining the water as solvent for his troubles. What had he done to deserve this string of back luck? Maybe it was punishment for the fact that he'd believed for too long in the Barnes family immunity to hardship.

If he had been another kind of person he would have been braying now, an unbridled rush of noise that would morph into keening, and he wouldn't cease making noise until he was fully emptied of oxygen and forced to collapse on the beach, curled in on himself like a mollusk without its shell. But he was George Caldecott Barnes and such behavior would have been beneath his dignity.

He made his way back to the sand, his wet clothes heavy, clinging indecently to belly and thighs. Something scuttled past him. A white toy poodle off its leash. When George turned, the poodle turned too, pivoting and trotting to George and gleefully licking his legs. George tried to sidestep out of reach, but the dog pursued him. *Goddamn dog.* He looked around for the owner, saw a woman far down the beach moving in his direction, but without any urgency.

"Can you call your dog off?" he said when she got within hearing range.

"She doesn't mean any harm," said the woman, who was tall and blond, with an oval face that belonged on a TV screen. Her youth and antiseptic prettiness irritated George, summing up everything he hated about Florida.

"Harm or no harm, I don't want her licking my legs."

"She's just trying to be friendly. You don't have to get all nasty about it."

"By the way, dogs are supposed to be leashed."

"Oh, go fuck yourself." She scooped the dog into her arms and strode past George without looking at him. "Get a life," she hissed.

He sank to his knees in the shallow water. He couldn't help himself and was beyond caring who saw and judged him. *Get a life.* What a disdainful thing to say. Had he ever said that to anyone? Not out loud, though he'd probably thought it. But the woman had it wrong. The challenge wasn't *getting* a life, it was *keeping* the life you had.

35

THE SOLES of your feet were hammered by asphalt. Your heels and toes blistered. Slabs of dead yellow skin detached and released their bubbles of liquid. Your head was a bowling ball dragging against muscles of neck and shoulders. Overworked calves and quads tightened into angry fists. Poison oak and insect bites covered your limbs with rashes and welts. Bruises everywhere: shoulders, knees, points of your pelvis, all ravaged by sleeping on hard surfaces.

Still, you walked on, converting the conference of pain to bearable white noise, drawn by your lodestar, the person at the center of your heart, your daughter. The longing fueled you. Your sense of direction had never been keener. You understood south.

Along the way you lost things you'd always thought you needed. Phone. Credit card. Wallet. Water bottle. Backpack. One by one these objects fell away without your noticing. These losses opened the door to other losses. Loss of access. Loss of dignity.

In the reflective glass of a 7-Eleven, you saw yourself, a person you barely recognized: shoulders hunched, face elongated, hair matted, clothes in tatters. No wonder you'd been prevented from using the

Arco restroom. No wonder a passing driver had given you the finger. You were no longer welcome in the places where other humans
congregated.

You had to eat. You discovered the largesse of dumpsters. Styrofoam
and cardboard boxes containing almost-full meals of Chinese food,
Indian food, sushi, half-consumed Big Macs, pizza slices, pizza
crusts, endless fries skinny and fat. Sometimes there were days-old
baked goods, dry but delicious, yogurt cups past their sell-by date,
fruit beginning to rot. Your years of gymnastics prepared you well
for dumpster diving. You were stealthy, nimble, could easily leap in,
forage, make yourself invisible when necessary. Pride was gone—or
its focus had shifted. You were proud of surviving.

There were long stretches in the dry hills between the north and
south of the state when you had to survive without any sustenance
at all for a couple of days. You endured, until you couldn't, and then
you sampled the vegetation and lapped water from the most meager
of puddles, hoping for the best.

As darkness fell you searched for places where you could sleep
undisturbed, away from the roads and hubbubs of commerce.
Sometimes a field, but sometimes the best you could do was settle
your bottom on a slab of cold asphalt and curl into yourself as
tightly as possible against a wall to sleep for a few hours, hoping no
one would chase you away.

During the long days of walking alone you rarely had the call to
speak. You opened your mouth, intoning vowel sounds. *Aa. Oo. Ee.*

You attempted syllables: *Glot. Pom. Liss. Schwill.* Your cheeks had gone slack. Your teeth had migrated. The sounds you made were not language, only gruff vocalizations. Whistling was out of reach, and you could no longer mold your lips into a smile. Speech, as you'd once known it, was evaporating.

So yes, there were losses, but there were compensations for the losses.

The startling ingenuity of your nose. Keener than ever before, you delighted in the pleasure and information it delivered. It led you to water, to food. It told you the history of a place, its recent visitors. Without your new capacity to smell, you would not have survived.

The world became newly vivid. You noticed and appreciated things you'd never seen before.

The bend and stretch of a speckled inchworm traversing your chest one morning as you awoke. The fat king snake that regarded you another morning, its body muscular, its tongue flicking in research. Cows. Their ease. Their liquid eyes. Their lack of haste and ignorance of judgment. The lustrous red bark of madrones. The myriad colors of sky. The fluidity of light. The endless flux of everything. Yourself included.

Dogs began to notice you. They smiled, happy to see you. *Hello, dogs, happy to see you too.*

36

THE SANTA ANA WINDS had put everyone on edge, scraping faces and eyeballs and tempers with their abrasive dryness. Dar was acutely aware of the widespread restlessness as he and Philippa traversed the campus looking for a private place to sit and talk.

They settled under a capacious magnolia tree in the empty law school courtyard. Distress seeped from her entire body, a trembling silence in which it was clear she was quartering something she couldn't tamp down for long. She had texted him an hour earlier, begging to see him. *Something happened*, she said cryptically. He had been on his way to another meeting, but he begged off, sensing her urgency.

Because she had summoned him, he waited for her to speak, curtailing his impulse toward nervous chitchat. Whatever she had to say, he was afraid his response would not be adequate. She lifted the lid of her coffee, squinted into it. He waited. He sipped his tea, scorching his tongue. Why was he so irrationally fond of this girl? A golf cart motored through with two maintenance men. Its passage created a breeze, so a swarm of broad leaves dislodged and clacked against one another in noisy descent. She looked up, brushed the leaves from her lap, rolled her shoulders, began to speak.

Her mother was gone. Disappeared. The cops had been called. Her absence was now official.

37

YOU SAT UNDER a tree in a park overlooking the ocean, which glittered below you, a heavenly blue. Kids somersaulted and pirouetted and spun in the grass.

Your daughter's magnetism vibrated up and down your spine. Knowing you were close—no more than a day or two—you were happier than ever before.

A dog approached you, a cocker spaniel. He sniffed your crotch, licked your face, barked, wanting to play. You barked back. His owner called, and he trotted away.

You laughed. At least the dogs were not turned off by you.

As you stood to continue on your journey, you happened to glance down. Your forearms were covered with tendrils of hair, a dark peach fuzz. Fur-like. You brought your nose and lips to your arms, sniffed, licked, began to groom yourself.

Later that same day you bedded down in a meadow, away from the fray, a slab of dumpster-rescued cardboard laid out in the tall grass making a luxurious nest, the quiet night doming around you, the only sounds some scrabbling voles and a few crows in the branches of nearby live oaks, the sky a miracle of clarity, a portal into the universe.

At dawn you jerked awake to see a man aiming a rifle at you from twenty feet away. Rage spooled from all his parts, from the tip of his rifle, the spread of his legs, the brim of his cowboy hat, but mostly from his bloviating mouth, whose shouts battered the peaceful landscape.

Git. Now.

He fired aloft into the clear morning air so everything around you shuddered, and resting birds took flight, and field mice scuttled away, and snakes slithered under rocks, and the grass quivered. A moment of local anarchy.

You jumped to your feet and hightailed it away from this man, away from his rage, away from his gun, his need for ownership, his apparent fear of you. You heard him stumbling through the tall grass behind you, but you didn't take time to look back. You ran fast, your breath coordinating with your limbs in the singular effort of escape. You arrived at the edge of a steep ravine, and you leaped without thinking, feeling the pleasure of being airborne, light and limber, almost birdlike. The final shredded remnants of your clothes sailed away as you landed on hands and knees, joints easy, hands splayed to absorb the impact, shoulders and spine realigning themselves, becoming looser. Without a second thought you continued into the incandescent morning on all fours.

Only much later did you think of the bloviating man with gratitude. What a blessing he unwittingly bestowed on you, his blast of anger severing you from a world you no longer needed.

38

LIFE DIDN'T STOP just because your mother had disappeared and you were beside yourself with dread. No, life had other ideas. It had selected you as a special target for bad luck. The bad luck now materialized in the form of Hurricane Zelda, which was careering up the Gulf Coast, leveling buildings, taking out power, causing monumental floods. Most galling to Philippa, flights out of Florida were canceled, and no one knew when they'd resume. Her father was stuck until who-knew-when. Even Grandma Linda, who had the ability to remain calm through everything, even she thought this was an unusual run of bad luck.

For several days Philippa texted her father nonstop (getting useless placating responses) and holed up in her apartment in a semidaze interrupted by long walks. She logged miles into the hills above Sunset Boulevard and to the beach in Santa Monica, putting one foot in front of another on the unforgiving pavement, *da-dum-da-dum-da-glum*, music tunneling through her earbuds to blunt the city's splenetic roar. What tortured her was there was nothing she could do, no action she could take, no magic words of a spell she could intone to locate her mother, or to bring her back, or to get her father on a plane. When Alice had disappeared, she could visit the shelters—not that it had helped, but at least she'd felt proactive. If only there were a shelter for lost mothers.

Her father, under pressure, had told Philippa about the smashed car, and now she couldn't wipe the grisly images from her mind. Her mother raped, or beaten, or even murdered, left to rot like anonymous roadkill. She refused to accept these scenarios as the truth of what had happened, but that didn't eradicate the images. She couldn't help thinking about the other disappearances, the artists and the fisherwomen especially, and the lunatic who was likely behind them. She had told Dar she thought those women had chosen to disappear, but she only half believed that.

She ignored her classes, except for zoology. Music theory, persuasive writing, American history—it had all become trivial to her. She was alone in a black tunnel, sealed off from the rest of the world. She went through the motions of emailing her professors as Dar had instructed her to do, telling them about her mother's absence and her father's unavailability, saying it was impossible to concentrate. They wrote back with rote condolences, telling her she would have to consider taking a withdrawal or an incomplete. There were a bunch of deadlines they cited associated with these options, but Philippa didn't have the energy to take the next step.

She had told Dar the whole story, for better or worse. Now she could tell he felt sorry for her. Because of this, and because of his kindness, she exited her tunnel and dragged herself to his class, but even his energetic lectures couldn't hold her attention. She only half listened to his Introduction to Vertebrates lecture. He took note of her presence and as she was leaving class, he called out to her, "Philippa!"

Several of the other students snickered—*You're in deep shit*, someone muttered—and she approached the podium hunching her shoulders, gaze on the floor.

"You okay?" he asked, his voice in a quieter register than his lecturing voice. A muscle in one of his cheeks pulsed with what she read as sadness, and it made it all the more difficult to contain her own sadness. She raised a skeptical eyebrow: *What do you think?*

"Well, let me know what I can do."

There was nothing he could possibly do. "If you can find my mother, that would be awesome . . . or maybe you could do something to stop the hurricane, and while you're at it, the fires too." She had meant to make a joke, but it came out sounding bitter. The lecture hall had emptied—it was only the two of them remaining.

"I can't keep coming to class. I'm sorry. I'm too preoccupied."

He nodded. "I get it. No worries." Another student had re-entered the room and was waiting to talk to him. As she turned to leave, she felt pathetic again, the deluded mime from her youth. His kindness was only professional.

You don't give up. This was something Cindy Blackman had said at the drumming clinic. From someone else such a statement might have sounded insipid, but it meant so much coming from her. *If there's something you really want, you don't give up.* It was the only thing Philippa could say that made her feel better, and she said it to herself repeatedly as she walked around the city, waiting for her father to call, taking in the multiple manic rhythms, and watching the citizens enjoying sushi and kombucha and bubble tea, or engaged in their regimens of running and yoga and weight lifting. Were they happy, she wondered, or were they only involved in a rigorous search for happiness? They certainly wore the shiny cloaks of apparent contentment. She wondered if her face ever sported the self-satisfaction theirs did. Their happiness, even if it was only an act, made her own seem unattainable, even though she knew they were unrelated, not contingent on one another, and even though it was not even happiness she sought, only the return of her mother, which was a necessary precondition for any modicum of satisfaction going forward. She had always had the sense that she wasn't really made for happiness as some people were.

She had, however, known moments of deep contentment when she and Alice cuddled together, and she had felt they were connected in some soulful way, wanting the exact same things for their bodies at that moment, to be enmeshed, Philippa's fingers lifting the loose skin around Alice's shoulders, the fur of Alice's back soft against Philippa's cheek and upper lip. Sometimes she would place her palm on the white fur of Alice's belly and feel Alice's heart trilling through the skin of her palm. Those moments were the closest she had ever come to understanding untainted happiness, but they had always been fleeting, and afterward she would return to being the same old girl wondering about the point of it all. She missed that bonded feeling, and it seemed unfathomable and pointlessly cruel that she still had no idea of Alice's whereabouts, if she had been adopted by some other family, or if she was dead.

Growing up, she'd had similar bonding moments with her mother, when they were out-of-control laughing about something, or both equally pissed off about the same thing, or when she was a younger kid and they had played with each other's hair and her father said they looked like grooming chimps. Their talks through most of high school had offered comfort—her mother listened better than anyone Philippa had known. God, the thought of it all being gone made her want to roar in protest.

Everyone loved Lu—Philippa couldn't imagine anyone who would have wanted to harm her.

Dar had emailed an article. *For some distraction*, read the subject line. "What If Individuals Don't Exist?" was the article's title. It was written by an environmental philosopher Philippa had never heard of. She saw immediately that it wasn't the kind of article one could comprehend by skimming, but she didn't have the concentration for deep reading, so she spot-read sentences here and there, gleaning what she could.

Who has moral standing? the article asked. *Are humans more important than animals? Are sentient animals who feel pain more important than those without such complex nervous systems? Do all living organisms, as well as nonconscious entities like trees and plants, have equal stature? What about the value of the entire biome? What if we were to move beyond an anthropocentric view of the world to embrace the well-being and diversity of the entire earth, living and nonliving?*

The article was diverting for ten minutes or so, but after that she couldn't focus. It occurred to her that she was going to flunk out of school if she didn't make some other arrangements. The thought should have bothered her, but it didn't.

She was composing an email to thank Dar when she was distracted by barking from the driveway. She stepped out onto the landing. At the bottom of the stairway was a furry black dog, a Labrador-like mutt. He barked up at her in great excitement. Philippa laughed and closed the door, thinking how upset Mrs. Marvel would be. Mrs. Marvel of the astute hearing. Now she would have to realize that a cat's meowing was a mere whisper in the forest compared to the barking of this dog. She was glad the dog wasn't her problem.

She returned to composing her email. *Dear Dar, It was kind of you to send that article. I guess what you're really trying to tell me is that I'm nothing but a bundle of microbial material, without a personality at all.*

The dog continued to bark. She continued to write her email.

She had a mischievous desire to mess with Dar a little. He had become the one bright spot in her life, even if he was only being nice for professional reasons. At least flirting made her feel a little more alive. *I've always thought of myself as more than a package of microbes, but maybe I've just been flattering myself.*

The dog's barking wouldn't let up, and it was beginning to make concentration impossible. She opened the door and stepped out again. "Be quiet!" she ordered the dog. "Go away. You've got the wrong house."

How terrible to be a dog, doomed to endless barking, unable to state the specifics of your need or desire. She went back inside, finished the email to Dar and sent it off, then collapsed on her bed, spent from anxiety.

A text from her father. Zelda was abating and he'd been able to snag a flight to San Francisco the following day. He would update her soon. She thought of their house on the hill and yearned to be back there in the safe, contained chaos of her childhood bedroom. Coddled back then, she'd been allowed to remain ignorant of the malevolence and danger she had come to understand lurked everywhere. It was immature to wish to be coddled again as she'd been as a child, but didn't everyone wish for that?

An absence of sound prompted her to rise and peer through the window of her door. The dog had come up the stairs and was curled on the landing. Feeling her gaze, he looked up, his expression lodging a plea to be let inside. What a strategic dog. She knew better than to allow him inside. Once a stray was gratified, it was impossible to eject him, especially for an animal lover like herself, and now was not the time to take on responsibility for a new animal. Plus, she still held out hope for Alice's return—wouldn't Alice be indignant to learn she'd been replaced by a dog? She moved away from the door, out of view, and the animal bounded up, placed his paws on the glass, and began to bark again, his voice loud and declarative, his intention clear.

She cracked open the door. The dog was standing on all fours now, raising his muzzle into the air where, between barks, his neck and head bobbed as if on a spring. "Shush. Be quiet." Amazingly, the dog obeyed. Despite the heat, she shivered and stepped onto the landing. She and the dog regarded each other. His thick black coat was dusty and matted with twigs and thistles. He was obviously a stray. He sniffed her feet, her legs, her crotch. She allowed herself to be smelled, struck by the dog's friendliness, resisting the urge to pet him. His buzzing energy threw static into the air.

She closed the door to her apartment and started down the steps, heading out for a few groceries. The dog followed. At the bottom of the steps she hesitated, not keen on being followed all the way to the store. The dog's eyes, big and brown and expectant, spooked her a little. She retraced her steps back up the stairs.

She tried to read Dar's article again, but without success. The dog wouldn't go away. It trotted up and down the staircase, nails clacking, barking ceaselessly. At some point he parked himself on the landing again and didn't shut up. Whining and barking, whining and barking. It was driving her nuts, but it gave her satisfaction to think that Mrs. Marvel was probably even more bothered, and if she was, *she* would have to find a solution because Philippa was too heartbroken to be a problem solver. She wouldn't take this on. She refused to try to quiet the dog again. Eventually he would have to leave.

She put in earbuds to dull the quagmire of her mind's looping images: her mother's body, broken, bloody, abandoned somewhere in the woods. Maybe her mother had been taken down by flames she couldn't outrun, suffocating on smoke, passing out, her skin searing, bubbling, turning black as briquette, until finally reduced to a few shards of bone.

The dog had escalated his entreaties so she could hear him through her earbuds scratching on the door. A relentless *scrtz-ts-scrtz-ts-scrtz-ts*. He was standing on his hind legs, forepaws on the door's window. When he saw her seeing him, his barking became desperate. And—fuck all—there was Mrs. Marvel coming up the top step behind the dog, pushing him out of the way with her knee and knocking on the window.

Philippa got up and opened the door just enough so she could speak through it. The dog was quiet now, and he tried to scuttle past Mrs. Marvel, but she kicked him hard. Philippa winced.

"Go on. Get out of here," Mrs. Marvel yelled. She turned to Philippa. "What's going on with you and these animals? I can't have this. It's disturbing the whole neighborhood."

"He's not my dog," Philippa said.

"Well, he seems to think he's yours."

Philippa shrugged. "What am I supposed to do? I have no idea who he belongs to."

"I don't care what you do, but do something." She flung her arm over her head dismissively as she made one of her usual abrupt exits, punctuating each step of her slow descent with a groaning expulsion of air.

Philippa watched. The dog also watched. While Pippa continued to monitor Mrs. Marvel's retreat, the dog scooted inside. For god's sake—*now* what was she supposed to do?

The dog sniffed her bare feet, uncovering an ecstasy of scents with his moist black nose and wagging his matted tail, as if he had won the lottery, as if he already knew of Philippa's soft spot for animals. She would *not* succumb. Disarming as he was, she wouldn't be keeping him.

The dog had no collar or tag, no number to call. Judging from the briars and bits of dirt clinging to his coat, he appeared to have been on the loose for quite a while. She coaxed him into her tiny bathroom and rubbed him down with a moist towel, which turned black with dirt. She plucked the briars from his back and legs. The dog did not resist these ministrations; he seemed to enjoy being groomed. As she moved around her apartment, locating her phone, finding the address of the closest shelter, calling a Lyft, the dog trailed in her wake. Being watched so closely aroused a flash of annoyance that made her feel bad about herself. She hoped the dog knew she would never bring harm to any animal, especially a dog like this with beautiful pleading eyes.

She had the odd feeling that she should contact Dar and tell him what was happening, but why? He wasn't her parent, or boyfriend, or even, technically, her friend. And calling Dar would prolong the situation when she felt an urgency to shed this dog as quickly as possible.

The Lyft driver was okay with taking an animal—he said he liked pets—but the dog refused to get in, resisted her efforts to lift him. Without a collar he couldn't be dragged. He slumped onto the street between the curb and the car, possum-like.

She apologized to the driver, a Middle Eastern man, who gave her a quick nod, lowering his brows, probably impatient. Looking down at the slumped dog, Philippa was overcome with quiet desperation. Now what? She perched on the edge of the seat, feet on the curb, the dog beneath her legs. The dog raised his head. Philippa pulled her legs inside, as if she planned to leave without him.

"Okay," she said to the driver.

The driver appeared dismayed. "You want to go. You leave the dog here?"

The dog jerked to his feet, leapt onto Philippa's lap, the fur of his back and tail bushing into her nose and mouth. She had hoped this would happen. "Okay. Now we can go."

"Your dog is okay?" the driver said, inserting himself into the drama.

"Yeah, he's fine."

The dog, newly quiet, adjusted himself on the seat beside her, his head in her lap. Periodically he lifted his head to glance up at her with the pleading look he had perfected, but she turned away and looked out the side window, determined to remain immune.

At the shelter, having no leash and afraid the dog might escape into the traffic, she carried him from the car to the building, straining under his dense weight. He allowed himself to be handled without resistance, his muzzle drooping onto her shoulder.

She had been at this shelter before when she came looking for Alice, but today it was staffed by different people. They were cheerful and righteous as missionaries. She filled out a form with a few details about where she had found the dog and her own contact information. The dog remained at her feet the entire time, vigilant, head uplifted, watching her. A middle-aged woman who looked Filipina, barely five feet tall, came around from behind the counter and crouched.

"What a beaut. You say *he*, but it looks like a *she* to me."

Philippa felt stupid, having wiped the dog down without correctly identifying her sex, though now she saw, of course she was a she. The woman went to a back room to fetch a collar and leash, but when she tried to buckle the collar around the dog's neck, the dog squirmed, resisted, growled.

"Hey there," the woman said. "It's only a collar." Skilled at handling fractious animals, she remained undaunted, petting the dog aggressively then taking her in a forceful hug and fastening the collar. "You're a feisty one, aren't you?" She hooked the leash onto the collar and turned to Philippa. "Thanks for bringing her by. I'm sure we'll find a good home for her, good-looking dog like this."

The woman started down the long corridor to the dog wing, but the dog had other ideas and fell into another slump on the floor. The woman yanked at the collar. "Come on, girl, stand up. That trick won't work."

Flooded with guilt, Philippa slipped out the front door, telling herself she had done what was necessary. The dog was no longer her responsibility. As soon as the shelter door closed behind her, the dog began to bark, a piercing bark that ascended the scale, amplifying as it went, a primal howl easily heard from the street.

Outside the wind had picked up. It jammed into signposts and rattled the glass doors of storefronts. *Pft-pft-pft.* Philippa jetted down the block, not running, but almost. She passed a FedEx, a Supercuts, a Starbucks, before she remembered Alice. She ought to go back and check again for Alice. She stood at a crosswalk in indecision, the wounded sound of the dog's barking still in her ears, indistinguishable from the braying of her own heart. She was about to summon a ride when she convinced herself to return.

She sealed her ears with her fingers, only half muffling the chorus of barking dogs, the black dog's voice clearly distinguishable from the others. The cat room was a high-volume, high-activity hive of its own, smelling of piss and wet concrete. She walked the rows, scanning each cage with adrenaline-sharpened acuity, only to confirm Alice was not there. Hurrying away, she exited the shelter a second time, passing by the front desk, where she noticed something different in the atmosphere. An aural emptiness. Not total silence, but the absence of the specific bark of the black dog. They couldn't have euthanized her for barking, could they? It was in a dog's nature to bark. But they might have tranquilized her.

Whatever they'd done, Philippa refused to worry. The people at the shelter were helpers, people who cared deeply about animals, not people who would do anything cruelly utilitarian. *You are only one person, Philippa. There is only so much you can do to stanch the world's pain.*

39

SHE BOLTED AWAKE, the morning sun storming through the front window. A scratching at the door. *Fuck*. The dog was back. The very same black dog she had dropped at the shelter just yesterday, now without its collar, looking up at her from the landing with an irritatingly winsome expression. Surprise outstripped her annoyance. She opened the door and the dog trotted in without pausing to greet her. It sat by the foot of the bed, regarding Philippa, cocking its head slightly as if to say, *Come on, you know I belong here.*

The two regarded each other. The sunlight, voyaging from orange to yellow, inched across the floorboards, warming the air and exposing volcanoes of dust. They were wrapped in the sun's aura, girl and dog, sharing a lagoon of warmth and silence.

"What do you want?" Philippa whispered.

Help me, the dog's mournful brown eyes whispered back.

Never had Philippa experienced such intention coming from an animal, such will. There was a sparking electric signal jetting between them, and it made Philippa afraid.

I'm not leaving.

Philippa crouched beside the dog, stroked the woolly heft of her coat. She lowered her face and sniffed the sweat of the dog's recent exertion, felt in her cheek the ongoing twitch of the animal's muscles, the beat of its athletic heart. The dog rested its muzzle on Philippa's shoulder.

Philippa tried to chronicle what must have happened. The dog, like some canine Houdini, had escaped from the shelter, traveled almost ten miles through a raucous, unfriendly city, and found the exact compass points of Philippa's apartment. How could she have done these things?

"Why me?" Philippa moaned, lifting her head to scrutinize the dog's eyes again. The dog whimpered—not a whine so much as a plea—and her eyes widened, and more sparking encoded messages whipped back and forth between them, retina to retina, brain to brain, heart to heart.

40

DAR WAS about to go for a run when a text came. *What do you know about dogs?* He stared at his phone, laughing to himself. He'd never met anyone who could be so straightforward and simultaneously cryptic.

He texted back: *300 million olfactory receptors. A dog can detect a teaspoon of sugar in the volume of water to fill 2 Olympic swimming pools.*

Leaving his phone at home, he headed out.

He ran his routine five-mile circuit faster than usual, but instead of energizing him as he'd hoped, the run reactivated his shin splints. Breathless, he limped the last half of his block feeling old. From several houses away, through the scrim of his sweat-blurred vision, he spotted Philippa on his front steps. She was hunched over a black dog, her face buried in its fur, the dog's face in her lap, two entangled bodies denoting devotion and despair.

He paused, wanting to watch without being seen, stunned by his immediate recognition of her body, how quickly she'd become familiar to him. *What do you know about dogs?* He was relieved to see the inquiry was practical, rather than an encoded question about the meaning of life. He came up the walkway laughing, heartened by the sight of her. She jerked up.

"You've adopted a dog."

"She adopted me."

The dog had been eyeing him, and now she approached him and sniffed his feet, his ankles, his sweaty shins, thighs, crotch.

"Hey there," he said, nudging her away from his crotch. He bent to pet the dog, an attractive specimen, and the dog angled her head around to lick his hand. "What's her name?"

"That's the thing."

"Oh? Meaning?"

"Can we go inside?"

How uncharacteristically forward she was. Letting her inside did not seem prudent, and yet here she was, needing something from him again. He had become, he understood, her go-to person.

"How did you find me?"

"I told my sob story to a woman in your department office and she took pity on me."

Probably Mindy, an older woman with a big heart. How resourceful of her to have tracked him down. He unlocked his door, remembering what a mess his house was—no messier than usual, but not fit for guests.

"Sorry for the chaos," he said, kicking an umbrella and shoes out of her path in the foyer.

"No worse than your office."

"True."

In the living room he rushed around, shoving papers and books into piles, gathering up a pair of trousers from the carpet, a hoodie from the couch, embarrassed by the wanton disrobing they suggested, ferrying them to his bedroom down the hall. It was silly to bother with tidying, as she'd already seen the chaos of his office and car but, unnerved, he couldn't help himself. As he went through these motions the dog remained at her side, her loyal bodyguard watching his every move.

"You don't have to do this," Philippa said.

"Force of habit."

She was the picture of ease, had stepped into his personal space with her dog without any apparent discomfort at all, as if it was the most natural thing in the world for her to be in his house. How was it that the power between them, until now weighted toward him, had shifted toward her right here on his own premises? How had she insinuated herself into his life in this intimate way? How had he allowed it to happen? It came to him in a sudden rush of understanding, what should have been obvious long ago: She had a crush on him, and though it was misguided, he couldn't help but be flattered.

In the kitchen he rinsed his sweaty face and filled two glasses with water, along with a bowl of water for the dog. He laid the water bowl on the floor, the glasses on the coffee table, and perched himself on the edge of the easy chair next to the couch where she sat with the dog, whose paws were on her lap. Girl/woman and dog were both still, watchful, waiting for him, the man of perpetual motion, to settle. He couldn't shake his self-consciousness. How funny that he understood her infatuation with him at a moment when he felt so old, hobbled by shin splints, pores still leaking sweat, wisps of his fine hair bothering his temples. He couldn't say who was regarding him with more intensity, the girl/woman or her dog.

"Alright," he said. "I'm here. Now tell me about this dog with no name."

"I can't name her."

The dog laid her head on Philippa's lap again, as if aware of being discussed.

"Because?" he said.

Where had she learned to sustain her gaze as she did? Most people conducted conversations while their attention was darting here and there, insect-like, but her attention was unrelenting. In some corners it would have been called rude.

He thought of his dying grandmother's gaze, how it had sucked him in. Philippa's gaze was doing the same now. "I'm all ears," he prompted, afraid of saying too much or speaking too loudly.

"You won't believe me," she said.

The dog's look, too, had become piercing, uncomfortable really. "I don't think your dog likes me."

"No. You're wrong. It's not what you think," she said. "This dog . . ." She peered down at the dog, and the dog jumped off the couch and came to him and laid her muzzle on his knees, slaying him with her preposterously intimate brown-eyed gaze.

Philippa dug into her jeans pocket and brought out a silver chain bearing a small silver pendant embossed with letters. "See this necklace?"

41

THE BANK WAS REQUIRED to wait for a period before repossessing the house and land belonging to the Michigan Nine, but they had made no interim plan for the animals, so Randy Walters stepped up and came by twice a day to feed and water them while he scouted around for other farmers who might be interested in taking them on permanently. Not everyone wanted more animals with all their attendant costs: grain, mash, hay, vet's bills, etc.

In Randy's opinion, the group had overextended themselves. The two horses, for example, seemed unnecessary. Horses were expensive to maintain, in part because of their sheer size, and they didn't contribute to the bottom line. The immediate value of the sheep seemed questionable too, since the group had never slaughtered the sheep for eating, only shorn them and spun their wool into yarn. Randy couldn't imagine the yarn business was profitable enough to offset the cost of raising sheep. Randy thought the group should have concentrated on raising cows and chickens. Possibly the pigs too, though he wasn't certain about pigs. But cows and chickens, with their reasonably high yields, were clearly useful. Milk, eggs, poultry—all items that could be consumed. Still, despite his opinions on the matter, Randy attended dutifully to all the animals. The two horses, five cows, six sheep, fifteen chickens, two roosters, seven pigs.

After the first couple of weeks, the hullabaloo died down and journalists lost interest in the disappearances as there was no new fodder for reporting. He couldn't stand how the worst of people emerged around an event like this. Speculation about psychotic rapists and alien abductions. It didn't sit well with him. *Calm down, people*, he wanted to say every time another reporter had tried to corral him for questioning. He was relieved that most of the paparazzi had left, less interested in the Michigan Nine now that more people had vanished in West Virginia, Montana, and Florida. Who knew why this was happening again and again—it wasn't for him to figure out.

Randy arrived every morning at dawn to make his rounds, then he returned again at dusk. At both ends of the day, it was exceptionally quiet, other than the chickens and roosters doing their usual clucking and crowing. It reminded Randy of what drew neophytes to farming life. The big barn housed the cows and sheep and the horses who spent the daylight hours grazing in the meadow and came in at night. The chickens had their own coop where they spent the night—during the day they roamed free. A new structure had recently been built for the pigs with an adjacent pen dedicated to them.

When Randy had made his impulsive offer to oversee the animals, he hadn't calculated how much work and time it would take. He had to keep track of the grain and hay and feed to make sure he didn't run out. He had to examine each animal regularly to make sure they were healthy. Sometimes herding them from the pasture or the yard into the barn or coop could be challenging; the chickens in particular seemed to have minds of their own and took time to gather. He was appreciative of the eggs he brought home to his wife, but he was glad he'd had the foresight to hire a young high school girl to do the morning milking, because he hadn't done enough milking to ever become competent.

Despite the extra work, he enjoyed those meditative morning and evening rituals. By himself on the farm in the half-light of dawn and dusk, he had thoughts he didn't have anywhere else. An unusual atmosphere entered him and expanded his heart. It was a little like being in church. An otherworldly hush. The animals lowing and grunting in their quiet way made him feel as if they were talking to him. It was utterly peaceful, not at all like a place where violence had happened, and he could feel the continuing presence of the commune members. He understood why they'd hung on so desperately when, given the financial stresses they were under, they probably wouldn't have been able to endure. They had loved this tough piece of land; they had loved their livestock; they had loved the challenge of trying to make a go of it. They were gentle people, perhaps too gentle to survive easily anywhere.

He tried not to speculate about what had happened to them— what was the point of speculating? Maybe the proponents of alien abduction were on to something. It didn't really matter—you chose an explanation and let the matter rest until something new was learned.

A few of the other animals, following the chickens' example, wouldn't stay put. He would arrive in the morning and some of the cows and sheep would be wandering around the driveway, coming right up to him and nudging his legs. A couple of the pigs were like that too. They would find a way to get outside the barn or the pen. Smart independent thinkers like their former owners. Luckily, they complied with his efforts to lead them back to where they were meant to be.

His main feeling about the group was that he felt sorry for them. He had observed them often enough at close range to see that, although they'd been determined, they had also been deficient in survival skills. Some of them showed signs of stress in their bodies, several with bad cases of acne, at least one girl anorexic. They were hypersensitive and too often derailed by sadness. So many things upset them. They didn't have a TV, but they listened to the radio. One day he had come into the kitchen and found two of the girls, Sophie and Claudia—he was supposed to call them women, but he had such a hard time thinking of such young people as women— sobbing over something they'd heard on a news program. A shooting somewhere, but far away on one of the coasts. They were right, it was sad that such things happened, but you couldn't let every little thing bring you down. Especially when you couldn't control it. People would always be dying. There would always be cruelty. You just had to learn to live with those things. Randy didn't think this was a harsh way to look at things, only practical.

He still hoped the group would reappear before he had to disband the animals, because the animals were a sensitive lot too, and it felt to Randy as if they missed their owners.

He hadn't entered the house since the day of the disappearance, even after the police had departed and the investigation had all but shut down. It would have felt like a violation to go inside. The house still belonged to them, and what if they were to come back and find him snooping? But one morning nature called, and he had no choice but to put his key to use and go inside to avail himself of the toilet.

Done with his business, he wandered around. Why not, since he was already inside? He wasn't searching for anything, just wandering, absorbing the atmosphere. All the other times he'd been inside the house he had been talking with them, giving them advice, and he'd been so focused on the people themselves, he hadn't registered the details of the rooms. Now he noticed more. He saw how they'd transported their youthful urban tastes with them: a fancy coffeemaker, herbal teas, biodegradable cleaning products. But what stood out to him most was the random clutter of the place. It was a place where young kids had roamed free without a lot of restriction, and none of the adults had taken much interest in domestic order. Randy thought of how the mess would horrify his wife, Ellie, who kept a tidy house and was always after him to pick up. Here, it was as if all the rooms served multiple purposes. He saw a bag of flour and a baking sheet on a bed. A spatula and trowel had migrated to the upstairs bathroom. Beside another bed was an axe next to a container of Dr. Bronner's liquid soap. There were crayons everywhere along with loose LEGO blocks. And, while there were no bookshelves, each room had stacks of books lined up against the walls: how-to farming books about living off the land, health-food books, books about the climate, a few novels and mysteries, lots of poetry collections.

He lifted a paperback splayed open on the living room couch to a Walt Whitman poem, "Song of Myself." "I think I could turn and live with animals, they are so placid and self-contain'd . . ."

He read the poem twice, chuckling. Yes, indeed, they loved their animals. Maybe they had chosen to go somewhere and live like animals. Well, wasn't that as likely as being abducted by aliens?

42

THEY DROVE NORTH to Sonoma, Dar at the wheel of his Volvo, Philippa in the passenger's seat, the black dog in the back. Philippa replayed in her mind what she'd told Dar, hearing how ridiculous it must have sounded to him. Downright insane. How she had found the silver chain embedded in the dog's matted coat—the *very same chain* her mother had always worn around her neck *every day*, embossed with the initials Lu had had when she was born, LMV, Lupe Maria Vasquez, her mother's surname instead of her father's because her grandmother wanted the Mexican heritage to be preserved. How many people had a chain like that with those very initials? Philippa thought the chain made a strong case, but she fully understood that it might be hard for Dar to buy—it had been a big leap for her too. But how else was she to understand what had happened? The sudden appearance of this female dog. Her uncanny escape from the shelter. How she'd been able to navigate her way back to Philippa's apartment. Her insistence on entering. And Philippa's own parallel feeling of being connected to this dog as she had only ever been connected to one person in her life, her mother. The sheer will of this dog was not ordinary. Her expressive capability was not ordinary. What Philippa was finally understanding was that the whole world was not ordinary anymore. Alice was gone and her mother was gone, but neither of them was really *gone* gone. Some incarnation of her mother was clearly here with her—and Alice might return too, in different skin maybe, but her unique soul still recognizable.

Dar had listened to what she said with unusually riveted focus, intent on every word, all of them data that would prove or disprove the veracity of her outlandish claim. His questions were measured, neutral-sounding. He had never exuded shock. *Other than the chain, what specific things do you see that link her with your mother? Have you ever known this to happen to anyone before? Do you think she's likely to turn back into what she was?* Although he never said so directly, she could hear some of his inquiry being directed to her state of mind—was she having a psychotic break?—but that was fine. The calm way he spoke had kept her from feeling defensive. He was the consummate scientist. At some point his questions stopped.

"Yes, I'll drive you home."

So here they were, driving to Sonoma. They had decided—*she* had decided—to call the dog Lu. Dar had no reason to object, and she would have felt weird calling the dog another random name, knowing what she knew. And Mother/Mom/Ma—those didn't seem right for a dog. Palm resting on the dog's back, she wished the dog could speak and describe what had happened. She thought of all the conversations she'd had with her mother over the years— would she ever adjust to a different kind of communication, one not based on words? It was hard to think about, hard to accept.

"Hey, Lu," Dar said, peering into the rearview mirror. "I have an idea. If we ask you something you can answer with one bark for yes, two for no. Does that work for you?"

Yip.

Dar laughed. And, after a startled moment, Philippa laughed too. "See, I told you she understands," she said.

"Yes, you told me."

At least he was game, she thought. She reclined against the seat back and closed her eyes. So much was uncertain, but it didn't matter. The love between and among them—she and her mother and Alice and even Dar—would thrive without words.

43

YOU SAT BEHIND THEM in the car, sniffing the pleasing musky scents of your daughter and one of her people. Their scents told you they matched. This man understood your daughter as few people did. He would not allow her to be harmed. And she adored him. How happy you were for them both.

You would have liked to be able to explain certain things to them, but maybe it didn't matter. Humans, you were coming to see, were slow to learn many things that animals understood from the get-go.

Sitting there in the pleasantly humming car, you began to recall wisps of stories from years ago, some you'd read and some that had been told to you. Back then you'd paid little attention, perpetual-motion machine that you were, but tidbits of those stories remained. There was one about a man who woke up as a bug. There was another about men who became pigs. In a third, a man became a donkey. There were so many of those stories. The transmutation of human cells. In what world did that happen? It occurred to you: Here. Now.

But, if you remembered correctly, most of those other transformations had been punishments. Had you been punished, too, for failing to live as a human being was supposed to live?

A memory swaddled you. Your daughter at three. Done reading

her a story, you were bidding her good night. You rose and turned out the light and came back to deliver a final kiss. She had rolled over and was snuggling beneath the covers. You bent to her exposed cheek and ear. *Good night*, you whispered. *We are not dogs*, she answered back in a clear, resonant voice. She nodded, somber and certain in her conclusion. You were confused. Where did this random thought come from—you had not been discussing dogs. You concluded it must be some independent strain of cognition she was born to, some throwback DNA. It didn't matter anyway, because such unusual ideas made her the unique girl she was. *That's right*, you said, *we are not dogs*. You lingered, waiting for what she'd say next but, hypothesis confirmed, she had no need to say more. She closed her eyes and gave herself over to the heavy breathing of sleep. It was years later that she behaved like a dog at school.

What you would have liked to say to her now: Sometimes it turns out that we *are* dogs. Sometimes we *prefer* being dogs.

44

DAR MULLIGAN HAD always liked to think of himself as an adventurer, a person cut from happily defiant cloth and living at the margins of the culture, but the truth (a truth he was only now confronting) was that though his mental life had been highly adventurous, his actual day-to-day physical life had been largely confined to the halls of academia and, as such, quite conventional. He had never taken the kind of leap he was being asked to take now: aiding and abetting the cockeyed beliefs of this young woman he had grown so fond of. He didn't actually *believe* her claim about the dog having once been her mother, but somehow he hadn't contradicted her and was allowing himself to play along.

He had no idea where this trip would lead him. When they left LA he had told himself he would drive Philippa home and deliver her and the dog into the hands of her father, but now that they were on the road he understood the mission might not be as simple as he had imagined. Would he stay long enough to listen to how Philippa described to her father what had happened? How far would he go in supporting her? Would he allow the father to believe that he, Dr. Dar Mulligan, a UCLA professor, a scientist, also believed that a woman had become a dog? The thought of being party to such a conversation made him panicky. The situation was further complicated by Philippa appearing to be her usual self, which was always, admittedly, a little *unusual*, but not psychotic. If only he didn't feel so fond of her.

They'd only been on the road for a little more than two hours when they both confessed to hunger. They purchased Subway sandwiches in a place called Lost Hills and brought them to a rest area. He sat at a table with the food and watched Philippa prancing with the dog. There was no denying their exceptional attunement. Philippa instructed the dog to position herself for optimal catching, then tossed a Frisbee, which the dog caught in her teeth, leaping into the air with astonishing agility. The dog trotted back to Philippa to deliver the Frisbee, and they hurled themselves at each other as if in a hug before resuming their game. This must be what it was like to be a father, he thought, taking exceptional pleasure in observing something so mundane.

The dog—Lu—devoured a bowl of dried food then ate half of Philippa's turkey sandwich, hand-fed by Philippa, bite by bite. If she was deluded, she was also happier than he'd ever seen her.

She texted her father to say she was on her way then offered to take the wheel. She was a relatively new driver and exceptionally cautious, driving below the speed limit and staying in the right lane, flinching each time a car passed her at too great a speed, or rode on her tail for too long. Such a contrast to his own manic driving style.

"Sorry," she kept saying to him. "I know I'm going too slow."

"You're doing fine," he replied each time. "Stay the course."

After an hour she couldn't continue. "My hands are numb," she said, pulling to the shoulder. "I think I've been gripping the wheel too hard." She massaged both hands, curled and uncurled her fingers.

"Weird." Bringing her hands to her nose, she sniffed. "Weird." She turned to him. "Do I smell funny?" She held out a hand.

"You're fine," he assured her, after an awkward perfunctory sniff revealed nothing unusual. Well aware she might not be fine at all, he took the wheel and encouraged her to sleep.

"Really?"

"Sure. Lie down in back with Lu."

She clambered to the back through the break in the seats. She was still such a kid. But then again, so was he.

"Sweet dreams," he said. He should have called Ivan before he made the offer to drive her north, but momentum got the better of him. He knew Ivan would have told him not to make this trip, but Ivan knew only part of the story.

Light snores rose from the back seat. The dog had taken the cue to sleep too. He drove past thirsty brown hills that flattened into the squared-off geometry of agricultural land, dark mountains limning the horizon, a beauty he acknowledged but was not native to him. The snoring dog and the sleeping girl put him in mind of a dream, as if everything beyond the windshield was a hallucination, neither permanent nor real. Life had never taken him to a more unusual place. He had always pictured his adventures as unspooling in the wilderness, not on a California freeway at the center of civilization. He imagined the conversation he would eventually have with Ivan, trying to describe how she'd told him about the silver chain embedded in the dog's matted coat, a chain she recognized from her mother. *That's when I knew for sure*, she told Dar. She had shown him a picture on her phone of her mother wearing the necklace. It was certainly a coincidence that the dog had been carrying such a chain, but it proved nothing. So why did he have this eerie countervailing feeling when he watched Philippa and the dog interact? Maybe . . . *Maybe what, Dar, come on!*

One way of looking at the situation was that it might not matter if Philippa's story was correct. Didn't everyone cling to certain delusions in order to power through life? Maybe he was finally allowing himself to become the nihilist he'd always been born to be.

Driving long distances had never been his strong suit—it demanded too much stillness, and his attention was best focused by moving; in driving too long he lost his sense of purpose. The exit signs beckoned him. Hovering just off the freeway were so many places he would have loved to explore. Monterey, Salinas, Gilroy. Who wouldn't love to see the garlic capital of the world? Mercey Hot Springs. He could barely resist the lure of a hot spring.

He had no time for detours. Today was Friday, a day he didn't teach, but he would have to get back to his classes by Monday, could only afford a day before he'd have to head back south. He would hand Philippa and the dog over to her father, find a cheap motel for the night, then turn around the next morning and retrace his steps. As for Philippa, he had no idea what her next steps would be. He had a hard time imagining her returning to school. Would she stay in touch with him, or would this be their last encounter? God, he hoped it wouldn't be.

Philippa and her dog were still sleeping when, just past Livermore, about to be devoured by Bay Area traffic, he decided to stop for a piss and a stretch. He exited at a small town called Dublin, thinking briefly of his unknown Irish ancestors. After driving a short distance, he came upon a small public park with a restroom. Not a single other car in sight. He parked, got out, stretched, did a few jumping jacks, reveling in the release and freedom of movement. He was hesitant to wake Philippa and her dog but imagined that they, too, would enjoy a stretch and a bathroom break. He peered through the back window, blinked to clarify his vision.

Two heads lifted, two pairs of eyes regarded him. He opened the door. Two dogs, one black, one brown, leapt to the pavement and rushed toward him, their torsos shuddering, their noses examining his legs like TSA officers.

"Philippa?" he said, scanning the parking lot, the grassy area beneath the trees. Where had she gone during his brief moments of inattention?

The world became airless, silent; he felt himself spinning through space, barely hanging on. Though he was not a praying man, he launched a prayer.

The dogs bothered his legs. Two dogs—not one, *two*.

He spun, jogged toward the restroom, away from the dogs' bustling bodies. Impossible to shake, they trotted in his wake. He broke into a full-on run, barreled through the restroom door, letting it slam behind him, closing the dogs out. They scratched at the door, whined. *Gah.*

Dizzy, he steadied himself with both hands on one of the sinks. His sweat was cold, his breath quick, ragged. He had never been called upon to question his own sanity; he'd always seen things more clearly than most, been less prone to subjective bias.

The dogs, just outside the door, wouldn't stop scratching. He splashed his face with water as well as he could from the stingy faucet. He looked for the urinal and, failing to find one, realized he'd entered the women's restroom. He peed in a stall, still dizzy, thinking for a moment he might pass out, the stream of his piss momentarily muffling the dogs' impatience. He flushed, sat on the toilet, coaching himself. How had he failed to keep track of what was happening in the few moments he'd been stretching? It was probably the uninterrupted hours of driving that had brought him to this precipice. It was good he'd thought to get out of the car, move his body, push reset. Now he needed to locate Philippa and find out where the second dog had come from. He would go back out there now and attack this problem with restored lucidity.

But he couldn't move. He sat there, still light-headed and lethargic, chiding himself. Maybe he needed water. He rose unsteadily. He wedged his head into the sink at an angle where a thin stream of water reached his mouth. Mouth full, he attempted to swallow, but he choked, and the choking made his eyes water, and he hoped he wasn't crying. He collapsed on the wet concrete floor, back against the wall, hoping no one would come in to find him there, collapsed like a derelict. The dogs were no longer making sounds, and suddenly their absence alarmed him as much as their presence had alarmed him earlier.

He took out his phone and pulled up Ivan's number. A single ring fired off, a sound belonging to the world outside his brain, jolting him. He canceled the call and forced himself to stand.

The dogs were sniffing around in the grass near the car, but as soon as he exited the restroom they hurried over to greet him. Scanning the rest area for Philippa, he didn't look down at them. Another car was parking beside his, a red Ford Fiesta. Two young women stepped out. Full of young-woman vitality and good cheer, they stooped to pet the dogs. "Hello there. Good dog. Pretty dog," one said.

"Your dogs are so friendly," the other one said.

"Yeah." Dull-witted and unresponsive, he half wished the young women would spirit the dogs away, solving his problems, but they disappeared to the restroom, leaving him alone. Philippa was nowhere to be seen. He was too embarrassed to call out for her.

He examined the car's back seat and floor. One side was filled with detritus he should have cleared out long ago—empty coffee cups and fast-food cartons, browning apple cores, his workout bag. On the other side were Philippa's clothes, her blue jeans and work shirt and the tiny shoulder bag she used as a purse. The gallon water jug he kept for emergencies had lost its top and spilled its contents over everything.

His own solidity dissolved yet again. The dogs were behind him, badgering his legs. He turned to them. The brown dog—a female, he saw—rose on hind legs, laid her paws on his belly, barked. He bent, took the dog's paws in his hands. "No," he said. "No." A sob burped up in him; he swallowed it down. "Please," he whispered.

The black dog watched as the brown dog continued to bark for attention. She insisted on keeping her paws on his waist, insisted on his regard. He urged the dogs into the back seat, where they went willingly and lapsed into silence. He closed the car doors and wandered to the single picnic table under the trees. He sat himself down, suddenly ancient. He pulled out his cell, dialed Ivan, let it ring.

"Hey, man. How's it going?"

"Ivan?"

"Dar? You okay? You don't sound good."

"I'm—"

"What's up?"

"I'm—on the road."

"Okay . . . ?"

"Exhausted."

"I hear that. Is this about the girl?"

"No . . . Well, yes and no."

"Uh-oh."

The young women were returning to their car, laughing, bringing their faces up to the window of Dar's car and waving to the dogs. "Bye-bye, cutie pies," one of them said. Dar turned away from them. Their youth and energy were too overwhelming.

"Look, things are happening. I've gotta go. I'll call you next week."

"Okay, hang in there. Don't do anything I wouldn't do, okay? And keep the faith, bro."

Dar laid his head on the picnic table, pressing his third eye against the splintered wood. He heard the young women opening their car doors, their ignition starting. He sprinted toward them, waving his arms overhead, knowing but not caring that he looked like a madman.

"Hey! Hello there! Wait!"

They stopped, and the driver rolled down her window partway, regarding him suspiciously. "What?"

"I was wondering—if you—I don't know, maybe you'd like to—take my dogs? They're wonderful dogs, but things have happened so I can't care for them."

The woman's face darkened, and she turned to her companion, signaling something, before turning back to him. "You're asking us to take your dogs?"

"Only because . . ." He was aware of the dogs watching from his car. The windows were closed so they probably couldn't hear him, but their expressions told him all he needed to know. "Never mind."

"I'm sure you'll do great," the girl said. She rolled up her window, and they drove off.

Feeling terrible pangs of guilt, he filled one of the empty coffee cups with water and offered it to the dogs, watching their rough pink tongues trying to finesse the cup's small opening. Did they know he'd been ready to give them away? He wrung out Philippa's soaked clothes and laid her small purse and cell on the dashboard to dry.

The phone, having sat in a pool of water for a while, was unlikely to function again.

He thought of Antonio Damasio, whose work he'd recently been reading. Damasio was a neuroscientist at the University of Southern California who studied the role of emotions in human consciousness and decision-making. Would Damasio say he, Dar, had wanted this to happen, had somehow willed it? Were these events springing from emotions at the depths of Dar's own brain?

No. Of course not.

The brown dog scuttled into the seat beside him; the black dog remained in back. They both had their ears pricked; their noses browsed the air.

What would Ivan do now? What would his grandmother do? What would his friend the octopus do? He turned to the brown dog, seized her muzzle in his hands, and stared into the spindles and facets of her gray eyes. *Go forth*, the eyes told him.

45

IT BROKE OUR HEARTS to see him like that. So uncertain. So unwilling to accept what he knew to be true. We did what we could to reassure him. We nudged him and licked him, trying to convey our love. But he resisted, couldn't let his guard down, couldn't give himself over to the moment.

He hit the freeway like a madman at top speed, and it wasn't long before tears streamed down his cheeks. The silent tears of someone too afraid to sob. It made us sad to see this lovely man in such despair, but we knew our limits. We fell silent to let him sit alone with his uncertainty. Maybe, in time, he'd work it through.

Meanwhile, sitting there, quietly sniffing, we learned so much about him. The candy bars and peanut butter sandwiches and McDonald's burgers he'd consumed in the car. The sodas and French fries. The weed he'd smoked. The sex he'd had right there on the back seat. So many delicious and revealing molecules were buried in the fibers of those seats, on the floor, on the dashboard and the doors. It was probably good he didn't know what we were learning—it might have embarrassed him. He had enough on his mind.

46

EVEN AFTER A WEEK back in her studio, Marley barely trusted what she saw right in front of her. She drifted through her studio lifting objects and placing them back down. Mugs, throw pillows, paintbrushes, blocks of wax for her encaustic work. This book had survived. This bed and its bedding. This table and all her canvasses. Pure luck. If the winds had been different, or if the firefighters' efforts had been less valiant, everything could have gone up in flames. Her clothing was still redolent of smoke, but everything else was intact and recognizable. How could she have been spared the loss so many others were facing? The imbalance wasn't fair or right—though who could expect fire to adhere to principles of fairness? This was what had happened. No sense could be made of it.

No sense could be made of the disappearance of Lu Barnes either. Marley tried to connect it to the other disappearances, but it didn't seem to fit. In those other cases people had disappeared in groups, whereas Lu had disappeared all alone. Marley hated to think of the violence that might have been involved. Lu was tough, but she was small and female, therefore vulnerable. Marley barely knew Lu, but still she missed her. Lu's spontaneous hug had conveyed so much genuine feeling. She was a rare person who could forgive. Marley knew they would be friends—if Lu returned.

~

There was no way of avoiding him. She was on her way to buy groceries, and they were the only two on the sidewalk, advancing toward each other. She spotted him first, about twenty feet away, the woolly beard, the dejected, downturned gaze, the plodding gait. Had he gained weight? He *did* look like Francis Ford Coppola, though not the triumphant version of the film director, more like Coppola after his *Cotton Club* failure. This was a different man from the confident, jocular aesthete she'd known this past summer, running his winery with such panache. The disappearance of his wife had carved troughs beneath his eyes, accentuated the sag of his jowls, slowed him down. He appeared to have aged almost a decade since she'd last seen him. By the time he noticed her they were within a few feet of each other. He shrugged and tried to mount a smile, but it didn't stick; even a smile required too much energy.

"What a surprise—I thought you were in Florida."

"I just flew in."

"Coffee?" Marley said, because something needed to be said, and it would have been cruel to simply move on and not inquire how he was. Her groceries could wait.

He shrugged his acquiescence, and they entered the nearest coffee shop, the Uncorked Café, an unpretentious community favorite serving hot drinks, wine, light food, and breakfast all day. They navigated to the only vacant table at the back, where George slapped his leather folder onto the circular table and collapsed into a chair as if he never expected to rise again.

"Regular?" she asked him.

He nodded, and she went to the counter and ordered two coffees and brought them back to the table along with cream and sugar. They busied themselves customizing their drinks.

"I guess you haven't found her?" Marley said.

He shook his head, already beyond speech, already weeping, head down. When he managed to speak, his voice was low and hoarse. "She's gone. The house is gone. The winery's gone. Everything. What am I now?" He looked up at her, terrified, gesturing and overturning his coffee cup so the scalding liquid flooded the table and overflowed into her lap. She leapt up for napkins and piled them on the table, ignoring her coffee-blotched lavender pants.

"See? Every damn thing I touch." His attempts at sounding swashbuckling did not begin to mask his sorrow.

"No worries. I've got this," she said, mopping and wiping. He waved off an offer of more coffee. Order restored, somewhat, she took her seat again.

"Is there anything I can do to help?" she said.

"Help?" His look of disgust was tempered by incredulity. "There's not a damn thing you, or anyone, can do. Some asshole has taken advantage of my wife, and these fires have us by the balls." He lifted his folder, waved it around. "Insurance? What a joke."

His rage flared and died, and she felt sorry for him. His phone vibrated, and he glanced at it. "My mother-in-law. She's about to descend on me. She isn't saying so straight out, but she's got some underlying attitude that tells me she thinks Lu's disappearance is my fault.

"My daughter is coming up here too. What am I supposed to do with my daughter? I'm staying in a room at the Best Western, for god's sake. She doesn't know the house is gone. How can I possibly break that news to her? She seems to have some expectation we're going to go out on foot searching for her mother." He looked up at the ceiling and closed his eyes, a momentary plea to higher powers she was sure he didn't believe in. "Aaaargh. The police have been useless. The only thing they've come up with is that a credit card of hers was used at a Super 8 Motel north of San Francisco. It must have been stolen. Lu would never stay at a Super 8 Motel. And they won't weigh in on whether her disappearance is related to all of those other people who have gone missing."

She had nothing to say. Nothing in her life, despite the hours she'd spent in therapy, had prepared her for this, for finding words that would make a difference to an eviscerated man. He had once ridden high, ruled over so much, believed he was untouchable. His loss seemed like too much for anyone to have to bear, though people all over the world suffered losses of this magnitude and greater all the time. She felt for him having to break the news to his daughter, having to console her. She watched him struggle to compose himself and thought of her own recent tears of relief and joy at seeing her world intact. Such a stark difference between their two fates.

"When will your daughter arrive?"

"Unclear. She's hitching a ride with someone. I don't know if I have it in me to expose her to all this. If I can't absorb it, how will she?"

She wondered if his ambition was quashed or if he would use whatever insurance funds he received to start another winery, here or elsewhere, and build another custom house. But those questions were premature to ask. So much would depend on whether Lu came back. It suddenly occurred to Marley—had Lu *chosen* to vanish? She turned the idea over as she watched George. Was it possible Lu had wanted to escape him and his power? Yet another question that couldn't be asked. So much had to be adjudicated in the privacy of one's mind.

His moment of candor had passed. He was battening down, preparing for whatever the next onslaught might be.

"Will you be seeing your house or the winery—what remains of them?"

"As soon as the fire officials let me in."

"It'll be good to see your daughter. You'll figure things out with her."

He raised his eyebrows in skepticism. This summer he had shown her pictures of his daughter. The girl's body was husky, her head half-shaved, and she looked into the lens without smiling. George claimed to be proud of her, but he also said he didn't understand her, and Marley had had the distinct impression that this wasn't the daughter he would have chosen for himself. She wondered if the daughter sensed it.

"I talked to your wife, you know. At the evacuation center. She's wonderful."

Alarm coursed through him; his privacy had been breached. "Why?"

"Why what? Why did we talk? You know how it is. We were there together with time to kill. Why wouldn't we?"

He nodded. "Look, I have to go."

She saw she still made him uncomfortable—she had humiliated him.

He rose, and she did not. "Well," he said. He leaned down for a quick awkward standing-up/sitting-down hug in which he gripped the balls of her shoulders and brought his face to some no-man's-land near hers, without allowing their skin to touch. Then he popped back up, the enactment of friendship complete.

"Thanks for, you know, listening," he said.

She watched him make his way to the exit as briskly as he could, performing strength. A man undone and pretending not to be. A man who kept his soul hidden. She understood the impulse to hide; it still swam too powerfully in herself. She hoped the arrival of his daughter would bring him some relief.

47

IT WAS DARK when Dar arrived at the center of town. He had stopped only once for gas and dog food. The smell of smoke was appalling, and yet the main street appeared elegant even in the midst of disaster. Everything was aglow with after-hours lighting that made it sparkle, glamorous as a movie set, so he almost had the feeling there might have been nothing at all beyond the enticing facades. Buildings of pink stucco or red brick with colorful awnings. Charcuteries and bakeries; gift shops and wine bars. Bulging flower baskets suspended from lampposts. If you didn't count the air, nothing here had been directly touched by fire, so why wasn't there a single human being in sight? It looked like a place where a plague had descended and people had been forced to vacate suddenly.

He had hoped to find somewhere to stay overnight, nothing fancy, simply a place to rest his head and refresh himself for decision-making, but nothing looked promising. He doubted any of the swank places he passed would take dogs. A short way out of town he pulled off on a gravel turnout and slept in the car, crimping his long body to fit the restricted space, relieved when the dogs took the cue to sleep too. They all dozed for a few hours, woke to reassemble their addled bones, then slept again.

He woke with the sun, under-rested, alarmed by the stench of the smoke, and worried about his next move. With Pippa's phone ruined by water, how was he supposed to find her father? He drove back to town and waited with the dogs on a bench under a catalpa tree for the Uncorked Café to open. He didn't normally drink coffee, but today he needed something to jolt him from his altered state. The dogs sat companionably on either side of his legs, and he stroked their heads. He was trying to be kind, still feeling guilty about trying to give them away. Whatever was happening to him was not their fault. Now that he was in public he had to curb his growing habit of speaking to them as if they understood him, though the truth was, they *did* appear to understand him. They obeyed readily, and they took an interest in everything he said. Though he couldn't pretend to know what their barking meant, it seemed to him like a crude form of speech. He wished it didn't seem that way. He wanted the dogs to ignore him, treat him like the different species he was.

The brown dog unnerved him more than the black dog did. He still couldn't allow himself to look at her directly. Everything about her filled him with unease: the sheen of her chocolate brown coat, the healthy pink of her tongue, her avid black nose. Her gray eyes especially disturbed him. He'd never seen a Labrador with gray eyes. He regretted telling Philippa about communicating with the octopus. It might have given her ideas. But even thinking such a thought layered more crazy over the substantial amount of crazy he already felt. Yes, it was best not to look into that dog's eyes.

Someone was unlocking the café's front door. A maternal-looking woman of middle age with a thick gray-brown braid and a smile that ruled her face.

"Desperate for coffee?" she said.

He nodded. "Morning."

"Oh, hon, tell me about it. Coffee won't fix the fires, but it sure makes the outlook better. Come on in and let's get you fueled up. Get you out of this damn smoke."

He rose, and the dogs rose too.

"Oh no," she said. "You'll have to leave the dogs outside. I'm sorry. Health code and all."

He hesitated. "I promise they'll behave."

She surveyed the street. Not a soul in sight. "What the hell. Who's gonna report me in times like this? Bring 'em in."

The coffee shop, remarkably unpretentious for an upscale town like this, doubled as a wine bar. The menu was handwritten on a giant chalkboard above the counter. The wooden tables and chairs didn't match. Beyond the red gingham curtains on the front window, there was no décor to speak of. Dar and the dogs settled at one of the tables along the wall, not immediately visible from the street, lest some passerby should object to the dogs. She brought him a regular coffee.

"How about some food?"

"I think I'm good for now."

"How about these beautiful dogs? Don't they need something?"

"They're fine."

Both dogs barked, and the woman laughed. "I think they need something." How readily she accepted that the dogs must understand her.

"Okay. Eggs."

"Highbrow dogs, aren't they!"

He found himself laughing and realized he hadn't laughed for days. "Oh yes, they are. Definitely highbrow."

She brought three plates of scrambled eggs, bacon, toast, laying two of the plates on the floor. "I figured why not give them the works? Every dog I've ever known loves bacon and toast. I'm Millie, by the way."

"Dar."

She lingered, watching the dogs, clearly keen on conversation. "You been hit bad by the fires?"

"Not me personally, but people I know."

"That's how it always is. Some get walloped. Some get off scot-free. No rhyme or reason. Maybe it would be good to believe in God at a time like this, but that's not my jam."

"Mine either," he said.

"Whereabouts do you live?"

"Actually, I live down in LA. I'm up here helping some people out. In fact, I'm looking for someone named George Barnes. You wouldn't know him, would you?"

"George Barnes of Barnes Winery? Sure, I know him. Not real well, but I know who he is. He was just in here yesterday. Poor man—he lost everything. House. Winery. Even his wife has gone missing. I feel so bad for that man."

Both dogs stood and began to whine.

"Hey, boys," Millie said. "Calm down."

"Girls."

"Calm down, girls."

The dogs' bodies writhed and shuddered. They'd devoured their eggs and were ready to move.

"You don't know where I could find him, do you? These dogs belong to him."

"I can't say where he is. But Marley probably knows. Like I said, they were in here together yesterday."

"Marley?"

"Oh, I forgot you're not from around here. Everyone knows Marley. She's an artist. I don't have her number, but you can find her at her studio about five miles out on Calendula Road. Cute little red barn she made into a studio. She lives there too."

Millie refilled his coffee, and he craved the extra uplift it promised, but the dogs were restless, trotting around the table, tails swishing, impatient to leave. Millie watched them in semi-alarm, afraid her leniency would be discovered, and he felt like a bad parent, incapable of discipline.

"I guess I need to go. The dogs call the shots. Would you mind putting this in a to-go cup?"

Millie brought him a cardboard cup along with the check. She hadn't charged him enough, and he began to object, but she cut him off.

"No worries, the dogs' food is on me. Crisis etiquette, you know? Different times."

Different times, he thought. If she only knew.

48

SHE HEARD THE CAR before she saw it. A beat-up kelly green Volvo charged up the dirt driveway, culling dust that permeated the already smoke-mucked, dun-yellow air. It was only a little after 9:30 in the morning, and she was still in her coral Japanese robe. When she had awakened almost two hours earlier, she had wandered in a dreamy daze to her studio, where she'd been lounging in an easy chair with coffee, trying to make sense of her luck. Survival had robbed her of forward motion and made her introspective. She wasn't sure when she'd be moved to make art again. Fortunately, a small grant from a foundation supporting female artists would allow a stretch of laziness, as she expected to be in the clutches of this sorrow-laced relief for some time to come. She'd been living in Sonoma for just over a decade, and each year, in the wake of the fires, everyone was unsettled for months, regardless of what had happened to them. The memories lingered like the monsters of childhood.

She stood at the window watching a gangly man step from the car with two dogs, both Labs, one black, the other brown. The dogs sniffed along the grassy area in front of the studio while the man looked around. He was tall and pale with large white blotches on his neck and arms, one of those people who appeared to be allergic to sun. Hesitant, he followed the brick path to the front door. Except for occasional studio visits, she rarely had visitors, let alone unexpected ones. She thought of her space as a private sanctum, and neither the living area nor the studio was built for accommodating guests. For a moment she thought this man might be here to tell her she had to evacuate again, but he didn't appear to be official. She opened the door before he knocked.

"Good morning." Her manner was clipped but cordial. "Sorry I'm not dressed. I wasn't expecting anyone."

"Marley?" The dogs stood at attention behind him, as if ready for a hunt. "I'm Dar Mulligan."

"How do you know who I am?"

"The woman at the Uncorked Café, Millie, she said you'd be here."

"Ah, Millie." If Millie had told him to come here, he couldn't be all bad. They shook hands.

"These are my dogs." He stood back and gestured to them, and they barked in unison. "Well, they're not really mine," he amended.

Marley laughed. "They're very polite."

"Millie said you're a friend of George Barnes."

She squinted at him.

"Do you know where I can find him? These are his dogs."

"George's dogs? Last I knew he didn't have dogs."

"Well—"

"How did you come by these dogs if they're his?"

"It's hard to explain," the man said. "Millie said he's lost his house. And his winery."

"Yes, I know. Terrible luck."

The black dog had sidled up to Marley and begun sniffing her robe. The dog looked up, its brown eyes gentle. "Hello there, buddy." She bent to stroke the dog's back.

"She's a she."

Marley laughed. "Strange, isn't it, how often people assume dogs are male and cats are female? Beautiful dog. Unusual eyes."

"Yes. They're both unusual dogs."

"So, you're looking for George?"

The man looked to his dogs as if to include them in the conversation. "Yes, we are."

The brown dog had come to join the black dog. Marley had always appreciated dogs from a distance but, having never been a pet owner, she often found dogs overwhelming.

"Would you like to come in?" she said on a whim, acting against her usual private impulses. Something about this anxious man aroused her pity. He needed some succor, and his dogs were polite.

"I don't want to bother you."

"It's not a bother. I was just about to make another pot of coffee. Come on in."

She turned to go inside, and both dogs trotted past her.

"Ladies, no," the man admonished. "You have to stay outside."

Marley laughed at his use of the word *ladies*. "I think they'll be fine. As long as they don't pee on things or chew on my canvases."

"You hear that, Lu? No peeing. No chewing."

"Lu? You call that dog Lu?"

The man, Dar, scratched his head with both hands. So many nervous tics.

"Do you know," Marley said, "that George Barnes's wife is named Lu?"

"Yes, I know."

The dogs were listening, ears pricked.

"Funny coincidence," Marley said.

The man nodded.

"Do you know that she's gone missing?"

"Yes, Millie told me that too."

"I'm confused. How do you know George Barnes?" Marley said. "I get the sense there's something here you're not saying."

Anguish wreaked havoc with the man's face. He looked around the studio as if making an exit plan. For a moment she thought he might cry. "It's impossible to explain."

"Try me."

He shook his head. "Oh god." He plucked the skin of his throat. "I'm a scientist, okay? A rationalist, you know? Not the least bit woo-woo."

"Okay, neither am I—so?"

"So, do you have an open mind, is what I'm saying? Can you hear something strange without judging?"

"An open mind might be the only real asset I have, Mr. Mulligan." She liked to think of herself as open-minded but, even as she said it, she suspected her claim was only half true.

"Dar, please."

"Dar. I'll make coffee while you and your dogs explore. Then we'll sit down and you can tell me this strange thing."

Once again the poor man looked as if he was disassembling on the spot. Her curiosity was piqued about the strange thing he wanted to tell her. He was an odd man, for sure, but she trusted him. She'd always been a good judge of character. He followed his dogs into the studio area, corralling them away from the easel, where a flicked tail could send paint and wax into orbit. Marley was glad she'd laid out her canvasses. It was like having a spontaneous open studio with a stranger, and she was always interested in the reactions of strangers. As she set about making coffee, the black dog, Lu, came up behind her and nosed her shins.

"What's wrong, honey? You hungry? I only have people food.

Maybe some water?" She laid a bowl of water on the floor, but after a single tongueful the dog was done with it, whimpering again, insistent on something. She crouched.

"Hey there, Lu, what do you want?" Saying the name invoked the real Lu, the absent one Marley thought of as her new friend. Vertigo halted her for a moment—the world looping around itself.

The dog was barking, licking Marley's hand and arm, diving in to nuzzle her neck and cheek. While Marley would normally have been turned off by a slobbering, licking dog, this licking was delicate, the tongue rough and dry, and it made her feel unexpectedly flattered, almost kissed.

"Okay, okay. I love you too. But can you stop now?"

The dog ceased its licking and held its gaze on Marley, its eyes beseeching. Marley couldn't look away—the creature's stillness combined with a knowing quality was, quite honestly, a bit unnerving.

She served the coffee in her studio, bringing an extra chair for Dar, where he sat with the brown dog beside him; Marley took the other chair with the black dog at her feet. Two chairs, two people, two dogs. It occurred to Marley this might be a good scene for a painting.

Dar turned his attention to her. His focus was absolute. He waited a long time before he began to speak, and during his attenuated preamble of silence she had the dizzying sense she was on the edge of a high-dive platform, butterflies in her belly, gazing down at the voluptuous blue below.

49

IT WAS long past midnight and Marley couldn't sleep; she blamed her sleeplessness on the presence of the dogs. They were perfectly quiet, lying on the floor beside the bed so at first she'd thought they were sleeping, but when she sat up to check on them she saw they were wide awake too, their eyes receptacles for the scraps of moonlight seeping into the studio. Their big eyes seemed not only a catchment for that light, but they seemed to be flaring it back out to Marley.

Were they still disturbed about Dar having left them? What had happened had been undeniably strange. One moment he was completely immersed in telling his story, the next minute he was desperate to leave. He acted as if he'd just confessed to some terrible crime and had to depart quickly before he was apprehended. Marley had wanted him to linger, discuss the ins and outs of his story. She had wanted to figure out what motivated him to tell such a story in the first place. But instead he had scribbled his contact information, thrust the silver necklace at her, along with Philippa's phone and some folded clothing—*Take these, please!*—and he ran to his car.

She didn't want to be saddled with the dogs, and the dogs clearly didn't want to be left. They had raced after him, barking emphatically and hurling themselves against the closed car doors, leaving scratches on the finish, but Dar paid no attention and drove off so quickly Marley had worried he might hurt the dogs. They tore down the driveway in the car's wake but couldn't keep up and returned to Marley's front door, barking to be let inside. What could she do but relent? She half expected Dar to return for them, but he didn't. She texted George: *Please come by. Something odd has happened.* But damn him, he wouldn't respond.

She had tried to make the best of things. She had no dog food and didn't feel like going to the market, so she fed them cold cereal and hunks of cheddar cheese and sliced ham. They nibbled a little but without much interest then wandered around the studio together, seeming aimless and depressed—if you could say such a thing about dogs. Occasionally the black dog came up to Marley to lodge a sniffing plea into her crotch.

If only they'd sleep. Awake and eyeballing her, they were making her self-conscious, even a little scared.

In leaving the dogs here, Dar had sloughed his problem and dumped it onto her, a problem that shouldn't really be hers. These weren't George's dogs—Marley was ninety-nine percent sure George had never had dogs. They had talked about the cat his daughter had taken to college, how empty the house had seemed without the presence of an animal. Though he'd confessed to not being an "animal person," he'd admitted to missing the cat. So no, he'd never had dogs. Marley liked these dogs well enough, but she certainly didn't plan to keep them. She couldn't accommodate two dogs in the studio. So far they'd been respectful enough, but they could so easily run roughshod over everything. Could she convince George to take them even if they weren't technically his? She tried to imagine how he'd respond to seeing the necklace. Probably the same way she herself had responded. It was a perfectly ordinary necklace, cheap. Yes, Marley recalled Lu wearing a similar necklace, but there were probably dozens of those necklaces out there in the world. The fact that Lu's initials were engraved on this one meant next to nothing.

She fell into a liminal state in which she half dreamed, half imagined she was in a dark fairy-tale forest. There were trees with gnarled branches that resembled the silhouettes of witches. There was a winding path. There was a darkness so complete and menacing it seemed to forbid walking. But then, sudden shafts of light shot out from between the branches, sparkling, shimmering, swaying, resembling the northern lights.

Awake again, she sat up, checked on the dogs. The brown dog was sleeping, thank god, but the black dog was wide awake with those eerie wide, light-shedding eyes. She lay back down and drifted again, went deeper into the fairy-tale forest.

She awakened again. It was still dark; she was stuck in unending night. The black dog had come onto the bed and had wedged herself against Marley's waist, her head on Marley's belly, her eyes wide open. "For god's sake," Marley said, "don't you need to sleep?"

The dog whimpered, as if to say *I'm not sleeping until you do.* Marley reached out to locate the necklace on the bedside table. She brought it down to the dog's face. "So what do you make of this?"

After a moment's hesitation that felt like consideration, the dog began licking Marley's hand, the hand holding the necklace. As she did this, her round brown eyes remained focused on Marley in the most undog-like way.

It hit her in an instant. Of course there was a soul flickering behind those eyes. A life force. A consciousness apprehending the world that was as valid and coherent and full of feeling as Marley's own. Not confined by biology, by species. It was a soul Marley not only *saw* but *recognized* as her new friend Lu.

50

A LIGHT RAIN had turned the ash to a thick, ankle-deep sludge. George stood in the middle of the lot he'd determined was the former location of his now-vanished house, his breathing shallow. The vaporizing of so much—the landscape, all the neighborhood's houses, certainty itself—made him feel the potential for his own disappearance. He hugged his forearms close to his chest, palpating his ribs, reminding himself his body was still there.

This had to be where his house had once been, but without the landmarks—the cluster of live oaks marking the bend in the road at the crest of Juniper Road, the expanse of meadow, the Montgomerys' house telling him to turn right onto Sunset Loop— he honestly had no idea if he was on the correct road. He would have thought his body's directional memory would place him in the correct location reliably, even without the visual cues, but apparently this was not so. The road leading up here was a disaster, the asphalt so buckled by heat it had threatened to ruin the tires of his BMW. The two sheriffs stationed at the base of the hill had warned him about this. It was like a war zone, they'd said, at the very least highly toxic. "I swear to god," said one of the sheriffs, "things melted in this fire you'd have counted on to be around for centuries."

George adjusted his mask and slowly walked the perimeter of the foundation, which, protected by dirt, was still discernible. He reached down to sift the ash, trying to wrap his mind around the enormity of not just the loss but the *change*. It was like a middle-school science class. Solids. Liquids. Gases. How things can transform through cooling and heat. But it was one thing to witness an ice cube melting into a liquid state, or a glass of water evaporating into gas, and another thing entirely to see your house and all its contents reduced to this gunk. The walls and windows of the house. The floors and countertops. The furniture and carpets and drapes. The shelving and books. The artwork. Everything reassembled and transposed into this singular disgusting glop. The impermanence of it was breathtaking, heartbreaking, mind-bending. It wasn't possible to live in a world holding so much uncertainty, despite what Keats said about embracing negative capability. How could it be that none of the house's glass remained? There'd been so much glass, and he couldn't even locate small pieces of it. The temperature would have had to have climbed to over 2552 degrees Fahrenheit for all that glass to melt. Everyone had said this fire had burned hotter than any of the fires that preceded it, but until now he hadn't bothered to consider what that meant. Tom, George had just learned this morning, had visited the winery on his own so he could prepare George for what to expect. The worst part, Tom reported, was seeing how the aging bottles of wine had exploded before they'd even had a chance to melt, spattering their exquisite hard-won vintages like blood.

Something leered up from the scrim of smoke ahead of him. The blackened husk of the Odyssey slumping into the ground, all its windows blasted out. George felt he was looking at the ruins of an ancient civilization, once prosperous but now brought to its knees, only rubble speaking to its former magnificence. He could see the blindness that had gone into the Odyssey's making, the hubris built into it from the start.

Now his eyes began to pick out other things: a bathroom sink and part of a toilet, both so misshapen by heat they resembled sculptures more than household fixtures, still recognizable for their former function, but long past usable. They were probably from Pippa's bathroom, but he couldn't be sure. He tripped on a scrap of metal that rose to the height of his knee. Drawing his fingers along its edge he realized it was his former file cabinet. All his records had lived in there. All his history since arriving in California almost thirty years earlier. He had digital records, but he'd never fully moved past the era of paper.

This was a fool's errand. There wasn't a single thing worth salvaging here. He was glad Lu wasn't here to see this. Looking around now, it was almost impossible for George to imagine them living here again. It wouldn't be habitable for years. And the return of beauty—that would take even longer.

He dreaded Pippa's arrival. She would be devastated seeing this, and further devastated when she learned how useless and distracted the police were turning out to be. He'd never been able to manage Pippa's bouts of angst and depression—navigating her run-ins with teachers when she thought they were exhibiting mean opinions, her difficulty choosing "acceptable" topics for school projects, her anxiety about being in the band back in middle school with all those older boys, the high school boy-crush who'd rejected her, the roller coaster involved in trying to select a college; he'd relied on Lu for all that. The thought of himself and Pippa stuck in his cheerless room at the Best Western together with no other place to go—well, it was untenable. Pippa had said she wanted to drive around looking for Lu. They would stop people on the street, she said, and show them pictures: *Have you seen this woman?* She wanted to get Linda involved, form a family search party. George would do anything to get Lu back, but this plan of Pippa's was grossly impractical, a shot in the dark, futile busywork to give them a false sense of agency. Linda had probably arrived at the Best Western by now, devastated by Lu's disappearance as they all were, but full of irrepressible forward motion and practical problem-solving plans. He was already overwhelmed by the thought of her energy, such a contrast to his own lassitude. And he could feel a rising competition between them over ownership of Lu—who was preeminent at a time like this, husband or mother?

Beneath his toes, something hard. He shouldn't be touching these things, poisonous as he knew the ash to be, but he couldn't help himself. He bent, scrabbled around. As soon as his fingers touched the stone, he knew what it was—one of the diamond-studded necklaces he'd given to Lu. The stones were caked in ash, but he would be able to clean them. What a find! On a mission now, he reached down again, dug around, and located two more necklaces, an earring, a couple of rings. His heart flew off on a tear. It wasn't as if his house had been saved, but it was *something* to find these heat-resistant objects, still intact, things he could present to Lu when she returned home. Wouldn't it make her happy? Didn't it seem like a sign that not everything could be destroyed? Evidence that sometimes, certain things really could survive? The question was—had Lu herself survived?

He tossed his haul onto the passenger's seat of his car and contemplated returning for more. How much was enough? It was only jewelry, after all. Decorative items. It had memories associated with it, but what good would jewelry do without Lu?

Another text arrived from Marley, along with one from Linda announcing her arrival. She was thrilled to report that she'd managed to book a room right next to his. He hadn't answered Marley's first two texts. He'd ignored her too long. Linda would have to wait.

51

NEITHER MARLEY NOR the dogs had been able to sleep at all, and now, in the light of day, Marley found herself in a daze, unsure of her next move, questioning the understanding she'd come to last night. The dogs were unusual dogs, exceptionally obedient, but that didn't mean they'd once been people. Marley had no interest in living with dogs, any dogs—it would be like having two over-involved roommates. She prized her solitude too much to incorporate two needy animals. She hoped George would take them off her hands. He was on his way over now, coming straight from the site of his decimated house.

The sun, still weakened by smoke, had crept overhead so it now shone down through the skylight, highlighting the three of them like a theatrical spot. On each of her thighs, a dog's head rested, heavy in relaxation, numbing her legs.

She stroked the dogs' heads. "Don't you wish you could talk?"

They rustled. The black dog—Lu-dog, Marley had been calling her—raised her head and licked Marley's hand. Did this mean: *Of course I wish I could speak*? Or did it mean: *I have no use for speech—I'm fine being mute*? What contentment the dogs exuded, their bodies given over to the pleasure of the sun's light and heat. She'd never seen a person, herself included, exuding such contentment.

The dogs pricked their ears, scuttled to the door, shivering, wagging, whining, barking. George's car was parking in the drive-way. She told the dogs to calm down and stay where they were, which they did. A moment of dizziness halted her, followed by a quiver of vanity. Why had she not thought to fix herself up? She was wearing the loose cotton pull-on pants and sweatshirt she often wore when painting, and she hadn't applied her face. For god's sake, she didn't still have to perform for George, did she?

She opened the front door, and he walked in without saying a word; neither did she. He didn't wait to be told where to settle—he took one of the two chairs in the studio, the chair Dar had sat in the day before. The dogs, jittery, sniffed his crotch.

"Dogs?" he said, nudging them away. "When did you decide to get dogs?"

"Was there anything still standing?" she said, buying time, still trying to figure out how to present the dogs.

"It's all gone. Demolished. Some jewelry survived, that's it. Small solace, but something, I guess."

She had meant to save the necklace for last, but now, on a whim, she dug it from her pocket and handed it to him.

He examined it closely, suspiciously. "Where did you get this?" His voice was harsh. "Do you know something about Lu? Is that why you've been texting me?"

Slowly, in barely more than a whisper, she began to tell him what she knew. Dar's arrival yesterday with the dogs. Dar, she ex-plained, was his daughter's professor, a scientist. She described how Dar had said the dogs had come into his possession, how the neck-lace had been embedded in the black dog's coat. When she came to relaying the rest stop transformation, she began to feel fraudulent, unsure of what she was saying. Who were these dogs? What did she herself believe? If Dar was a crackpot, as she was portraying him to be, maybe she was too. Dar had been simultaneously dubious and believing. She forced herself to stop speaking. The dogs had inched closer to George's legs. He reached down to pet them absently, his face remote, unreadable.

Hyperventilating, she stood quickly. "I know. I know exactly how outlandish this sounds."

"You're telling me a lunatic has abducted my wife and daughter. Either that or—or you're going off the deep end."

"Look, I have no idea what happened. But he didn't seem like a bad man. My instincts are good. He wasn't irrational. Or acting like a criminal."

"It's always like that. People always say perpetrators seemed so gentle before they inflicted their violence."

"He gave me his number. He wouldn't have done that if he was a criminal, would he? Wait, there's something else."

The clothing Dar had left lay folded in a pile on the kitchen island, the phone on top. She extended the pile to him. "He left these."

George was still, slumped, boneless, blinking at what she held, but making no effort to accept it.

"Your daughter's things. You don't recognize them?"

His catatonia was absolute. She found it irritating. "George."

He said nothing. The dogs were scratching at the French doors. She unfurled the jeans and the blue work shirt and flattened them out on the floor in front of him, the phone on top of the shirt. It was not lost on her that the shape on the floor resembled a policeman's chalk outline.

"I'm going to take them for a quick walk," Marley said.

He held to his silence as she stepped out. What a relief to be outdoors, away from the cloud of his bitterness and self-absorption.

She couldn't blame him for feeling bleak, but it didn't mean it was pleasant to be marooned in the midst of it.

The day had a sultry Indian summer feel, the sun exceptionally large and mango-colored against the smoky sky. It would have been beautiful were it not for her knowledge of the fires still at work, the stultifying scent of burning a reminder. Could a thing be beautiful if it was caused by something so damaging? Could beauty and ugliness coexist in the same space? It seemed as if that convergence was happening so often of late. There would always be ugliness at large in the world, but would there always be beauty? Her art making seemed like an uphill struggle. Weren't there times when beauty in all its manifestations—especially love and kindness—disappeared all over the planet?

She couldn't accept that. She wouldn't.

The dogs completed their business and cavorted around each other, nipping each other's butts, their bodies strikingly similar to each other but for their different coloration. She loved the way they investigated the world, traveling in each other's orbit, sutured together like twin stars, or like some couples she knew, part of the same system, molecular or planetary.

Now they raced to the crumbling chicken coop and sniffed its collapsing moss-covered siding. She had ignored this building for too long, allowing it to succumb to entropy.

They pushed inside, unbothered by the decay, and disappeared from view.

Something was causing them to bark furiously. She peered inside and saw them, side by side, tails raised on high alert, like workers reporting for duty. It took her a moment to spot the object of their attention: a fat snake in the shadows, lifting its head, starting to rattle.

"Dogs! Lu! Come out here right now!"

They came to her, agitated, shivering, and she corralled them away from the shed, kneeling in the grass to stroke them.

"I'm so sorry about that. I had no idea there was a snake in there. I hope there's not more than one. I need to fix that place up. I should never have let it go like that. But don't go in there now. We don't want to rile the rattlesnakes."

The dogs listened, and their quivering bodies began to relax, toned muscles releasing their tension. She stroked their luxurious coats, at home now with their doggy smell. She couldn't remember ever having had such an immediate effect on anyone (could they be considered someones?). She had clearly comforted them, and she could see they were appreciative. She almost wept. Then, still stroking, she did weep.

"Who are you dogs?"

They licked her face, and she allowed them to lick. It didn't occur to her to think of their tongues as unhygienic.

"Are you happy?"

They hurled themselves against her, both of them at the same time, so she toppled back into the prickly grass, and the three rolled around together, all of their bodies hot and tremulous, incandescently alive. Love encircled Marley, a tidal force. She thought of her understanding last night that these dogs had souls. Of course they did.

She laughed as she had never laughed before, delight cleansing her limbs. After a few minutes the rolling stopped, and they all lay there, panting and content. How could she possibly let these dogs go?

"You are so—so much yourselves, aren't you? You're so unstuck, whoever you are."

It would be a brave new life with these dogs. They would keep her honest.

~

Inside George was standing at the kitchen island, staring down at his phone. "The cops have me on hold. Look at this bastard." He angled the screen to her; it displayed a photo of Dar on the UCLA faculty website. "You send your daughter to college and she ends up studying with a madman, an incipient criminal. Who the fuck knew?"

Marley wished she could help him, but if there were words that would comfort him, she wasn't privy to them. Had he digested any of the things she'd said to him? They appeared to have made no impression at all.

"I'm happy to keep the dogs. In fact, I'd *like* to keep them."

"Oh no. They're coming with me."

"Seriously, George, you don't even have a home."

"They're coming with me," he repeated. He scrolled through his phone, his chiding finger bearing an astonishing payload of anger. "What?" He lifted the phone to his ear. "Dammit, they cut me off."

"You don't even like animals. You said that."

He was ignoring her, redialing, ignoring the dogs who had become frantic; they swerved between the two of them, without barking, alert to the tenuousness of their fate. She reached down to reassure them, stilling them for a moment and cradling one head then the other. She felt such a powerful connection to them, but it occurred to her she didn't really know what they wanted for themselves. They loved her, that was clear, but maybe their rightful place was with George? If only they could speak.

George was pocketing his phone. "I've got to get going. I'm meeting Tom at the winery—what's left of it. Then I've got to go find my mother-in-law. Come on, guys." He beckoned to the dogs. They stood their ground between the two humans, unsure of their alliances.

"Why not leave them with me, George? I've got all this space."

"I can't. They're evidence."

"Evidence of what?"

"Whatever this man did. The clothes. The necklace. The phone. All of it." He bent toward the dogs, coaxing them with an outstretched palm, a tad less gruff. "Come on."

The black dog went to him. The brown dog hesitated.

"Will you be nice to them? You won't hurt them?"

"Oh, for god's sake, what do you take me for?"

"But you have to treat them better than fine. Exquisitely. Tenderly. Will you?"

"Yes, of course."

She walked them to the car. It was hard to say goodbye to the dogs. They licked her again, their love overwhelming, unconditional, matching no love she had ever experienced before. George loaded them into the back seat of the BMW. She hoped he could keep his rage in check.

After they drove off she was bereft, restless. It would take months for her to understand this, years maybe. She would miss the dogs acutely, but the mystery of their presence would linger.

But now—how to go forward? She laughed at herself—the question was, as yet, unanswerable.

First, shower and dress.

The bathroom mirror commanded her to look. It reflected back to her a collage of a human being. Overlays of all the people she'd been over the years. Stripped down to her essential self. No makeup, but still a raw, bold-featured beauty shone through. She could become attached to this unvarnished version of herself, a more honest Marley.

52

THE LONG ASPHALT ROAD uphill to the winery had become like a path of lava rocks, forcing him to drive slowly. The poplar trees that had lined the road like a welcoming committee had been reduced to blackened stumps. The dogs were peering out the side windows, their quiet whining in sync with his own inner whine.

He pulled up next to Tom's red truck. Tom was nowhere in sight. The dogs were chafing to get out, and when he opened the back door they sprang from the seat and tore off, diving over the gravel into dirt and blackened stubble, disappearing past the lip of the hill and down the slope that had once been home to bountiful grape vines, his best Cabernet. He called out to them briefly, but they didn't come. He had no idea how to summon them back. It was becoming apparent they had minds of their own.

He leaned against the car, trying to summon the energy to go forth. He would pay whatever ransom the professor wanted to get his wife and daughter back, but what if they were already dead? The thought impaled him, and he pushed it away. The sight he looked out on—the absence of everything he had built and grown—was yet another gut-punch, even more of a gut-punch than the ruins of his house had been. Years had gone into creating a profitable business on this acreage. Years of research about viticulture. Years of planting the grapes and constructing the buildings. Years of mental focus, waiting for certain vintages to age, trying and failing and trying again. He'd had a vision, and he'd been able to manifest that vision. People had loved coming here. People had loved drinking his wine. Even people in faraway places bought and drank and praised his wine. It was—he was—by all accounts a success. Now what he saw directly in front of him didn't resemble anything that could be called successful. It didn't even seem as if it still belonged to him. It was ruined. Nothing remained of the buildings but heaps of concrete and blackened metal. The tasting room's two chimneys rose up from the moribund landscape like lunar outposts. As for the land itself—he feared the soil was no longer nutritive enough to grow anything.

He trudged toward the hill where the dogs had gone. The stink of the air was bad, a smell he'd never encountered despite all the fires he'd lived through. He hated to think of the dangerous chemicals he was breathing, was glad he'd thought to bring a mask, part of his kit bag in this new world.

The view out over the valley, once so prized, was now an ugly thing, decimated and devoid of variety and nuance in the way of a clearcut. Partway down the hill stood Tom, in his brown canvas jacket, feet planted firmly in the soil like the most indestructible of trees. He was sniffing something, a handful of dirt. George came up beside him, and Tom brought the soil to George's nose. George sniffed. This was a habit of Tom's, sniffing the soil, his nose a litmus test informing him of the soil's nutrient composition. George's nose had never been sensitive enough to glean what Tom gleaned. Now, however, his nose reported a great deal, just what he'd feared: The dirt smelled acrid, smoky, not remotely life-giving. You wouldn't want to trust dirt like this with a grape seedling. It would be like giving a newborn an acid bath.

"I'll run some tests," Tom said, "but the nitrogen, the

microorganisms . . ." He shook his head in his slow, ever-thoughtful way. Nothing hastened or alarmed him, even now. This quality had made him a critical ballast for George over the years.

"You mean we're fucked?"

"We'll watch it. See how quickly it changes. But now, we'd be doing no one any favors by planting here."

The dogs were running back up the hill toward them, the brown one in the lead, both barking, excited by who-knew-what. They stopped in front of George and ceased barking, watching him, waiting for something in a way that made him uneasy. What did they want? Why weren't they paying any attention to Tom, who adored animals? Yes, they were good dogs, special dogs he supposed as Marley had insisted, but they were also a damn nuisance.

"Where did the dogs come from?" Tom asked.

"Oh god." George flapped his hand to let Tom know he didn't plan to tell the story. To tell Tom about the professor would make the situation too real. For now he had to put it aside.

The brown dog tapped George's shoe with her paw. *Thump-thump. Thump-thump-thump.* She parted her mouth, exposing her lanky pink tongue.

"She wants something," Tom said, laughing a little.

"Yeah, well . . ." George shrugged. He bent to pet the animal, feeling deficient in his understanding of beasts.

Tom was laughing now, and George was confused. The dogs wanted to play, he guessed, and they appeared almost gleeful. What a concept—that anyone, even a dog, could feel glee amid such devastation.

"Throw a stick," Tom said.

But there were no sticks. A gust of wind blew over the hillside, stirring up feathers of ash that floated back to the ground, rejoining the carpet of grayish-black. The brown dog wouldn't leave him alone. She lifted a paw to his shin in clumsy nudging. *Thump-thump. Thump-thump-thump.* A shiver passed through him, bearing a somatic memory of Pippa and the game they used to play. *Try this, Dad. Try this!* Her palm nimble and quick. *Dah-dum, dah-dum. Dum-dum-dum-diddy-dum.* Easy at first then increasing in difficulty. Most of what she tapped he couldn't possibly replicate. She was always one step ahead of him, her hands facile with syncopation. Life had strange resonances. One tried to make sense of the connections between things, even when there were no connections.

"If we don't rebuild, what will you do?" George said.

Tom shrugged. "Might be time for the woods again."

George couldn't imagine living as Tom had, relying on ingenuity and knowledge of the natural world. He'd left that life behind for reasons George hadn't dared to ask about, and he'd made peace grudgingly with the first-world values and commitments of the winery, using a phone only when George bought him one and insisted he use it. Until this fire he'd been living in a minimalist cabin on the winery's acreage, constructed by George expressly for him. But that had burned too, so he, like George, was now homeless.

"You're welcome to come with me." Tom laughed at the absurdity of his suggestion, knowing George's predilection for comfort.

"I don't know if Lu would cotton to that."

Lu, the proverbial elephant in the room, the ghost on his shoulder, the absent woman, possibly dead, without whom . . .

Tom nodded. "She'll come back. I'm sure they'll find her. You'll rebuild somewhere. It will be fine."

Both men understood Tom was saying what had to be said, regardless of its dubious truth. He was a kind man.

The dogs barked.

"They want us to play with them," Tom said.

"I'm not exactly in a playing mood."

The dogs had figured this out and, bearing no grudges, they turned to each other in chase, a dyad of spinning energy, needing nothing but each other. Their self-sufficiency impressed George. Humbled him.

"I can't do anything. Even if I could think of what to do, I wouldn't be able to pull it off."

Tom swiveled, a quick and almost violent pivot toward George. "Hey! You're still here, right? You *survived*. Okay?"

Breath ratcheted through George's windpipe. Noisy. Disturbed. He hadn't been slapped, but he felt slapped. He tamped down a spur of annoyance at Tom, who had been so good to him for so long. Still, it was out of line for Tom to be harsh when George had lost so much. He was still alive, yes, still cycling breath and blood, but there had to be more to life than the ebb and flow of blood and breath. He thought enviously of the way the dogs had looked traveling up the hill, enthralled with themselves and each other. They took up energy and happiness so easily. How did they accomplish that? He wanted such energy, even a fraction of it.

Tom was watching him, maybe contrite, maybe not. The dogs were out of sight again, exploring the rubble.

"Dogs!" George called. "Come here, dogs!"

Either they did not hear him, or they chose to disobey. They did not come.

53

DAR DROVE THROUGH the night, a madman at the wheel, sparring with the other cars, outgunning them until he was off the freeway and alone, a solo vehicle brazening up and down circuitous mountain roads, through moraines of darkness and light, fueled by confusion. Haunted. Away. Away.

He couldn't have said he was going to the desert, but each exit and turn he chose led him there. He drove fast with athletic prowess, commanding the reluctant Volvo easily even on these serpentine roads. Through craggy canyons. Past looming shadows of undulant rock. After hours of driving, the road broke straight and flat, delivering him into a dark barren valley, sandy land stretching out to an obscured horizon.

His mind hammered on. *The dogs. The dogs.* He pictured them as they'd looked sprinting to his car, almost airborne, leaping against the Volvo's door as he rocketed off, praying he wouldn't run over them. He had to leave. If he hadn't left he might have disintegrated, and there was an imperative to save himself. But those dogs, those dear dogs, how guilty he felt. He hoped they understood.

But they wouldn't let go, those crazy-making dogs. They had crept into the car, usurping his concentration. He saw them in the rearview mirror, approaching to lick his neck. Licking brought them to his brain's portal, and they barged in, barking and whining, ceaseless and insistent. The monomania of those dogs. They had taken over his whole being, a new form of energy, previously unknown to him.

The desert's night chill seeped into the car and turned his sweat icy. He stopped for gas at an all-night mom-and-pop store, where he filled his water jug and bought a Bigfoot sweatshirt and surprised himself with his own speech.

A single car approached from the other direction, the first car he'd seen for hours, its headlights alarmingly bright. It seemed they should acknowledge each other, but the car sped by, disinterested. There was no cell service out here, the loneliest of outposts.

The sky began to lighten, revealing a stunning no-man's land. Sandy soil stippled with scrub grass and creosote. The gracious silhouettes of low mountains on all sides. The sky blared pink, purple, orange, fuchsia, the colors of abandon. His arms trembled with fatigue. He wondered what was happening with the dogs. Marley had appeared to be perfectly nice, but he shouldn't have trusted her. He hadn't been able to sense what she knew. Would she give the dogs to Philippa's father? He worried for them, for Philippa, for Lu.

Hands numb from gripping too long and hard, he pulled to the side of the road, got out for a quick stretch, then conked out in the back seat.

The dogs visited his dreams, no longer obstreperous, but silent, gazing at him with their depthless eyes. His grandmother's eyes, *yes, no, yes*, the sentient eyes of the octopus, who had seemed to have eyes throughout its curious arms. Everywhere eyes, a whirl of wise eyes and eyes full of questions but without need. Eyes gifting him with sensibilities he didn't fully understand, but he needed to understand. *Who are you, Dar? What kind of life do you want?*

When he woke the sun was at its zenith. The extravagance of dawn had ceded to a uniform white. He unfolded himself and stepped from the car, stiff, slick with sweat, only half-rested, squinting against the startle of light. Heat drummed down from overhead, and pulsed through everything, rolling over the asphalt, the sandy soil, the scrappy vegetation. Mirages everywhere, as if he was still dreaming. Visible energy. The air beautifully redolent of sage.

He stretched, cracked his knuckles, remembered his dreams as he assessed himself. He was tired, but he wasn't crazy. He had guided himself to Death Valley not in order to die, but to find the clarity that sometimes lies at the lonely doorstep of death. He perched on the hood of his car, its hot steel scorching his thighs, and gulped from his jug. He wouldn't be able to tolerate this sun and heat for long. It had to be at least a hundred and ten out here, maybe hotter.

A truck materialized in the distance, first a mere pinprick of glinting silver, then gaining in heft and understandable shape. A Chevron tractor-trailer crashed past him, a bluster of combustion engine and loose clanging metal, engulfing him in its din and exhaust. It honked as it passed, a greeting of sorts, then disappeared from sight. On the other side of the road a few desert rats, flushed from the underbrush, scurried away. When the truck's clatter subsided its presence remained, a blot on Dar's brain.

A smoldering patch of grass corralled his attention. Exactly where the rats had been. Within seconds the smoldering ignited into orange flame.

He sprinted across the road, emptied the contents of his jug over the conflagration. He stamped and stamped, hoping the soles of his shoes wouldn't melt.

The fire sputtered and dwindled into a small plume of smoke.

Disaster averted. The only remaining evidence was a small patch of blackened grass and his own double-time heartbeat. What if he hadn't been here? A spark must have been ignited from the truck's loose metal scraping the asphalt. A sagging muffler perhaps? The truck had passed too quickly for him to say for sure. Was this truck catalyzing fires wherever it drove? It was the nature of energy to leap from place to place, finding new venues for expressing itself. Labile. Insuppressible. That was the abiding way of the world, and Dar knew it well.

A huff of hot wind. The shadow of a hawk. The suffocating heat. He held still, trying to understand what had happened, pondering the transfer of energy he had just witnessed, its speed and unpredictability. The dogs. The way their eyes had looked in his dream. The way they'd established a presence in his body, awake and asleep, the fullness of their being a radical new energy he'd never known before.

The combustion he'd just witnessed repeated itself in his heart, birthing a singular thought. He had to get to those dogs. How could he have turned his back on them after he'd seen what he'd seen, after the mystery of their transformation had entered his body and mind, posing so many questions? What a coward he was to see but refuse to look, to understand but refuse to embrace. He was no better than the close-minded men occupying the seats of power and the halls of academia, those who clung to the outdated knowledge and bigoted views that had brought them success. How could he claim to be a man who understood and celebrated animal consciousness, who'd shared such memorable intimacy with a cephalopod, but who could not handle the sentience of those dogs? And worse—how could he have neglected to honor the unexpected affection he'd felt for Philippa, a girl with a soul like his?

So much was unknown, yes. The only chance of knowing those

things was to return to the dogs. *I'm going to the dogs*, he said to himself. The resonances of that phrase made him chuckle.

He couldn't move quickly enough. He sprinted back across the road to his car, the soot of complacency, the contagion of doubt, all evaporating. He made a wide U-turn in the throbbing desert heat. *I'm coming*, he whispered. *Wait for me.*

54

WHEN THEY WERE deep in conversation, their backs turned, we bounded into the blackened underbrush at the perimeter of the pasture. We ran fast, side by side, enthralled with movement, and with each other, and with the leap to freedom we had made. Molecules flew past our nostrils: pollen, dirt, musk of other animals, scents of fescue and madrone and eucalyptus and bay, along with the smoke. A new world for us to explore.

We heard them calling out for us, but the sound of their voices had become a weak leash; they had no effect on us, could no longer pull us back to their orbit. We were fully ourselves now, and we knew they could survive without us. They would find others to love them and soothe their burdens.

We left because it was the only choice that seemed available to us. We loved those people, even knowing their foibles, and they had always been good to us, but we saw no way to help them arrive at the place of simplicity we had come to occupy. We couldn't bear to stand by and witness our people being slowly diminished, even destroyed, by all those forces we abhorred. Locked in endless anxiety. Dreading the future. Regretting the past. And loneliness. A downward path for most people. If we had stayed to watch them degraded by life, we knew we might be taken down into that chasm too. We might channel their anxieties. We couldn't risk it.

Without regret we bounded into the world, dashing up hillsides and through copses of live oaks, meeting the wilderness of our new lives to be lived at the margins of the human world. Scavenging, playing, sleeping—doing these things not because it was the time to do them, but because we were moved to do them. No planning. No second-guessing others.

We felt sorry for our humans, but they would survive too, stumbling along with varying degrees of happiness. Marley already knew how to forge a new path boldly. George had resources, which always helped. And Dar was young and self-examining; he would do fine too—maybe one day he would come to join us.

We descended a hill and wiggled under a fence into a field of grazing cows who lowed softly when they saw us. The calls of our people faded into the smoke. They might look for us, but they wouldn't find us. We were fast and knew how to camouflage ourselves. We would become for them a memory, or a dream they could not make sense of and would ponder again and again, trying to understand. They would wonder why this strange thing had happened to them. What did it mean about them, or about us, or about the world in general? We imagined them wishing that they, too, might someday sample the satisfactions of a stripped and simple life.

No grasping, no greed, no ambition, no malice.

Enough. Gone. Full stop.

Sniff the glorious world.

Author's Note

I began to write *Unleashed* at the beginning of the pandemic, when I had also just started to notice there was something wrong with my voice. I couldn't control its inflections, and it was sounding gruff, though no one noticed these changes but me. I didn't go out much that spring and summer. Instead, I hurled myself into writing, feeling the strangeness of what I was working on, the likelihood it might never see the light of day. I didn't care; I had to write whatever this was, and it poured out like an opium-induced dream. Meanwhile, the doctors I visited had no idea what was wrong with my voice.

I finished a draft in September 2020, when my husband and I were staying for a month in a cottage on the coast of one of the San Juan islands. We were steps from the beach, and every day we immersed ourselves in the natural world, kayaking in the bay, watching the cavorting seals, the otters skittering across the beach, the eagles in the treetops waiting to swoop for fish. My voice was notably compromised by then, a matter of concern for our host-friends and my husband. And me too. I had begun to sound, to everyone's ears, somewhat like an animal.

It wasn't until months later, after several revisions of the novel, just before I was given a diagnosis of bulbar-onset ALS, that I understood something about what I'd written: it was my body's chronicle of a developing disease, a metaphorical autobiography of sorts, though nothing about it borrowed anything from my actual life.

My body was wiser than my conscious mind. I say this as if mind and body are separate entities, the Cartesian dichotomy persisting in my mind though I know well that mind and body are inextricable. Still, it surprised me to see the way this work took shape as if my conscious mind were not involved.

I summoned the hutzpah to send the novel to my agent, Deborah Schneider, and I am full of gratitude that she and my editor at Dutton, Lexy Cassola, have worked hard to speed up the publication schedule.

I am doing fine as of this writing in December 2021. Though I can't speak intelligibly, I can walk and write, and I expect to be around for a while. I hope you have been as engaged by reading *Unleashed* as I was in the writing of it.

Acknowledgments

Writing a novel during the first year of the pandemic was a solitary experience. During the months it took to come up with the first draft, I didn't do any face-to-face research, and I saw few people other than my husband. But once that draft was completed, I might never have moved through the next seven or eight drafts without what was offered by numerous people who provided everything from manuscript critiques to friendship and moral support.

Some of these people are: my terrific tiny writing group pals, Miriam Gershow and Debra Gwartney; Andrea Schwartz-Feit and Becky Dusseau, who gave me early reads; Lanie McMullin and Michelle Sosin, who gave us extra time to write in their wonderful cottage on Lopez Island when fire was moving toward our home.

Love and support came from near and far in response to my ALS diagnosis and it was very meaningful in keeping me going. There are too many people to list here, but I am extremely grateful for the words and offers of help that came from every one of you. Feeling this network of love and support has made it possible to sustain the hope and passion necessary for writing.

My doctors and the whole medical team at OHSU have been an unexpected gift. Dr. Nizar Chahin, Dr. Orly Moshe-Lilie, Yvel Maspinas, and many others have been so remarkable in their availability, their continuous offers of valuable help, and most of all their positive attitude, which affects everything they do and infects everyone around them. And a special shoutout to my dentist, Laleh Rezaee, who has taken an interest in my medical situation when she didn't have to.

I have been blessed to work with my extraordinary agent and friend, Deborah Schneider, for over two decades, and I'm delighted that she found a home for this book with an editor at Dutton, Lexy Cassola, who is so astute and with whom I feel so simpatico.

My sisters, Ebe Emmons and Patty Emmons, what can I say? We have never been closer or loved one another more.

Ben, you have been so present and devoted during this time that it moves me to tears. I adore you.

And Paul, my hayati, there are simply no words to thank you for all the love you've given me over the years. It has shown through in everything: our conversations about our work, the stellar meals you make, our shared laughter. Even now, though I'm afflicted with this irreversible disease, life with you couldn't get any better.

About the Author

Cai Emmons is the author of six novels—*His Mother's Son*, *The Stylist*, *Weather Woman*, *Sinking Islands*, *Unleashed*, and *Livid*—and a story collection, *Vanishing*. She holds a BA from Yale University and two MFAs, one from New York University in film and the other from the University of Oregon in fiction. Before turning to fiction, Emmons wrote plays and screenplays. Winner of a Student Academy Award, an Oregon Book Award, and the Leapfrog Fiction Prize, and a finalist for the *Narrative*, *Missouri Review*, and Sarton fiction prizes, she has taught at a variety of institutions, most recently in the Creative Writing Program at the University of Oregon. She lives in Eugene, Oregon.